A *Strange* AND BITTER *Crop*

E. L. Wyrick

St. Martin's Press New York

Design by Basha Zapatka

Library of Congress Cataloging-in-Publication Data

Wyrick, E. L.
    A strange and bitter crop / E. L. Wyrick.
        p.   cm.
    "A Thomas Dunne Book."
    ISBN 0-312-11075-8
    1. Women lawyers—Georgia—Fiction.   I. Title.
PS3573.Y68S77   1994
813'.54—dc20   94-1112
                                                                      CIP

First edition: July 1994

10 9 8 7 6 5 4 3 2 1

For Mom and Dad

Your unyielding faith and support
made this effort possible.

Acknowledgments

◗ ◗ ◗ ◗ ◗ ◗ ◗ ◗ ◗ ◗ ◗ ◗ ◗

The author wishes to thank the following people for their invaluable help: Attorneys Jenny Turner and Rick Dickson; psychotherapist Sherryl Richier; Georgia Bureau of Investigation forensic anthropologist Dr. Karen Burns; Jackson County, Georgia, sheriff Stan Evans; Gwinnett County, Georgia, policeman John Hobson; Instructor of nursing Benna Cunningham; and a special woman who shared her pain, but wishes to remain unnamed.

Also, thanks to several people who read and responded to the manuscript: Pete McCommons, Elizabeth Exley Paulsen, Shirley Daniel, Bob Hall, Betsy Lindsey, Harriet Austin and the members of her writers' workshop, John Dagley, Peggy Dagley, Gary Siegel, Herman and Betty Greenway, Jane Scales, Judy Saye Flemming, Ted Goetz, Cathy Miller, Frances Brooks, Sharon Aronson, Judy Steuer, Melissa Blackstone, and Mary Downs Dixon.

Special appreciation goes to Donna Willer Wenzel, who copyedited this work countless times. Every author needs a friend like Donna.

Finally, I want to thank Pat, and my daughters, Heather, Kalli, and Mariah, all of whom understand my absence as I am squirreled away tapping on the keyboard.

A *Strange* AND BITTER *Crop*

Chapter 1

Within ten days I killed two men. Both deserved it. For the first time in my life, I hope my mother's right and there is a hell. The savagery I suffered demands that those men now scream in horrible pain.

When Dan suggested *de malo, bonus*—from evil, good—I reacted with anger. And yet, the truth is, I feel more alive than I ever have. I don't know yet how to reconcile that. Perhaps it's because I've finally begun to shed the restrictions I used to blame on Mama. Now I realize those strictures were self-imposed. But that revelation didn't come because I was attacked. My awakening came because I did something about it.

It started, I think, with the Mustang. Ten o'clock had come and gone when I parked my four-year-old yellow Yugo in front of Professor Gatlin's house. The delicate light from the full moon seeped through the canopy of water oaks that sheltered Farris Street. I climbed out of the car and was hit by the hot, clammy Georgia air. Despite the darkness, the temperature remained above ninety.

I stretched and yawned deeply. The syrupy fragrance of honeysuckle brought back memories of long-gone summer nights back home in Maytown. I leaned against the car and, in the dead stillness of the night, pictured Daddy and me sitting on the front porch swing, the honeysuckle fighting a losing battle with Daddy's cigarettes and his breath, which reeked of Jim Beam. Once again, I wondered what demons had tormented this man who tried to protect me from Mama's never-ending demands and censures backed by the screaming Sunday sermons at the Congregational Holiness.

And once again, I fought the demons that roused my own anger toward that most important man.

My reverie was broken by a sound. A slight sound, but one that echoed through the muted, darkened street. I stood away from the Yugo and looked around. I thought I saw, but couldn't be sure, movement within an old Mustang sitting across the street, a couple of houses away. I picked up my briefcase and walked quickly between the two huge magnolias that hid the professor's century-old, rambling house from the street. I stepped across the screened wraparound veranda and unlocked the front door.

As I entered the wide central hall, the phone was ringing in the room on my right that I'd made my sleeping quarters. I let my answering machine take the call. I turned on the small room air conditioner and stripped to my bra and panties before doing anything else.

After my taped message ended, I heard, "Counselor Randall, this is Lucas Anderson . . ."

I picked up the phone and interrupted him. "What's this 'Counselor Randall' stuff?"

"My mother taught me to be polite."

Because it's easier to give advice than take it, I said, "Get over it, Lucas."

"If you say so, Tammi. You know the Bond Street murders?"

"Of course. It's hard not to know with all the stories in the *Herald*." The bodies of Dr. Gary Reeves and his wife had been found two weeks ago in their home. They were both descendants of old-time, influential Patsboro families. Old-time, influential Patsboro family members do not get murdered. It simply isn't done, and the community was in shock.

"We got the guy," Lucas said.

"That's great. Who is he?"

"Fifteen-year-old kid from Stony Bottom named James Cleveland."

"Fifteen?" I repeated while arranging the phone cord so I could sit on the floor underneath the air conditioner.

"Yeah. No doubt he did it. Prints match what we found in the house. He still had the baseball bat he used."

I paused, thinking about a baseball bat as a weapon. It was a gruesome thought. "I'm glad you got him. People in Patsboro will be relieved."

I was wondering why he'd phoned to tell me. I work at the Teal County Legal Aid Society, but I wasn't on call that night. While Lucas and I were more than mere acquaintances, we weren't bosom buddies who called and chatted.

Lucas answered the question without my asking. "He says he wants you to be his lawyer."

"Me? Why?"

"Don't know. Just said he wanted to talk to you. Specifically. So I called. He's watched enough television, I guess, to know not to talk. Only thing he's said is he wants to talk to you."

I straightened my legs in front of me and slid farther down the wall. My long day, coupled with the life-sucking humidity, had exhausted me. Part of me just wanted to take a bath and collapse into bed. Because I wasn't on call, I could have done just that. On the other hand, in the past year my cases had consisted of defending drunk drivers, shoplifters, and an occasional housing project resident who had been caught with an illegal substance. The most stimulating aspect about most of those cases was keeping my clients quiet long enough so that I could bargain some kind of a plea. Defending an accused murderer would be a new challenge.

There was another consideration. Being from Stony Bottom meant the boy was black and more than impoverished. Stony Bottom was the pits, even compared to the housing projects where most of my clients lived. I'd chosen to work for legal aid because I'd grown up watching poor people in Maytown getting short shrift from the legal system.

After telling Lucas I'd be there soon, I put on fresh pants and a blouse. As I changed clothes, I wondered why James Cleveland had asked for me. Maybe I'd defended a relative of his.

After taking a quick look in the mirror, I headed out the door, then paused. A fifteen-year-old, I thought. I returned to the telephone and dialed. Dan's fourteen-year-old daughter answered.

"Hi, Samantha. This is Tammi. Is your dad around?"

"Yeah. He's down in his workshop. I'll get him."

While waiting for Dan to answer, I looked at the Habitrail complex sitting on a stand on the far side of the room. Inside was the gerbil that Samantha and her two sisters had given me a year ago for a graduation present. At the time I thought it was a strange gift, but I'd grown to love the critter.

I also thought about Samantha and her phone call to her dad when he and I were in a hotel in New Orleans four years ago. Her call to say good night had stopped us from making a major mistake. At least I keep telling myself it would have been a major mistake.

Dan came to the phone. I told him about the call from Lucas Anderson. "You know the kid?"

"James Cleveland," he mused. "Nope, doesn't ring a bell. But you know how I am with names. Meg has to put tags on the children every morning so I know what to call them."

I chuckled. "I was wondering if you'd come with me to talk with him. My experience with fifteen-year-olds is limited." My bachelor's degree in psychology helped, but Dan, as a counselor at Teal County High School, had plenty of experience with teenagers. And during the summer he also had plenty of time.

He said, "Shouldn't be a problem. Let me check with Meg. Hold on."

Meg was Dan's wife. She and I got along well, but I sometimes wondered if she knew what we almost did.

Dan was back. "OK. But my VW's in the shop. Can you pick me up?"

"Are you getting a new engine or body?"

"They're welding the rust together."

"I'll be there in ten minutes."

At the magnolias, I stopped, remembering the car I'd seen

parked across the street. Standing in the leafy shadows, I shook myself. This wasn't New York City. It was Patsboro, Georgia. I started to move, then stopped again. *And* I was on my way to meet an accused murderer. I ducked under the low-lying limbs of the magnolia and looked toward the street where the Mustang had been.

It was gone.

Chapter 2

Dan was sitting on his front porch eating a Fudgsicle when I arrived. After squeezing into my diminutive Yugo, he could almost rest his chin on his knees.

"Dessert?" I said.

"Meg bought 'em today. Won't last long when the kids find out. Have to strike while they're hot—so to speak."

He was wearing jeans, low-cut canvas Asahi tennis shoes, and a loose-fitting cotton cargo shirt. A ship was emblazoned on the right side of the shirt, and underneath the ship were the words *Pacific Basin Tropical Cruise.*

Five minutes later, we were on the Monroe Highway heading into town. "When did you go on a cruise?" I asked.

"Cruise?"

I nodded toward his shirt.

"Oh. Got this when I cruised up to Commerce to the outlet mall. Cost me five-ninety-five." We were approaching the overpass that was being built for the new bypass around town. The road made a sharp turn because of the construction. "Nice, though, to sit on our deck and pretend. . . ."

Headlights flashed to my left. I turned sharply to the right, but it was too late. There was a strangely quiet thud, followed by the world outside my windshield whirling as the car spun twice. When the Yugo stopped in the middle of the road, I sat trying to figure out what had happened. I looked at Dan. He was staring at his Fudgsicle, which was bent from being jammed into the windshield. "You OK?"

"Yeah. But my dessert is totaled."

"Insurance will cover it," I said as I looked to my left. A dark, large sedan was sitting twenty feet away in the middle of the road. Smoke was rising from its hood. The driver's door was open, but with only the dim illumination from the moon, I couldn't see inside. I tried to open my door, but it was jammed. As I pushed harder, a thin black man emerged from the passenger side of the sedan. His short-sleeved shirt was unbuttoned to his belt and half the shirt's tail was hanging out of his pants. He moved toward us and tapped on my window. I tried to roll it down, but it would only drop a couple of inches.

The man leaned toward the opening and slurred, "Hey . . . you got a cigarette?"

"No," I said emphatically, then rolled up the window.

"Nice to know he's concerned about our possible injuries," Dan said.

"I don't believe it was the milk of human kindness I smelled on him. Let's get out. I can't open my door."

Dan tried his and it worked. I climbed over the gearshift, glad to be released from the tiny space of the Yugo. I looked over at the sedan again. A woman crawled out the driver's side, on her hands and knees, and pulled herself up by the rear door handle. She stood unsteadily, then headed for us. She wore short, straightened hair above her stocky, short body. Her immense breasts flopped under a tight T-shirt as she managed to round the front of the Yugo. She walked straight to me, put her hand on my arm, squinched her eyes, and said, "Lady, you got a cigarette?"

Dan released a small giggle.

"No," I said. "Are you all right?"

The woman closed her eyes tightly and shook her head slightly. Suddenly her eyes opened wide and she screamed in my face, "Bobby done wrecked my car! . . . Baa*ah*beeee done *wrecked* my car!"

I reeled backward from the impact of the incredibly loud sound and the gush of whiskey-filled breath she expelled. Dan was standing behind me, and my sudden movement caught him off guard. I heard him grunt and turned to see him spread-eagled on the ground. When I bent down to see if he was all right, the woman grabbed my blouse and howled, "Bobby done wrecked my car!"

"Yes, lady. Bobby wrecked your car," I said softly and slowly as I wrenched her hand off my blouse. "Now, *shut up!*"

I looked past her and saw a Patsboro Police car with flashing lights pull to a stop between my car and the sedan. A huge police officer, at least six-eight, got out and walked toward us holding a clipboard. I looked back at Dan, who was sitting up, his arms crossed, his hands rubbing his elbows.

"Ouch," he said.

As the policeman approached, the woman lunged toward him and screamed again. This time it was, "Bobby done *stole* my car!"

The policeman looked down at her and said in a firm voice, "Essie, you see those steps right there?" He pointed to a darkened vacuum-cleaner store across the street. "You walk over to those steps and sit down."

Essie looked up at the hulking man, her eyes swimming.

"Now!"

The woman turned and stumbled across the street, still mumbling, "Bobby done *stole* my car."

The policeman looked at me. " 'Evening, Miss Randall."

I'd seen him around, but didn't know his name. The nameplate on his shirt said he was McDaniel. "Have we met?"

"I've seen you in court, ma'am, and if you'll excuse my being forward, you're easy to remember."

In the coursework for my psychology degree, I learned that early experiences have a lifelong impact. My surprise at McDaniel's comment is concrete evidence of that.

As a child I was a tubbo. Early junior high was a daily experience in humiliation. By ninth grade, though, two things happened. One was a natural growth that lengthened my frame and the other was a determination not to let the fat catch up. I read everything I could on proper nutrition and exercise. I followed the prescriptions. It's still a struggle.

When I reached tenth grade, Lilly McClain filled out an application for me to try out for the cheerleading squad and gave it to the sponsor without my knowledge. When I found out, I told Lilly I'd die before putting my fat legs on display for all to see. When Mama found out what Lilly had done, she told me only harlots went half-naked in front of people. But Daddy said I ought to try out. I made the squad. I figured there was a quota system: eight perfect bodies, a black, and a tubbo.

I continue to be amazed when people make comments like McDaniel's. I still feel fat. My ankles are too big and my legs seem like thunder thighs. On that night I still worried about my image as compared to the prototypical ideal American woman.

I don't anymore.

McDaniel looked at the two wrecked cars. "Looks like y'all had a little problem here." He looked at Dan, who was still sitting on the ground. "Do you need some help, sir?"

Dan stood and wiped blood off his left arm with his right index finger. "I'll make it. Always thought elbows were an overrated part of the anatomy anyway."

I looked at McDaniel and nodded toward Essie. "You know her?"

"Oh yeah. She's one of the Dillards. If you ever read the paper, you know the Dillards. At least one of 'em gets arrested every weekend. Though usually they're hitting each other."

I nodded. The family was famous among public defenders. I'd wondered when my turn was going to come to defend one of them. Not this time.

McDaniel continued, "I've called a couple of wreckers so I'd better get the report before they get here. Tell me what happened." I described the events as best I could and when I finished, he asked, "Who was driving?"

"I don't know." Looking now at the steps where Essie was sitting, I said, "I didn't look over at their car for a while. When I did, the driver's door was open." I pointed toward the two. "He got out of the passenger side. She came out the driver's side but it looked like she crawled from the middle. I don't think she was driving."

McDaniel looked over the barren mounds of red clay between us and the bypass. "Driver might have run." He pointed to Essie and her companion. "I'll go talk to them." As he walked across the road, the wreckers arrived.

When the wrecker driver completed hooking up the sedan, he yelled at McDaniel. "Hey, there's another guy in here."

McDaniel walked across the asphalt and opened the rear door, reached in, and shook the man in the back. Another black man stumbled out of the car. It was obvious he had no idea what was going on. McDaniel walked back to Essie.

As the backseat passenger approached us, Dan suggested, "Ten dollars?"

I looked up at him. "Can't afford it, and besides, you'll win."

"Aw, c'mon. How about a dollar? Make it interesting."

"This has bored you?"

"Fifty cents?" Dan pleaded.

"OK! OK! When you win, I'll replace your Fudgsicle."

The backseat passenger arrived. He said to Dan, "Hey man, you got a cigarette?"

Dan looked at me. "I know a deal's a deal, but I really wanted an Eskimo Pie."

"I can handle it. Barely."

Failing in his mission with us, the man wobbled toward the others. Dan and I sat quietly on the curb until McDaniel walked over to us. "I'm taking these three in. Public drunk. How about if I call a taxi for you?"

"That'd be fine," I said. "Actually, we're on the way to the police station. But I'd just as soon not ride with them."

"Don't blame you. Essie'll probably puke before we get there."

McDaniel looked around at the cars being towed away. "You were mighty lucky, ma'am. Barely avoided a direct hit on your door and that big old car would have creamed you, no doubt."

"I've thought about that," I said, and shivered. "You figure out who was driving? Guy named Bobby, apparently."

"Yeah. Essie says Bobby's been hanging around Sable's for a couple of weeks."

"The bar?"

"Right. Just down the road there." He pointed across the bypass. "He told them he'd buy them some Krystal hamburgers, but he had to drive."

"Should have offered cigarettes," Dan said.

McDaniel looked at him.

Dan shook his head. "Never mind."

Pointing under the overpass bridge, McDaniel said, "He stopped at the Russell gas station and they had an argument. They wanted Krystals and he wanted to sit. Essie says Bobby all of a sudden took off and ran right into you two. Essie said they hollered at him, but he didn't listen."

"Is Bobby one of the Dillards?" I asked.

"Doubt it seriously."

"Why?"

"She says Bobby's white."

Chapter 3

"What kind of white guy hangs around Sable's?" Dan asked.

"Either one with a lot of guts or one who's just plain crazy," I said as we walked up the Patsboro Police Department's front steps, which were flanked by lamps meant to look like the gaslights of old. These were electric. A sickening stench hit us when we walked in the lobby. A work-farm trustee, dressed in white except for a black stripe down the legs, was sprinkling sawdust over the worn hardwood floor. I asked the uniformed woman behind the counter for Lucas Anderson.

The lanky detective emerged through a swinging door next to the counter. He was wearing a rumpled white shirt with a brown-and-blue tie and brown pants. He stopped short and wrinkled his beaked nose. "Jesus Christ!" he exclaimed.

The woman behind the counter said, "Essie Dillard. Just had to wait till she got inside to barf."

Dan said, "Look at those french fries. Makes you wonder why she wanted to go to the Krystal."

"Sheeeit," the trustee said from behind us.

Lucas said, "Let's go to my office. Good to breathe and I can't do it in here."

We followed Lucas through the swinging door and down a dark hall. His office was a tiny room that barely held a gray metal desk and one chair for visitors. An ancient air conditioner was groaning and clanking in the window behind the desk. Lucas squeezed around the desk. Dan and I stood and looked at the metal chair with green padding.

"You take it," Dan said.

Normally I would have argued, but I was too tired to fight for my right to stand. I sat heavily and Dan closed the door and squatted, leaning against it.

"McDaniel called your situation in. Y'all OK?" Lucas asked.

"Mostly," I said. "Dan's elbows took some damage in the aftermath and my poor Yugo's on its way to intensive care."

"Don't ask me to arm wrestle," Dan said in response to Lucas's look. "But I'll live."

Lucas's affection for Dan was obvious. That was partly because Dan had been one of Lucas's high school teachers, but that wasn't all. Four years ago, when Lucas was a Teal County deputy, Dan, Mitch Griffith, and I handed him Gerald "Jink" Jarvis, along with Jink's taped confession. As a consequence, Lucas had the opportunity to be a primary player on a prosecution team that included the Georgia Bureau of Investigation, the Treasury Department, and the FBI. That hadn't hurt his career.

Lucas leaned back as far as he could in his chair, which wasn't very far, and moved his eyes to me. "We got your client cold."

"My client?"

"Well, your potential client. Like I said, he asked for you, and knowing you . . ."

"Why'd he ask for me?"

Lucas shrugged.

"What do you have?"

"Fingerprints, for one. We found a bunch of the Reeves' stuff, silver and so on, laid out in the garage. Looked like he was trying to steal the car, but couldn't get in it. His prints were all over everything. The match is perfect."

"You said something about a baseball bat on the phone."

"Yeah. We found it in his grandma's house, where he stays a lot. Looks like he tried to wash it off, but it appears bits of dried blood and other, uh, residue were on it. Fits the profile of the wounds. Ten to one the blood matches. It'll be going to the lab in Atlanta tomorrow."

Dan asked, "How'd you find him? Fingerprints on file?"

Lucas had to lean forward to see Dan, who was close to lying on the floor. "Nope. Happened like most cases do. Somebody phoned it in."

"Tip?" I asked.

"That's it. Truth is that's how we solve most of them. People just can't keep quiet."

"Who called?" Dan asked.

"Anonymous. But it wasn't hard getting his prints, and they matched. With that, a warrant was easy. The bat confirmed it."

"This going before Judge Evans?" I asked. He was the juvenile judge.

"Not this one." Lucas leaned forward on his elbows. "If he'd have done somebody in Rat Row he would be, but this is a biggie. District attorney's going for trying him as an adult. He'll get it, too."

I rose wearily from the chair and said, ". . . and equal justice for all."

Lucas shrugged. "Way it is."

"Shouldn't be," I said as I walked out the door.

Dan and I followed Lucas to a room that contained a carved-up wooden table with four chairs on each side, and a large mirror in one wall.

"This has to be private, Lucas."

"Normal lawyer rooms are filled right now. Usual Friday night crowd. I figured you'd trust me on this."

He was right. I did trust him. If it was anybody else, I would have waited. But this was Lucas.

"All right, but I'd like the light on in there anyway," I said, nodding toward the mirror.

Lucas looked at me.

"I have to do my job right. You don't want a mistrial on ineffective assistance of counsel."

"OK. The kid'll be here in a minute." He left the way we had come.

Dan and I sat on opposite sides of the table and said nothing. I watched the mirror, and it suddenly became a window as Lucas turned on the light and waved. Another minute passed before the door opened again and James Cleveland entered. Kevin Spurlock, one of two other detectives in the Patsboro Police Department, was behind him. The detective was dressed in plaid polyester pants that matched his loosened tie.

James stopped and Spurlock shoved him hard. "Get on in there, boy."

The teenager bowed his back and half-swung his right elbow reflexively. Spurlock jumped a step and brought his right forearm around James's chest, then moved his arm up into a choke hold.

Dan and I were both out of our chairs when Lucas appeared behind Spurlock. Lucas grabbed the detective's arm. "For God's sake, Kevin, let go of him." Lucas pulled on Spurlock's arm and it slipped above James's neck.

Detective Spurlock screamed.

Chapter 4

"The son of a bitch bit me!" Spurlock exclaimed. He held his arm midway between his elbow and wrist.

James stood shrunken in the corner next to the door, a look of terror in his eyes.

Lucas grabbed Spurlock, pushed his shoulders against the wall, and held him there. Lucas said slowly, "Kevin, you better start praying that boy has never had contact with admitted homosexuals, bisexuals, intravenous drug users, prostitutes or persons from Haiti, or, God help you, San Francisco."

The portly detective breathed hard as he stared up at Lucas.

Lucas nodded toward James. "This one's mine. Lay off him."

Spurlock pushed away Lucas's hands and stalked out the door, still holding his wound.

"I want charges brought against that jerk," I said.

Lucas was at the door. "Spurlock won't say anything unless you do, but he's got a wound. Chances are they'd side with him. Could make it worse for your client."

I knew he was right. "Keep him away from James."

"Do my best," Lucas said and left.

I looked at James, pulled out a chair to my left, and said, "Have a seat." The teenager edged toward the chair and sat.

He didn't look fifteen. He looked more like twelve. He was built like Essie Dillard: short, about five feet, and stocky. His ears protruded from his close-cropped hair. BEAR had been carved in the hair on the left side of his head. He had a silver stud earring in his left ear.

"Bear," Dan said in recognition. "If they'd have said Bear Cleveland, I would have remembered you."

James said nothing.

"I'm Dr. Bushnell. We met at the Alternative School."

James looked at him, then at me. "You Miss Randall?"

"Yes, James. I asked Dr. Bushnell to come with me. I thought he might be able to help."

James slowly gazed back at Dan. The teenager was scared. Some clients were belligerent, haughty. Some were despondent. A lot were drunk or stoned during the first interview. James was scared.

In a barely audible voice he said, "Yeah, I 'member the Doc. He all right."

I leaned forward and placed my elbows on the table. I said as sternly as I could, "You've been charged with a serious crime. Very serious. Do you know what they think you did?" Stern didn't come easily for me then. I think it'll be easier now.

"Yes, ma'am. They say I kill some people."

I leaned closer to him. "Now I'm going to ask you a very important question. If I am going to help you, you must tell me the truth. If you lie, I can't. It's as simple as that."

James just stared at me.

"Did you hurt those people? Dr. Reeves and his wife?"

James was sitting ramrod straight. Both hands were palms down on the table. "No," he said, trying to say it firmly, but I could detect a tremble underneath. "I did not."

I glanced at Dan. He was leaning back, slouching in his chair with his legs crossed. His wound must have been feeling better because his left elbow was on the arm of his chair and he was resting his chin on his thumb with two fingers supporting the side of his face. Dan's eyebrows arched slightly. "Your fingerprints were found on their things in the garage. Your bat may have been used to kill them." He moved his hand away from his face, palm up. His other hand went palm up, too.

James looked at his lap and mumbled something I couldn't understand.

"What?" Dan asked sharply.

"I was there. But I didn't kill no white folk."

"You scared, Bear?"

James nodded his head with two quick movements.

Dan leaned forward. "I don't blame you. Anybody would be. It's OK." He resumed his former position, lying almost all the way down in his chair.

That's why I wanted Dan with me. When I worked for him, I'd seen him deal with kids and he knew when to be hard and when to back off. I was still learning with kids. Actually, I was still learning with everybody.

"Why were you there?" I asked.

James kept his head down. "I was goin' home from Cardinal and this dude come up to me."

"Cardinal?"

"Park," Dan clarified.

"Oh yeah," I said. "Go on."

"This dude come up and say some jive. I jive back. He say do I want to make some scratch." James stopped and looked up at me.

"How?"

"Ma'am?"

"What'd he want you to do?"

James looked down again. "Say he gonna go in a house and take some stuff."

Dan said firmly, "Steal, Bear. You mean steal. Steal somebody else's stuff. Not take."

A barely perceptible smile crossed the teenager's face. "Yeah, I 'member, Doc. Say what you mean." The smile faded as quickly as it came.

I looked at Dan. He shrugged. "Force of habit."

"So what happened then?" I asked, trying to get James back on track.

James looked down again. "I say, 'No way, man,' but . . ."

"Go on, James."

"He say somethin' make me mad."

"What?" Dan asked.

James looked up at me. "He say, 'You ain't nothin' but a chickenshit nigger.' I say, 'I ain't chickenshit and no white man better call me a nigger.' "

"The guy was white?" I asked.

"Both of 'em was."

"Both of them?"

"Yeah. I say I go with 'em. We walk back to a car and get in. There's another white guy in the back. I could tell he white by the way he talk."

"You didn't see him?" Dan asked.

"Say not to look around. I did anyway, sort of. But it was dark."

"So you're in the car. What happened after that?" I asked.

I was getting impatient. That's something I've got to work on. Getting as many facts as possible is imperative during the first meeting. That's because clients charged with crimes tend to lie a bit. Actually, they tend to lie a lot. There's nothing I love more than being in the middle of a cross-examination, ready to score a major point, and then finding out the client lied to me. Getting as much information from them when they are the most vulnerable—and just having been put in jail makes most people vulnerable—allows me to make veracity checks later when they've forgotten their fear, like ten minutes after bond is posted. The clients I had represented during the first year of my career tended to have short memories.

"Man drive down a couple of streets and stop at this big house. He take my hat and tell me to wait. I say, 'Why, man? I ain't scared.' Man look in the car. He take a toothpick out of his mouth and poke me with it. He say, real mean, 'I said wait.' "

A chilling image from the recesses of my mind flashed momentarily. It was too quick to grasp. "So what'd you do?"

James looked at me like I was stupid. "I wait."

I nodded my head. "You see anything while you waited?"

"Nothin'. The guy come back and say to go with him. So I go."

"Which one?" Dan asked.

"First one."

"How long did you wait?" I asked.

James shrugged. He looked down again. His hands remained palms down on the table in front of him.

I said, "And . . ."

"We go inside. He tell me to take stuff out to the garage. I say, 'Where the garage, man?' He say the buildin' out back. So I start takin' stuff out there."

"What'd the other man do?" Dan asked.

James shrugged again. "Never seen him."

"You didn't see him at all?" I asked.

James shook his head.

Dan said, "So you took stuff out to the garage. How many times did you go out there, Bear?"

James looked up. "A bunch. Man say we gonna take . . ." He paused and looked at Dan. "Man say we gonna steal the car. One time he say, 'Wait in the garage,' so I do. I wait and wait. Nobody come so I get pissed and go back out. Nobody there. My bat layin' against the back door. I get scared, go get the bat, and get pissed again. It all wet." He looked down.

"And . . ." I said.

James said quietly, "I go home."

"And the police got you tonight," Dan said.

"Yeah." He looked at Dan. "I didn't do nothin'."

"Yes you did, Bear."

"I mean I didn't steal nothin'. And I didn't kill nobody. Never even see nobody."

"Why'd you ask for me?" I asked. "How'd you know my name?"

James shifted his eyes to me. "Policeman bring me a letter. It say you a lawyer. I know my rights. I say I want to talk to you."

I sat back. Why would somebody send him my name? Maybe somebody who knows I work for legal aid and figures he needs help. Makes sense.

Dan said, "What'd the man look like? I mean the one you saw."

James squeezed his eyes shut and moved his head up. "He tall, like you," he said, opening his eyes and indicating Dan. "Only he skinny."

"Hair?" Dan asked.

"Ain't got none hardly, but what he got be white."

"White?" I asked.

"You know, yellow."

"Blond," I said.

"Anything else?" Dan asked.

James shook his head, then said, "Oh yeah. His teeth be messed up."

"What do you mean?" I asked.

"All brown and stuff."

"Rotten?" Another momentary flash.

James nodded.

"Did he tell you his name?" Dan asked.

"No. But the man in back say his name."

"What'd he say?" I asked.

"Buddy."

My stomach flipped. It was the feeling you get when you hear things like that the space shuttle just blew up. The mental image that was evoked earlier returned, blurring my vision for a split second. I refocused on Dan.

Dan was looking at me. He looked back at James.

I shut my eyes.

Dan said, "The Evil One?"

Chapter 5

"Chances are, it's just coincidence. He'd be nuts to come back here," Lucas said. We were back in his office.

Dan, sitting on the floor now rather than squatting, said, "Bear didn't see the scar."

I said, "It was dark. James was scared."

Four years ago Dan was directing a federally funded program to reduce suspensions in Teal County schools. He had hired Mitch and me to be part-time secretaries for his program. He really only wanted an answering machine, but the funding guidelines wouldn't allow him to buy equipment and the federal program director for the schools had written a secretary's position into the budget. Finding it impossible to fight the waste, he decided to hire two Catledge University students who needed financial help. Mitch was a senior in business school and I was in my first year of law school.

The father of one of Dan's students had disappeared. The family lived in Elysian Fields, where it wasn't unusual for people to run off, but Dan wanted to try to find the father for the student's sake. Mitch and I helped and we ended up accidentally uncovering an elaborate smuggling scheme that was directed by Jink Jarvis. Buddy Crowe was one of the truck drivers and was the only person involved in the plot who had not been caught. Back then I dubbed him "the Evil One."

I heard Lucas saying, "The search for Crowe is continuing. We got word from Oregon a year ago that he may have been seen in a little town outside of Eugene. He's elusive, not identifiable. I just can't believe he'd come back here."

"I guess you're right," I said without conviction.

"Besides, I think Bear made it up. He had some time to think while he was waiting for you."

"Lots of Buddys in the world," Dan said.

I stood. "Yeah, you're right. It's just that the build and hair fit . . . along with the name. And the teeth and toothpick." I shook my head. "Anyway, Lucas, I want to see the crime scene. Tomorrow, if that's possible."

Lucas stood and squeezed around his desk. "No problem. How about one o'clock? I've got to go to the Calvary Baptist Church in the morning and interrogate some chicken thieves."

"Chicken thieves?" Dan asked. "At the church?"

"Well, receivers of stolen chicken, anyway. Seems the preacher, secretary, youth minister, choir director, and several other members have been buying boneless chicken breasts from a kid in the congregation. Buck a pound."

"That's cheap," I said.

Lucas was standing in his door now. "Too cheap. The kid's uncle works for a processing plant and was helping himself to the stuff now and then. Apparently been doing it for years."

"You going to arrest them? The church people, I mean."

"Nah. Just scare 'em. Need to think twice before buying stuff off the back of a truck."

"Love to be there for that," Dan said with a chuckle.

"It ought to be . . . amusing," Lucas said.

"Give them my card," I said.

"You look worn out," Dan said.

We were riding in the same taxi that had taken us to the station an hour earlier. That wasn't surprising, since it was one of only four in Patsboro. The sixties-vintage Pontiac appeared to have been cleaned last about the time the Vietnam War ended. I wanted to lay my head on the backseat, but didn't dare. Instead,

I looked at Dan. The passing streetlights reflected off the splotch of pure white that hung incongruously amid the rest of his deep black hair.

"I'm exhausted. I finished up a court case late this afternoon then went to a meeting of the Anti-Airport Coalition. I'd just gotten home when I get the call from Lucas. We have a wreck with a bunch of drunks, interview a murder suspect after he's attacked by a detective, and find out Buddy Crowe may be in town. Tends to wear one out."

"Like I said, no reason to think it was him."

I nodded. I didn't want to talk about it anymore.

Dan said, "Why's the coalition still meeting? The airport's a done deal."

Happy to be able to talk, and think, about something else, I said, "The coalition doesn't think so. They're gonna fight it until planes start landing, I guess."

Patsboro is located eighty miles northeast of Atlanta. The airlines had outgrown Hartsfield International, and the Atlanta Regional Commission had chosen Teal County as the site of a new airport. Athens and Gainesville residents had successfully kept their counties from being selected, but were delighted that an airport would be located in nearby Teal. They figured to reap the economic benefits without having to put up with noise and pollution.

Dan was looking out the cab's filthy window. "Sure is going to change things around here."

"No doubt about it. Farmers can't possibly recover money invested in chicken houses and pastureland. Eventually, somebody'll make a killing on that land, but not the farmers. Too much lag time between development and the rising property taxes. They're scared to death." We sat quietly for a moment. "Got one piece of good news tonight, though."

"What's that?" Dan asked through a yawn.

"New member of the coalition. Michael Hutcheson."

"Hutcheson? Of Hutcheson Mills?"

"That's the one."

"Seems like he'd want it. Be good for business."

I shrugged. "Maybe he figures his business is doing well enough. He was on the United Way campaign committee I worked with in January. We never really talked, but I was impressed with him. He was particularly interested in the Boys Club."

The truth was that I was more than just impressed with him, but that was too embarrassing to mention.

"Hutcheson might help, but I still think it's too late."

"You wouldn't think so to hear him talk. Mitch said he must be sniffing mushrooms."

"Mitch there too?" asked Dan.

"Yeah. Says he moved down here from Newark to get away from concrete."

The taxi was pulling up in front of my house. Dan said, "Let me know when you have your next meeting. I'd like to go."

I nodded. "Talk to you tomorrow." Before closing the door, I leaned in and said, "Thanks."

"No problem." He took my hand.

I looked down at my hand in his.

"Don't worry about it." He gave my hand a light squeeze. "Crowe's long gone."

For the second time that night I walked wearily up the steps to the veranda. Wishing I had left the porch lights on, I groped in my purse for the key. As I edged toward the door, my foot hit something and I heard a clunk. After opening the door, I switched on the lights and looked down. A glass vase containing a single red rose lay on its side. Water flowed from the vase onto the floor of the porch. I picked up the vase and looked at the attached card.

It was blank.

Chapter 6

The phone was ringing. I knew it was, but making my body move to answer it seemed impossible. One eye finally agreed to open and I glimpsed at the clock radio sitting next to my bed. The blurred red image indicated that it was 10:03. Next to it was another blurred red image. The rose. I sat up straight and reached for the phone. The male voice said, "I'm sorry. Sounds like I woke you up."

I tried to figure out whose voice it was as I covered my head with the plain white sheet that covered the bed. The plain white sheets that were still hanging on the floor-to-ceiling windows didn't block much light. My eyes hurt.

"Long night last night," I replied.

"I heard your name on the radio this morning. They said you were defending the kid who was arrested for the Bond Street murders."

The voice evoked an image. It was Michael Hutcheson. "Yeah. I was at the courthouse till two."

I pictured him from the meeting the night before. He'd been dressed in a charcoal pin-striped suit, white shirt with thin maroon stripes, and a diamond-patterned chestnut tie. Everything fit perfectly. His smooth face and perfectly combed full head of sandy hair made him look younger than he was. From what I knew of him, he was in his early forties. I was impressed with his eloquence in describing his passion to maintain the quality of life of Teal County despite his company's financial gain if an airport came.

"Sounds like it might be a challenge, from what they said." He hesitated and I didn't say anything. Why was he calling? "After last night's meeting I had some further thoughts on the airport. I was wondering if you might be free to have dinner tomorrow night so I can run them by you."

I cleared my throat . . . mostly to delay. It'd been a long time since I'd been out. At least with a man that I . . . Was I? Attracted to him?

Ten years ago I had decided that all men were mean, manipulative, oversexed, self-centered jerks—or drunks—and shut down that part of my life. But Dan had changed that. A little, anyway. At least he opened the possibility of there being a decent guy or two out there.

I was saved by the beep of the call-waiting signal. Feigning despair, I asked Michael to hold on. Lucas Anderson was on the other line.

"How'd it go with the Baptists?" I asked.

"Preacher has a new topic for his sermon tomorrow. Reap hot chickens and you sow some time downtown."

I chuckled and reached for the vase with the rose.

"Anyway, I need to postpone our visit to the Reeves place. Had a shooting at Sable's right after you left the station and I was fortunate enough to be drawn to investigate."

"Sable's? That's where the Dillards were last night."

"It's a popular place. Anyway, this looks like your typical shooting over there. Happens all the time, but we still need to look into it."

"Later this afternoon, then?" I sniffed the rose. It had no fragrance.

Lucas hesitated. "Can't. I have to be in Atlanta." He didn't elaborate.

"I want to see the scene before the prelim Monday. How about tomorrow?"

"Could try it about one again."

I agreed, said good-bye, and put the rose back on the night-stand. I clicked back to Michael.

During the conversation with Lucas, I'd had time to think. It didn't help. I didn't know what to think.

"Michael, I'm sorry. That was a detective about the Reeveses' murders."

"I know you're busy. I shouldn't have asked on such short notice."

He's not asking me out, I thought. It's just business. I know now that thought was my way of dealing with the grain of excitement that was forming in my guts, the feeling I remembered vaguely from high school, the sensation that was rekindled briefly four years ago.

"No, that'd be fine. What time?"

We made arrangements and disconnected, which was kind of how I felt inside. I wasn't sure about how I felt about Michael Hutcheson, but the disappointment about postponing the visit to the Reeveses' was definitely there. In school, I started on term papers the day they were assigned. That compulsion remains with me in my work.

But the crime scene wasn't going anywhere and I had plenty to do. First, I called Essie Dillard's insurance agent and told him about the accident. After that, I started on the old house.

I was here because soon after my former professor had purchased the home, with its labyrinth of rooms and hallways, he had accepted a visiting teaching position at Harvard Law School. Given the limited salary paid by the Legal Aid Society, I had jumped at the chance to house-sit while he was away.

Professor Gatlin and his wife hadn't had time to do anything to it before they left town. I wanted to make the place livable. I spent the day cleaning the kitchen. The kitchen and my bedroom were all I planned to use.

At the time, which seems so long ago, I thought that was all I needed.

Chapter 7

Sweat. The July humidity sucked it out like a sponge, leaving my white blouse transparent. Maybe nobody would notice.

Mitch emerged from his baby blue Mercedes. He was wearing a pearl gray vested suit of summer wool. The perfect tailoring made him look taller than his five feet six inches. Oversize horn-rim sunglasses sat in front of protruding eyes.

I pulled the clinging blouse away from my body.

"Kind of reminds me of the Cheetah III Lounge . . . in Atlanta. 'Course, I only been there once, a long, long time ago."

"Yuck," I said, and gave up on modesty, letting the sodden fabric fall back against me. "Did Dan call you?"

"Come by the sto' dis mo'ning. Say dere be dis picyniny yo' be defendin'. Say yo' might be needin' the services of a truly bona-fide *African American* what can relate to the chile in question."

Vintage Mitch. His imitations had been instrumental in nailing Jink Jarvis.

After Mitch graduated, he went to work as a salesman for an appliance store here in Patsboro. Six months later, none other than Austin P. Maugham came in to buy his daughter a minirefrigerator for her dorm room at Catledge University. After spending an hour with Mitch, Maugham found his car loaded with a television, a VCR, a stereo system, and no room for the refrigerator. Mitch delivered that himself.

Maugham had made his fortune mining kaolin near Macon. He had recently returned to his plantation after serving two terms as governor and knew a can't-miss business opportunity when he saw it. Two weeks after the shopping spree, Mitch received a visit from a Maugham man who offered to set up Mitch in his own store. Two years later Mitch bought out Maugham, and had two additional stores in Atlanta. The Mercedes was a long way from the New Jersey ghetto where he was raised.

"That'd be great, Mitch, if you have time."

He sat on the hood of my rented Geo, his feet resting on the bumper, his arms on his knees, and his fingers intertwined. In a deep resonance he said, "Everything under heaven has its time. A time to be born and a time to die, a time to plant and a time to uproot, and"—he took off his sunglasses and his protruding eyes opened wide—"always a time for you."

Dan's tan VW bus turned the corner. Dan pulled up and said, "Hi, guys." He stretched through the van's sliding door. Like my blouse sticking to me, his knit polo shirt stuck to his trim chest and stomach. He breathed in the humid heat and gazed at the hazy sky. "Hot enough for you?"

Mitch crossed his arms over his chest and said slowly, "It is a good day to die."

"Or be in a pool, whichever comes first," I added.

Dan looked toward the house in front of us. "Looks awfully peaceful for a crime scene."

I moved next to him. "True," I said while gazing at the white wooden house with four two-story columns fronting it. Like Madison to the south, Patsboro had been spared when Sherman marched to the sea. The story goes that he had a second cousin here. This neighborhood predated the Civil War. A sterling tea set was visible through the lace curtains in the window to the right of the double doors. Yellow tape with the legend CRIME SCENE—DO NOT ENTER was stretched across the doors.

"Remember that, Mitch. Money ain't everything," Dan said as Mitch moved next to us on the sidewalk.

"Got a point, but it sure do help while you're—" Mitch was

interrupted by Lucas Anderson, who appeared on the wrap-around veranda.

"Afternoon," Lucas said from the railing. "Y'all come on up." We stepped onto the porch. "Thought you ought to know, the lab confirmed the blood type that was on the bat. Matched the Reeveses'. DNA stuff'll probably confirm it's their blood."

I leaned against the railing. A lot of evidence. Too much evidence? Bear admitted he was there . . . the bat . . . blood and fingerprints.

I had defended some folks I knew were guilty, but it had been piddling stuff. I just made sure their rights under the law were protected. But murder?

"Let's look inside," I said.

Lucas pulled down the yellow tape and unlocked the door. Pent-up heat poured from the house. Dan, who was in front of me, stepped back. "First to faint loses," he quipped.

Mitch stepped in front of Dan and went inside. "Feels just like home."

Lucas followed Mitch, and I entered last. The stale air smelled like . . . death. I shuddered despite the heat.

Death was not a total stranger to me. My father died when I was a senior in high school. Various relatives of age went the natural way, and a couple of school friends did not survive the teenage Friday nights on rural south Georgia roads.

Daddy and the relatives had died in the hospital, where they should, and the closest I'd gotten to my friends' locus of leaving this life was a quick ride past Schneider's junk yard to gawk at the twisted piles of pin-striped metal that had been the foundation of their self-esteem.

I'd never been in a death house. As I walked through the pristine living room, I thought of the Tony Hillerman novel sitting on my nightstand. This is a death-hogan, I thought. I felt the presence of dissatisfied spirits wrapping themselves around my sodden clothing.

"Let's go out back, first," Lucas called from over his shoulder as he moved through a swinging door at the rear of the room.

We walked through a large kitchen equipped with the kind of stainless-steel appliances usually found in restaurants.

"Must have entertained a lot," Dan said while rubbing his finger across the shiny stove.

"Not no mo'," Mitch responded.

The house had been built before the days of attached garages. Lucas led us toward a white frame building with swinging double doors. Inside was a dark blue, almost black but not quite, Lincoln. It dominated the space designed originally for a four-passenger buggy.

"This is where Bear stayed," Dan said from where he had squeezed between the front of the car and the far wall.

Lucas stood just outside the open doors with his hands on his hips.

"You said he had stuff from the house ready to be put in the car," I reminded Lucas. "Where was it? Not much room in here."

"Most of it was lined up between the driver's side and the wall. Some was sitting out here in back."

"What'd he have here?" Mitch asked.

"Mostly silver. Don't know how he missed the tea set in the window up there, but he found everything else. Candlesticks, silver trays, utensils. All kinds of stuff. Had a painting, too."

Mitch grunted. I looked at him. He was shaking his head.

I moved to the driver's door. The metal was scratched and dented as though somebody had tried to pry it open. "You figure he tried to get in, but couldn't?"

"Yep."

Feeling the sharpened metal that was pulled away from the frame, I asked, "What do you think he used to do this?" I turned to Lucas.

He shrugged. "Maybe a crowbar."

"Where is it?"

Lucas shrugged again.

"Seems kind of dumb to me. Why didn't he just get the key from inside?"

"Hey, we're not talking about a mastermind who attempted the crime of the century. Bear ain't that bright."

"Everybody's ignorant, only on different subjects," Mitch said in a midwestern twang. We all looked at him.

"Will Rogers," Lucas said.

Mitch nodded. "Bear may not read real well, but from what Dan told me, he'd know enough not to try to do that." Mitch pointed at the dented door.

I left the garage and looked at the house. An asphalt parking area filled the entire space between the two buildings. I guessed that it was for guests when the Reeveses entertained. Not much chance of finding footprints, but I asked anyway. Lucas confirmed my suspicion.

We walked back to the house. "How'd he get in?" I asked. "Presumably."

"No sign of forced entry. Door must have been unlocked. The evening was still young."

I shook my head.

"It's not unusual. You could check any one of these houses at two in the morning and find a door unlocked . . . at least till this happened."

Dan agreed. "Gonna take Patsboro folks a while to get used to locking up. Hasn't been necessary."

"I know," I said, thinking of the chill I'd felt on that dark street the night before. "It just makes me sad that it's changing."

"You ready to go up?" Lucas asked while pointing to the second floor.

I wasn't. But I had to. We followed Lucas through the kitchen, the dining room, the living room, and up the surprisingly narrow carpeted staircase. A foyer at the top of the stairs held four doors. Lucas pointed out the doors to two bedrooms and a bathroom.

"This big ol' house only have two bedrooms?" Mitch asked.

"Three, actually," Lucas said. "This room, the murder room, was converted to a study. It's the largest room in the house." He opened the door and we went in.

The paneled room *was* large. The floor was covered by a maroon carpet that seemed to envelop me as I walked across it. A small fireplace with a mantel stood at the far end, fronted by a large, white oak desk. Matching bookshelves flanked the fireplace. Windows were to the right and left, providing both the front and the back of the house with a view. There, in front of me, tape marked the outlines of the Reeveses.

If the downstairs was oppressive, the atmosphere in this room was dense with death. I stood and stared at the markings on the floor. Their size amazed me. I remembered the Reeveses as large people. The diagrams looked Lilliputian. Dark stains were visible beside both markings. For some reason, I thought of my blouse, stuck to my body. I'd forgotten about its condition, but now I felt naked again. Not hot, naked.

I walked around the misshapen blots on the floor and moved to the bookshelves. One side was filled with books on genetics. That made sense. Reeves was a professor of genetics at Catledge. I moved to the other side. The top two shelves held hardback fiction, mostly classics. The bottom shelves contained reference books—encyclopedias, dictionaries, bird books, shell identifiers, that sort of thing. The third shelf surprised me.

It was at eye level and filled with tomes from the sixties. All focused on civil rights, everything from Martin Luther King to Malcolm X. And a set of videotapes—the complete set of "Eyes on the Prize." Unusual collection for a man from an old-time, white, Patsboro, Georgia, family. I turned toward the death marks and looked at the detective.

"How'd he manage it, Lucas?"

"Manage what?"

"Killing them. I mean Bear's a small fifteen and Reeves was a big man. How'd he manage to do it?"

"Coroner says they were sitting. We think he surprised them. Had the bat and told them to sit down. They did it, as much in surprise as anything else. Then he whacked them."

"He was an artist," Dan said from across the room. He was standing in front of a painting on the wall. "They're all signed *Reeves.*"

I hadn't noticed the artwork. Most were scenes of swamps. Sort of. Not swamps like the Okefenokee, something else. Dan answered my unspoken question about what kind of swamps they were. "Must have liked beaver ponds." He moved behind the desk to the fireplace. "Except for this one. Got into modern stuff."

I looked over the desk. Above the mantel was a multicolored piece with splotches of green, brown, blue, and a patch of absolute black in the middle. Random markings were scattered throughout. For some reason the picture seemed familiar. I decided that's what makes abstracts popular. Each viewer creates her own reality.

Lucas moved behind the desk next to Dan to look at the painting. I moved to a wing-backed chair and sat. Mitch sat in the matching chair next to me. He leaned over and said quietly, "Tidiest project kid I ever heard of—and the weirdest."

I mouthed, "What?"

"Too neat in here. Should've torn up the place looking for cash or pills. And stealing silver candlesticks? Look over there." I followed his gaze to a television with a Mitsubishi VCR on top. "That's what he'd take. Not candlesticks. How in the hell is he gonna get rid of candlesticks?"

Mitch was right, of course. The problem was, Bear possessed the murder weapon. Selling the jury on Bear not being stupid enough to steal dumb stuff would be tough. More than tough.

"Wanna see anything else?" Lucas was standing in front of me. I hadn't noticed him till he spoke.

Standing up, I said, "Guess not." I looked at Mitch and Dan. "What do you think?"

They both shook their heads. That was fine with me, I wanted to get out of there.

On the porch I asked Lucas, "Who inherits?"

"Wondered when you'd ask. They have two children—a son, twenty-one, and a daughter, twenty. Both had already been left plenty by grandparents. First thing we checked. Absolutely no motive for them, either financial or anything else."

" 'Plenty' is not enough for some people."

Lucas shook his head. "Believe me. There was no rancor among them. On that, I'm certain."

"And you're certain James did this?" I nodded toward the house.

"Jury decides that. All I do is collect evidence."

"Yes," I said. And I thought but did not say, It all points in one direction.

Chapter 8

After Lucas left, Mitch, Dan, and I stood under a pecan tree in the front yard. The light breeze was a relief as it cooled my dank clothes. I asked Mitch if Dan had told him Bear's story.

"Yeah. Two white guys did it."

"And ..."

"And one of them was named Buddy but didn't have a scar."

"Didn't remember seeing it," I clarified.

Mitch sat on a root at the base of the tree. "Coincidence. Why would Buddy Crowe come back here?"

"Right," Dan said. He was leaning with one hand on the tree. It was hard to keep standing under the weight of the atmosphere. "Crowe is from New Orleans. The only thing connecting him to here is Jarvis, and Jarvis is in the Atlanta federal pen."

I settled on my knees with my skirt spread around me. "Which leaves us ..."

Mitch finished the sentence. "Which leaves us with either, one: we have a coincidence; or two: Buddy Crowe's doing something for Jarvis."

"Or the other white guy," Dan added.

"Yeah. What about him?" I asked.

Dan let go of the tree and stood straight. "He's the key, if Bear's telling the truth—"

Mitch interrupted, "Bear didn't do that," nodding toward the house, "by himself. Like I told Tammi."

Dan nodded in agreement. "So *if* Buddy Crowe is in town and *if* Bear is telling the truth, then the other white guy *must* be connected to Jarvis too."

"I learned in law school to never say 'must.' Just 'may be.' "

"OK. *May* be connected to Jarvis. He still in Atlanta?"

"Last I heard," I said.

"Be interesting to see if he's had any visitors," Mitch pondered.

"We can do that. Go up there and see," I said.

"When?" Dan asked.

"How about Tuesday morning? I've got James Cleveland's prelim tomorrow and you never know how long that'll go."

"Leave about eleven? That'll get us there by two. Want to go, Mitch?"

"Can't. Got a new store opening in Augusta Tuesday. Got to be there."

"OK, Rockefeller. We'll report to you," Dan said.

"Better Rocky than Reverend Bakker," Mitch said as he headed for his Mercedes. "Yesss, my children, the Lord *will* provide. *You* provide for the reverend, and the *Lord* will provide for you." Mitch opened the car door and stood with both feet on the edge. He pounded the roof and said, "In the *promised* land, you will find a home *filled* with riches. The *riches* of *love* and *redemption.*" He bowed his head, sighed, and said softly, "But, till then . . ." He raised both arms and screamed, "Gimme! Gimme! Gimme!"

At home, I ripped off my sopping clothes and drew a cool bath. Michael Hutcheson was due in an hour. I lay with my head on the bath pillow and stared at the cracked ceiling twelve feet above. I hadn't yet shaken from my consciousness the image of the taped markings and bloodstained carpeting on the floor of Dr. Reeves's study. I lifted my arm and looked at the bluish veins coursing through my wrist, picturing in my mind life blood pouring out into the water. An immense sense of loneliness overwhelmed me.

Gary Reeves and his wife had been in their early forties. They had a son and a daughter. Their lives were over, but in those lives they had loved and been loved. Where would I be in ten years?

The only people I talked to much at all, other than the necessary interaction at work, were Dan, Dan's family, and Mitch. Somehow the fear and excitement of trying to figure out the Jarvis deal had broken down the barrier I held before me. With my father dead, my brother being long gone to Saudi Arabia, and my mother being, well, who my mother is, Dan and Mitch had become my family.

Other than the relationship Dan and I formed during that tense time, the only other male I'd become close to was Paul Starling. That ended when I was seventeen in the back of his Trans Am. My father had just died, and I was looking for something to hold on to.

Paul was the captain of the football team and I was the captain of the cheerleaders. He'd been trying to get me to go to bed with him for a year. Maybe being in a bed would have been better.

Mostly what I remember is pain. Rough hands grabbing my breasts and digging between my legs. My trying to move in the confines of the tiny backseat, thinking, Maybe if he had more room it wouldn't hurt so much. He either mistook my groans of pain for passion or didn't care. Once he did it, it was over in thirty seconds, thirty seconds that led to weeks of worry until my period started.

But the pain and anxiety didn't compare to the guilt that was rooted in Mama's Congregational Holiness injunctions.

After that I sublimated any desire to get involved with another man. I buried myself in schoolwork and the swim team at Georgia Southern, then law school here. It was Dan who opened me up to the possibility that all men weren't jerks. But he was married and . . .

Had to quit thinking about that.

And tonight I had a date, sort of. Michael wanted to talk about the airport. But who knows? He seemed nice and wasn't married. At least, not anymore. Of that I was sure. I had checked.

And I was twenty-seven and tired of being alone and of being so . . . abnormal.

I shut my eyes as the heavy hand of the Congregational Holiness pushed my head underwater.

Chapter 9

I sucked in air when I saw him. I pushed the door closed to the ersatz outhouse and leaned against it. The door bumped against me and I slammed it back. I thought of Michael waiting for me in the dining room.

Michael had chosen the Pine Lake Lodge for dinner. I'd heard about it, but had never been here. The complex was made up of log buildings scattered among spindly pines on the hilly terrain. We sat next to a picture window that afforded a view of a large wheel turning swiftly from the force of water falling from a trough above it. The water fell off the wheel and traveled down a winding stream to the lake that gave the lodge its name.

The buffet was filled with fried catfish and perch, barbecued pork, Brunswick stew, fried chicken, hush puppies, and french fries. Michael sat across from me, dressed in a peach Ralph Lauren Polo shirt and white pants with Docksides, no socks. I was in jeans with an emerald green T-shirt, and was wearing my entire collection of gold: a bracelet and hoop earrings. Without doubt, we were both overdressed. As we raised our cholesterol to intolerable levels, Michael talked about the airport.

"Communities south of Atlanta are still fighting for it," he said as he dipped a piece of catfish in the pile of tartar sauce on his plate. "We have to convince the governor of the need for economic development there."

"That argument's been made since the beginning," I said. "Both from the folks there and letters we've written."

"There's a new dimension now. The Olympics."

"Mmmm," I said in an effort to respond. I had to wash down a hush puppy with iced tea before I could continue. Finally, the cornmeal concoction was gone. "How does that make a difference?"

"The main venues are going to be in the center of the city. But several are going to be south or southeast. Shooting, for example. Better reviews will surface if the airport's convenient, and reviews are what Atlanta wanted the games for in the first place."

"But the airlines won't agree. They want the airport where the money is—to the north," I said while peeling a piece of perch off its bones. This was real fish.

"The airlines are only part of the equation. I'm going to talk to the governor myself."

"That'd be helpful if you can get to him."

"Oh, he'll see me. Hutcheson Mills contributions helped him get there," he said matter-of-factly. He wasn't bragging, just stating a fact.

"That's the kind of punch we haven't had. We've been able to see him on his 'little people' days, but it didn't make any difference."

"I should've become involved earlier. I'm afraid I was concentrating on other things till the final site selection was made. I was surprised at the announcement."

"It surprised everybody. I went to the meeting for the coalition when the announcement was made. Mainly just to go. We were fifth on the list. I was astounded when the guy said Teal County." I ate the last of my Brunswick stew. "I would think you'd want it. Be good for business."

"Oh, it'd help us. Help us grow, anyway. But there are more important things in life than getting bigger. That's what impressed me so much when I read about your group. In a way, the airport would help your clients more than any other. More jobs and all. But they'd rather have that," he said, nodding toward the lake out the window, "than a nicer car."

"That's another direction we're going in. The commission's meeting in a couple of weeks to explain how the airport will fit into the ecosystem. We think that will be hard for them to do. I hope you can come."

He nodded and we sat quietly for a moment. I broke the silence. "I shouldn't, but I think I'm going to get some more Brunswick stew. Reminds me of the Fourth of July in Maytown." To get back to the buffet, I had to walk through two other eating areas, each a level up from where we were sitting. I was standing in line, looking at the display of rusty implements, animal skins, and ancient advertisements that covered the walls from floor to ceiling, when I felt a tap on my shoulder. It was Peter Landry.

Landry was one of the two other attorneys at the Legal Aid Society, and, if the truth be told, I didn't like him much. Mitigating that, though, was his talent as a lawyer. His clients were well served by him. In court, anyway. The problem was he didn't really give a whit about them.

He was from California and had come to Georgia to get elected to public office. He said the field was too crowded in his home state. But it was obvious what he really thought was that southerners were naturally stupid. He kept saying, "If Jimmy Carter could get elected here, anybody can." I've never been sure what that said about the rest of the country.

He also said that the only thing missing to solidify his political position was a wife. Unfortunately, he had picked me. Being raised southern meant biting my tongue to keep from telling him that getting a personality should be his first priority. We're taught to be polite, no matter what the cost.

Of course, Landry's problem could be genetic. Before he arrived in town, his mother had written and asked if Patsboro had paved roads and electricity.

"Hi, Landry," I said without enthusiasm.

"Hey, babe. Pretty highfalutin company you're keeping."

He reached to my plate to grab a hush puppy and I popped his hand. "We're talking business. The airport."

"Losing proposition. But hey, I wouldn't mind talking about it if I'd known it'd get you out."

I didn't respond to that, but another thought occurred to me. I tested it by saying, "Thanks for the flower."

He looked startled. "No big deal." He added something curious: "All work and no play makes for a dull girl, Tammi."

I was going to ask what he meant when I saw Michael coming across the room.

Peter followed my eyes. "Here comes Sir Galahad. See you tomorrow," he said and left.

So that solved the mystery of the rose.

"Thought I'd get some more stew, too," Michael said when he arrived carrying his plate. He looked back at Landry. "Guess I shouldn't leave such an attractive young lady alone."

"That's just Landry. Peter Landry. He's at Legal Aid too."

"Mmm." He nodded. "Speaking of legal aid, it looks like I'll be reading about you for a while. Reeves case, I mean." We were at the buffet and I didn't respond while we dipped stew. On the way back to our table Michael said, "You think the kid's innocent."

"I think James Cleveland was there. I don't think he killed the Reeveses."

"Why not?"

We were at the table and sat. I reviewed the case for him, including the visit to the crime scene earlier that day. I didn't mention Buddy Crowe. I didn't want to appear paranoid.

As I talked, his total attention was focused on what I was saying. No "me too" stories or wandering eyes. I liked that.

"So a principal point, you think, is the two white guys. You say he saw one but not the other?"

"Right. We're going to have him look at some mug shots tomorrow. See if he can recognize the one he saw."

"Think he will?"

I shrugged. "Hard to say. One guy in particular we're interested in."

"Who's that?"

"Guy with a history of that kind of violence." I still didn't want to get into Buddy Crowe. I pushed away my plate and said, *"No mas. No mas.* That's enough."

"Don't want any cobbler?"

"Of course, I do. But there's no way it'd fit." *Fatty, Fatty* echoed in my mind. I sighed. "I need to find the ladies' room."

"It's out back," he said, nodding toward a door across the room that led to a wooden deck. "A covered walkway leads to the outhouse, so to speak."

My watch said it was 8:25, but the late summer sun was out of sight behind the hills and trees as I walked through a door with a half-moon painted on it.

When I opened the door a few minutes later, I saw him.

Chapter 10

The walkway had dim, bare bulbs spaced twenty feet apart. He was leaning on the wooden railing in the shadows between the bulbs. His arms were crossed and he was wearing boots, jeans, and a white T-shirt. A toothpick was in his mouth. I stepped back into the ladies' room, shut the door, and leaned against it.

Was it him? I visualized the first time I had seen Buddy Crowe. He had been leaning on the cab of a purple tractor trailer. It was January and a bitter wind was blowing. He was wearing boots, jeans, and a light windbreaker with the sleeves pushed up. A toothpick bobbed in his mouth as he stared at Dan and me. His blond hair had been long then, and tied in a ponytail.

I made myself slow down my breathing. I was facing the mirror over the sink across the room. When I focused on my reflection, I whispered, "You're crazy, Tammi. Buddy Crowe's not here. Bear's guy happened to be a Buddy. Like Dan said, 'Lots of Buddys in the world.'"

The night we got Jink Jarvis, Jarvis and Rambo Williams had taken me from my apartment. On the way to the meeting with Dan, Rambo had said, "Man, Buddy'd like to get some of that," as he looked at me in the backseat. Through a laugh, he had added, "And Buddy generally gets what he wants." He was saying, "You know what Buddy said about her . . ." when Jink cut him off.

The door bumped against my back. I made a noise, turned, and lunged against it. The door was being pushed. I yelled, "No! Go away!"

A woman said loudly, "Look, I gotta get in there. Now! Open the goddamn door!"

Still leaning against the door, I stretched my neck back and forth. "Jesus," I said to myself and moved away.

The door flew open and two very large women burst in. Each wore stretch knit pants and identical T-shirts that said KISS MY BUTTONS. A button was sewed on each breast and the backs of both T-shirts were imprinted with large, red lips. The women looked like twins, except one was wearing glasses.

The one without glasses said, "Goddamn, lady, I'm gonna piss all over myself. What's wrong with you?"

"Sorry," I mumbled and stepped out the door. He was gone. Out of sight, anyway. I didn't want to go up the walkway by myself.

I stood next to the bathroom door until it started to open, but it was slapped shut. Through the door, I heard one of the women say, "Where'd you find these fuckin' dickheads anyways?"

"You callin' Jamie a dickhead?"

"Yeah, I'm callin' him a dickhead. What you gonna do about it?"

"You call him a dickhead again and I'm gonna whup your ass."

When the door opened, the one with glasses was saying, "Dickhead, dickhead, dickhead. Jamie's a goddamn dickhead."

I followed them down the walk. Even Buddy Crowe would think twice about messing with these women.

When I arrived at our table, Michael said, "Is something wrong? I was getting worried."

I picked up my purse. "I'm fine. Do you mind if we leave now?" Without waiting for a reply, I headed toward the front.

At the entrance Michael said, "Wait a minute, Tammi. I've

got to pay." On the way to the parking lot, he said, "Are you sure you're OK?"

I stopped, looked at him, and took another deep breath. "I'm fine. Just felt kind of ill. I'm all right now."

His face held a concerned expression.

"Really. There's no problem," I said.

He looked at his watch. "How about a walk around the lake?"

I turned toward the lake. The open space allowed the remaining sunlight to illuminate the area. Other couples were walking or sitting on benches. Besides, Michael would be with me.

And a bigger "besides" was that I felt stupid. That was *not* Buddy Crowe, I thought.

We walked along a path of pine bark that led to the lake. The sun created a pleasant twilight. Lightning bugs flickered at the lake's edge. Swimming ducks made a quiet clucking sound as they paddled in search of their evening meal.

We approached a small boardwalk that extended fifty feet into the lake. Michael turned on it and we moved to the end and sat on a bench. He leaned against the railing and breathed deeply. "This is nice."

"It is beautiful," I said, watching the water ripple and feeling a soft breeze coming across the lake. The oppressive heat seemed to be diminished by the water.

We talked about our past, surface stuff. The conversation was light and pleasant until I asked him about his family.

He extended his legs, crossed them, and slid down the railing. "My father . . ." He hesitated, then shook his head. "He died a couple of years ago." He stared straight ahead again.

"You miss him?"

"He was a son of a bitch."

I wasn't sure how to respond, so I said, "Oh."

He sighed. "I try not to think about him." After a pause, he continued, "Lots of things I've tried not to think about. At least, until recently. It's easy to go through life without thinking. Money, possessions, reputation . . . and friends. Especially friends." He put both hands in his pockets and slid farther down the bench.

I had no idea what he was talking about, so I said nothing.

He said, more to himself than to me, "I guess you get to a certain age, you got to start thinking."

I rested an elbow on the railing and pulled one leg under me. "If you don't mind my asking, how old are you?"

"Forty-two. Last December. How about you?"

"I'm in my twenty-eighth year," I said, and immediately regretted it. That was true, but in the terms we all understand, I was twenty-seven. Why did I want to seem older? Of course, I knew. I just didn't want to admit it.

"Hmm. You seem older than that."

I laughed. "I think I'm supposed to resent that."

He sat straight. "Oh, I didn't mean how you look. My God, you look great. I meant the way you act. You've got a seriousness tempered with a knowledge of the real world that's unusual for a twenty-eight-year-old." His funk seemed to be over.

"Twenty-seven." Might as well get it over with.

"I thought you said . . ."

"I said I was in my twenty-eighth year. I turned twenty-seven on my last birthday."

"Oh. That's even more remarkable."

"Nothing remarkable," I said. "I got in touch with the real world pretty early. Dealing with my dad . . . he drank. And my mother worked. I took care of my brother. It didn't leave a lot of playtime."

Michael nodded. "I always wanted a brother or a sister."

I threw a leaf in the water. "My brother left when he was eighteen. Got a job with Aramco in Saudi Arabia." The leaf was floating slowly away. "I suspect he chose a place to live where a three-minute phone call would cost my mother dearly."

Michael looked at me.

"Oh, it's not that Mama's so bad, she just has a way of driving you crazy."

"Know what you mean." The sun was well down and the stars were filling the sky. Michael looked at his watch. "I guess I'd better be getting you home."

"Yeah, I guess so." As we walked along the path our hands brushed.

Michael looked down and took my hand in his. "Do you mind?"

I shook my head. He intertwined his fingers in mine.

We talked about the airport again in his Porsche on the way to my house. With the top down, the breeze felt wonderful. I pulled the pins from my hair so the wind could blow through it, like in the commercials. It seemed sort of stupid, though. I could hardly see anything with my hair in my eyes all the time. It was absolutely dark when we arrived, and he walked me to my door.

We stood awkwardly for a moment. "Listen, do you enjoy the symphony?"

"I suppose so. I like the recordings anyway. I've never actually attended a concert."

"The Atlanta Symphony's going to be at the civic center in Athens Friday night. Would you like to go?"

I stared toward the street. A little proper hesitation, I thought. But not too long.

"Sure," I said. We set a time and he left.

I went inside, unsnapped my jeans, and headed to the kitchen for some Pepto-Bismol to counteract the mixture of barbecue and fish that was rolling in my stomach. After downing a swig, I took the bottle with me to my bedroom.

I threw my clothes on the bed and immediately did what I always do after overeating—I stood before the mirror to see how fat I'd gotten. I was determining whether I could pinch an inch on my protruding stomach when I noticed the smell.

The odor was slight, but it was sickening all the same. I put on my nightgown and walked around sniffing, but couldn't find its source. I gave up, opened a window, took another dollop of the pink medicine, and lay down with my Hillerman novel. After a few minutes, I put down the book.

What *is* that horrid smell? I wondered.

Chapter 11

Lilly McClain had a beautiful start. She'd stand on the block waiting for the gun to sound, just like all the other swimmers. But somehow her inner clock beat the others just enough to get that hundredth-of-a-second head start she needed to beat them all. She tried to explain it to me when we raced in the community pool in Maytown and again during our practices at Georgia Southern, but she couldn't. It was something she had within herself that couldn't be shared, a quirk of timing. It was also a quirk of timing that put her in a wheelchair.

Lilly wouldn't talk about it, but her mother did. The family was at its retreat on Lake Lanier. They had run out of coffee, and Lilly decided to take the boat to the marina to get some. Just as she got to the dock, her mother called to her from the kitchen window. She reminded Lilly to get Chock Full o' Nuts. The marina store had just started stocking it, and it was the family's favorite. Ten, maybe fifteen seconds went by.

As Lilly rounded the pier that led to the marina, a twelve-year-old boy who had sneaked his daddy's boat from its mooring plowed into her.

Ten, maybe fifteen seconds. A quirk of timing.

This Monday morning it was my turn for a quirk of timing.

* * *

It was eight o'clock when I walked into the reception area of the Teal County Legal Aid Society. Mrs. Thompson was sitting at her desk reading her morning devotional. Her thinly drawn face was bent down and her black-rimmed cat's-eye glasses drooped near the end of her nose. She kept her age a secret, but the stories she told indicated she had to be at least seventy. Her first name was Alva, but none of us ever called her by her first name.

Mrs. Thompson was our secretary. She had been a fixture in the mayor's office for years, but shortly after I arrived, the mayor bartered continued funding for the society in exchange for our taking Mrs. Thompson. I'd wondered about that until it became apparent that she couldn't type and was unable to figure out how to use the telephone.

"Good morning, Mrs. Thompson," I said.

"Morning," she sang back, lifting her eyes. They were full of merriment. "I guess you heard the news."

"What news?"

"Preacher Rothchild and the whole bunch of newcomers at Calvary Baptist were caught with stolen chicken. I knew he was bad news first time he preached. It was on the civil rights bill Congress passed. He said it was a good thing. I knew then he was going to be a bad one."

"You mean the bill that was vetoed last year?"

"No. The one when President Johnson was in office. Never heard of a Baptist preacher called Rothchild anyway," she said happily.

I went to the conference room, poured a cup of coffee, and moved into my office. I stopped and stared at a vase with a wilted red carnation sitting in the middle of my desk. Placing my briefcase and purse on the floor, I picked up the card and read it. *To the future first lady.*

"Landry," I heard from behind me. I turned in time to see Mrs. Thompson's upper right lip curl back in response to her saying the name. Like me, she did not like Peter Landry.

I moved the flower to the top of the file cabinet behind the desk. "A rose, and now this."

"What rose?"

"Oh, nothing." I didn't want to get into it with her. I thought I heard a "harrumph" as she left.

The first order of business was to call Essie Dillard's insurance agent again. As I reached for the telephone the outer office door slammed, followed by a booming "Good morning, Mrs. Thompson."

"Morning, Bernard. 'Spose you heard about Preacher Rothchild."

"Indeed, Mrs. Thompson. I know you'll be pleased to learn only the thief is being charged. Preacher and his people are being set free."

I smiled at the thought of the frown that must have set on Mrs. Thompson's face. All her good news was blown away in that one sentence.

I went to greet our senior member at Legal Aid, Bernard Fuchs. He was semiretired from a lucrative Atlanta practice and had come to Patsboro two years ago to raise horses. To have him in a legal aid society, even part time, was nothing short of a miracle.

I entered the reception area as he was putting his Stetson on the coat rack in the corner. He was dressed in a tan, western-cut coat with a string tie that featured a large turquoise stone on the clasp. On his feet were what he called his court boots: dark green alligator that came to a sharp point. Bernard is a true humanitarian, but those warm and fuzzy feelings don't extend to all animals. He is an avid hunter and fisherman, and had caught the alligator himself.

"Bernard, I need to talk to you when you have a moment," I said.

"And good morning to you, Tammi," he replied with a bow.

"Sorry. There's a lot going on. When you can."

"No need to apologize. I was once young and full of vim and vinegar, sweetheart. No time for niceties. Remember those days, Mrs. Thompson?"

Mrs. Thompson raised her head from her devotional with her thin lips pressed together. "Young people these days don't know the first thing about niceties."

"Now, now. We do tend to forget how it was to be young, you know." He looked at me and held up his leather briefcase. "Let me put this away."

"Thanks," I said and retreated to my office. From my purse I retrieved the name of Essie Dillard's insurance agent and called his number.

"Eric Fain Insurance," I heard on the other end.

"Mr. Fain, please."

"Speaking."

"This is Tammi Randall. I talked to you Saturday about Essie Dillard running into me."

"Yes, Miss Randall. I'm afraid we have a problem."

Here it comes, I thought. I had noticed his ad in the Sunday paper that said *We Insure Anybody*. Bad sign.

"What's that?"

"Well, it seems the Dillards claim the car was stolen. If that's true, we, of course, wouldn't be responsible for damage incurred."

"*Stolen?*" I said in a raised voice. "What do you mean, *stolen?*"

"Just that, Miss Randall. Essie Dillard says the car was stolen."

I was incredulous. "With *her* in it?"

"We need to investigate. Until then, I'm afraid nothing can be done."

I sat back and took a deep breath. Bernard stuck his head in my door and I nodded toward the seat in front of the desk.

"Listen, I've got to have a car. Your company is contractually obligated to the Dillards and I am entitled to a rental for loss of use. I rented a car this weekend and will expect you to pay for it as well as the damages."

"Again, as I said, we must investigate their claim. How can I get in touch with you if we need to?"

I gave him my home and work numbers. "That's the Teal County Legal Aid Society," I added with some pleasure.

"Legal aid? What is your position there?"

"Attorney, Mr. Fain."

"Oh," he said.

"I assume I'll be hearing from you soon."

"As soon as possible, Miss Randall."

When I hung up, Bernard crossed his legs with one boot resting on the opposite knee and his jowly chin resting on his chest. He arched his eyebrows.

"Got run into Friday night. Insurance company's fooling around."

"What company is involved?"

"Cotton Land Consortium. Eric Fain Insurance handles it."

"I have never heard of it."

"Car's owned by one of the Dillards of Nitaville."

Bernard nodded. "Enough said."

"Essie Dillard says the car was stolen. The fact that she was in the car at the time sort of makes me doubt that. Agent Fain says the company may not be responsible."

"Indeed. Who was driving?"

I shrugged. "Took off after the accident. I didn't see him. Doesn't really matter, though. The insurance follows the car, not the driver." I didn't tell him about the driver being white. It didn't seem important at the time.

Bernard nodded again while pursing his lips. I knew what he was thinking. Better get on the stick or the company will drag the thing out forever.

"There were two other passengers. One of them was out of it—asleep in the back. But the guy in front would be good to talk to. Think I will."

"That might be of some use," Bernard said doubtfully.

I had rocked my desk chair back when the phone chirped from the reception room. Bernard leaped from his chair and I lunged forward. Over the phone, our hands collided with a fury that caused us both to wince. It was too late. The chirping stopped.

Miss Thompson shouted, "Call on line one, Miss Randall!" I looked at the instrument and found no lights flashing.

"I'll get it," I said to Bernard, who sat back in his chair. I sat with my hands poised on the phone. At the first sound of a chirp, I picked it up.

"Legal Aid Society, Tammi Randall speaking."

There was no response, but someone was on the line.

"Helloooo," I said.

I heard a cough and a throat clear. A female voice drawled, "Miss Randall, I would like to talk to you."

"I'd be happy to, ma'am."

"Uh, not on the phone."

"Would you like to make an appointment?"

"Yes. I, uh, am tied up today, though."

"How about tomorrow?"

"Yes. Tomorrow would be much better." There was relief in her voice.

"What time tomorrow would be convenient, Mrs. . . ."

"Hildegarde. Minerva Hildegarde. Would ten o'clock be satisfactory?"

"Should be fine. Could you tell me what you wish to talk about?"

"It's about . . . James Cleveland. The paper said you were representing him. I, uh, might have something that would be of interest to you. I don't know for sure. It just might."

"Mrs. Hildegarde, I'd be very interested in anything you might have to say." And I was. Her accent was dignified and sounded old South. I couldn't imagine that she'd have much in common with Bear Cleveland.

"I'll be there at ten," she replied and hung up.

"Busy day, already," Bernard said.

"Yeah. And it's going to get busier. Did you hear the news about the Bond Street murders?"

"Arrested a juvenile, I understand," he said as he shifted his legs. "You were called."

"We were on the way to the police station when my poor Yugo got creamed,"

"We?"

"Dan Bushnell was with me."

"Ah." I had told Bernard about Jarvis. He had met Dan a couple of times.

"Anyway, the boy, James Cleveland's his name, asked for me to be his attorney."

"Why you? Had you worked with him before?"

"No. He says somebody gave him my name. He insists he didn't do it. Says he was there and has a story about two white men who enticed him to the scene."

"You believe him?"

I shrugged. "Dan thinks he's telling the truth. That's why I brought Dan with me—his experience with kids. Anyway, the first appearance is this morning at ten o'clock . . . before Judge Turner. I'd like to get him in juvenile court first, but Judge Evans is out of town till tomorrow. I checked Saturday morning."

Bernard slid farther down in his chair, resting his neck on the back of the chair. "Georgia Code Annotated, section 24A-2501, is the reference." He recited from memory, " 'If a child from thirteen years of age until his seventeenth birthday is charged with committing a capital felony, superior and juvenile court have concurrent jurisdiction. However, whichever court first takes jurisdiction retains the jurisdiction.' " He looked at me. "And, it's a whole lot easier to get the kid moved from Juvenile than the other way around."

"I guess I ought to petition to go to Juvenile anyway," I said with a sigh, knowing what was coming.

"That ought to delay the process about ten minutes. Superior court hears the petition. Superior judge wants the case. Superior judge gets the case. Then, of course, there is the evidence."

"There's that."

"Was the paper correct? They have fingerprints and the murder weapon?"

"Appears to be the case."

"I would forget Juvenile. It will never happen," Bernard said as he rose. He added, "And, Tammi, you must realize that you face obstacles in this case. Your client is a perfect suspect."

"Yes." I told Bernard about the incident with Detective Spurlock, ending with, ". . . and James bit him."

"Grand."

"Have you met Spurlock?"

Bernard stroked his chin. "We have met." He paused. "My

supposition is Detective Spurlock . . . enjoys the authority appended to his position."

"I adhere to the same supposition."

Bernard put his hands behind his back. "However, I have observed him behaving in a judicious and fair manner from time to time. All of us, I believe, do have our moments." He turned to find Peter Landry standing at my door. "Good morning, Peter. And what news from the polls do we have this Monday morning?"

"Looking good, looking good," Landry said as the two negotiated the doorway. After Bernard had left the office, Landry looked at me. "Have a big time last night?"

"Oh, yeah. After we worked out how to stop the airport, I took Michael to my house and gave him the full treatment—whips and Jell-O. It was great."

Peter closed his eyes, sucked in his breath, and said, "Ooooooh."

"What do you want, Landry?" I don't normally call people by their last names, not without a title in front. I think I did it with him in order to keep some distance between us.

"Just saying good morning, darling." He glanced at the flower.

"Thanks for the flower. Anything else?"

"You're a hard one, babe. What's it going to take to turn you around?"

"You can start by cutting out the 'babe' stuff."

He sighed deeply, for effect, I suspect, and turned to leave.

"Wait a minute," I said.

He stopped and faced me.

"Last night you made some comment about all work and no play. What'd you mean?"

He looked puzzled.

"When I thanked you for the flower."

"Oh . . . that. Figured if you saw it, you were in here over the weekend. Left it late Friday afternoon."

"Then the rose . . . ?"

"Rose?"

"At my house."

"Not me. Gonna have to be a little more forthcoming, ba— uh, Tammi, to get roses. Why?"

"Oh, it's nothing."

"Miss Randall, you have a visitor!" Mrs. Thompson yelled from the reception room. "He has been waiting for *some* time."

Peter winced. "Such elegance," he whispered and turned again to leave. He was scared to death of Mrs. Thompson. Figured she could cost him half the county's votes. He didn't know it was already a lost cause.

Michael Hutcheson walked in the door.

"Hi," I said in surprise.

"I was in the area and wanted to let you know I have an appointment with the governor for later in the week."

"That was quick."

"He's an early riser. When I told him what I wanted to talk about, he wasn't too excited. But he did agree to see me."

"Well, you never know. Worth a shot, anyway."

"Yeah." He stood silently for a moment. "Anyway, just thought I'd mention it. I know you're busy. I'll let you get back to work. See you Friday at six-thirty?"

"I'll be ready." He turned to leave and I added, "Thanks, Michael. For your efforts, I mean."

"Glad to," he said and left. He seemed distracted.

Mrs. Thompson was in the doorway as Michael shut the outer door. "That Michael Hutcheson, he's a good boy. I've known him since he was born. You could do a lot worse than him."

"We're just trying to stop the airport, Mrs. Thompson," I said while straightening the papers on my desk.

"Time moves on, Miss Randall," she said with a sigh and left.

For once, Mrs. Thompson was right.

Chapter 12

Bernard Fuchs was usually right, but he was wrong about my petition to move James Cleveland's case out of superior court to Juvenile. It didn't take ten minutes to be turned down. It took ten seconds. In fact, the whole arraignment took ten minutes. Detective Lucas Anderson testified about the bat and that was it. The case would stay in Superior and the boy would be tried as an adult. Bond was set at a hundred thousand. James would stay in jail.

I caught Lucas in the lobby and asked a favor. I wanted James Cleveland to look at some pictures. Mug shots. I wanted Buddy Crowe's to be among those pictures.

Lucas agreed to do it that afternoon. I asked another favor. I wanted the name of the front-seat passenger in Essie Dillard's car. He said he'd call me as soon as he got back to the station, which he did. The passenger's name was Willie Moon. He lived in the Ivy Street Projects, building J, apartment 4. I called Dan and asked him if he could be at the police station at two, and asked him to call Mitch. I drove the rented Geo to Ivy Street.

It wasn't easy finding J-4. The Ivy Street Projects were fairly new and built away from the city in an effort to integrate the residents into a more pastoral setting than the inner city. It didn't work. The effects of poverty and hopelessness don't stop at the city limits. Ivy Street was no different from any other public housing project. The street signs were obliterated. The letters identifying buildings and numbers over apartment doors were gone. That made it more difficult for repossessors, policemen, and school officials to find the people they were looking for.

Two-story buildings were scattered throughout the gridded streets. They were bricked halfway and topped with Masonite siding. Some residents obviously paid their bills and remained within the law, because they had spray-painted their addresses on the bricks. I wandered around using those occasional clues and my knowledge of the alphabet until I came to what I assumed was building J. It appeared that the apartments were numbered from left to right, so I weaved around bikes, wagons, and about ten preschool-aged kids to reach the screen door to the far right, and knocked.

Someone hollered, "Come on in." I entered a living room that held a sofa and a recliner. A small kitchen was on the left and stairs lined the left wall behind the kitchen. Three large black women were sitting on the sofa and another, even larger, black woman was leaning back in the recliner. A fan was rotating in the corner. Across the room, under the stairs, Oprah Winfrey was on a nineteen-inch television set. The room was stifling.

"Hello," I said and was greeted with silence.

Four pudgy, black faces stared at me.

"My name is Tammi Randall and I'm looking for Willie Moon. Is he here?"

No response.

"I just need to talk to him."

"Willie ain't here." It came from the woman in the recliner.

"You know where I can find him?"

No reply.

"Listen, I work with the Legal Aid Society, but that's not why I'm here. Willie was in a car that ran into me Friday night. I just want to ask him some questions. He's not in trouble or anything."

"You work with Legal Aid?" the same woman asked.

"Yes. I'm an attorney."

She reached to her right, pulled a lever that lowered the footrest of the recliner, and put her massive arms on the recliner's armrests. "Willie!" she shouted, "Get down here. Now!"

The sound of a door opening came from upstairs. Willie appeared at the top of the stairs.

"Come on down," the woman ordered.

Willie descended and stood at the foot of the stairs. He appeared to be in his early twenties and was thin with short-cropped hair. He was wearing shorts and a sleeveless, mesh T-shirt. The whites of his eyes were splotched with red lines.

The woman waved her hand toward the sofa. "Sit down, honey. Willie'll talk to you."

The three women on the sofa got up and moved to chairs surrounding a small table in the kitchen area. I sat on the sofa. Willie ambled over and sat between me and the woman I assumed was his mother.

The woman said sternly, "Willie, you in some kind of accident Friday night?"

"Yes 'um."

I said, "Willie, my name is Tammi Randall. I was driving the other car. I just want to ask you some questions."

"And you answer 'em," his mother ordered.

"Yes 'um," Willie replied, nodding.

"I need to know a couple of things. First of all—"

"We hads the light."

"The light?" I said in puzzlement. "What do you mean, you had the light?"

"The light be green." He was looking at the floor.

"Where'd this happen?" his mother asked.

I looked at her. "On the Monroe Highway, ma'am. Right where they're working on the bypass."

"Willie! Fool Willie! They ain't no light there! Now you best be tellin' the truth. You hear me?"

"Yes 'um."

"You ain't too old for me to take the strap to you."

"Yes 'um."

"Willie," I said, "Essie Dillard's claiming the car was stolen. She was in the car, between you and the guy driving it. That means if the car was stolen, she had to be kidnapped. And you're looking at some kind of trouble if she keeps saying stuff like that. You understand that?"

He moved his eyes to mine. "Car never got stole. Essie 'uz too drunk to drive. Man say he 'ud drive us to the Krystal. He be crazy, too. Pull over and just sits. We keep sayin' 'Move on, man,' but he just sits. All'a sudden he say, 'Goddammit we going...' "

His mother reached out and whopped him across the head with her meaty hands. "You watch your mouth, boy."

Willie rubbed his head. "I just sayin' what the man say."

"Don't have to say everything he say."

"Yes 'um. Well, he say ... that ... then he take off. I scream 'look out' when I sees you, but it be too late. He run right into you."

"Tell me about the driver. The white man."

"White man?" his mother asked.

"Yes 'um. He be a white man. He be over at Sable's."

"Double fool, Willie! What you doin' ridin' 'round with a white man?"

"I don't know," Willie whined.

"What'd he look like?" I asked.

Willie shrugged. "Like a white man. Tall, skinny. Didn't have no hair. Not much anyways. It be blond."

"Blond?"

"Yeah."

His mother whacked him across his head again.

"Yes 'um," he said quickly.

"And his name was Bobby?" I asked.

"No 'm. Wasn't no Bobby. That's what Essie kept callin' him."

"What was it?"

"Say his name was Buddy."

That feeling again. Stomach emptying up my throat.

Buddy. Buddy! Sitting there waiting. Waiting! Suddenly takes off. Runs right into me. Driver's side.

What had Officer McDaniel said? *You were mighty lucky,*

ma'am. Barely avoided a direct hit on your door and that big old car would've creamed you.

I looked up to see Willie's mother staring at me. I looked at Willie. "I need one other thing. I need you to be at the Patsboro Police Station this afternoon at two. I want you to look at some pictures."

"He'll be there," his mother said and put her hand on my shoulder.

I believed her.

Chapter 13

"This guy didn't get born," Mitch said as he leaned over the carved-up table in what served as a conference room in the Patsboro Police Station. "Must'a been laid in a packet." He was staring at Buddy Crowe's picture.

I looked at him questioningly.

"Roaches lay packets," Dan explained. He was sitting across the table. Or I should say reclining. Dan never really sat in a chair. He sort of lay in it.

"The exterminators must have missed him," Mitch said. "Somebody should've sued."

I shivered. Visualizing Buddy Crowe crawling from a bag of garbage didn't require Franz Kafka's narration. He just emanated . . . filth. No. More than filth. Ooze. Buddy Crowe oozed.

A few minutes before, I'd asked Lucas, "Is that the best shot you got?"

"Crowe's never been arrested. We don't have any real mug shots. Got this from his mother in New Orleans. Had to blow up the face to make it look like the others."

Lucas picked up Crowe's picture and put it in a plastic sleeve in a thick book that was a family album of crime. Or suspected crime. I had to keep remembering that. A good many of these people had never been convicted. But I had no doubt that Buddy Crowe was guilty of accessory to kidnapping. I was the victim.

He was, I knew, also guilty of smuggling and at least accessory to murder, if not murder itself.

Why would he come back to Patsboro? Surely he wouldn't. Surely another Buddy just happened to intersect with my life a couple of times in the last few days.

Surely there is a Santa Claus.

The dizziness started again but I stopped it. "Let's get James in here and have him look."

Lucas walked around the table and knocked twice on the door across the room. It opened and James Cleveland, dressed in a white shirt and white pants with a black stripe down them, came into the room.

"Hey, Bear," Dan said.

James nodded and stood with his wrists together as though he were cuffed. He wasn't.

"Come on, James. Over here," I said, indicating the chair in front of me. As he walked toward me, I tried to imagine this smallish boy beating two adults with a baseball bat. I couldn't. I looked at Mitch. He shook his head. He was thinking the same thing.

"Sit down," Lucas said as James reached the chair. Lucas pushed the book in front of him. "This is very important. We want you to look through this book and tell us if you find anybody you recognize." Did I hear sarcasm there? Or was I looking for it? I had to remind myself that this was Lucas. He wanted the truth.

I was leaning against the wall behind the boy. Dan was still reclining in the chair across the table. Mitch was at the window examining Water Street. Lucas had warned us that he'd have to testify to any coaching from any of us. Nobody moved.

James flipped through the book and went right past Buddy Crowe. He closed it and looked up at Lucas.

"Nobody?"

"No, sir."

Lucas nodded and James got up and moved toward the door. "Hang in there, Bear," Dan said.

James stopped and turned. "You ever been in jail, Doc?"

Dan surprised me. "Only once. Weird little deal down in Warner Robins for one night. Not the same thing, though."

"No, sir."

"Nuts," I said when he was gone. Why did I want it to be Crowe? Lord knows, I wanted to believe in Santa Claus.

The desk officer came in the room and said that Willie Moon and his mother were outside. The officer wanted to know if they should come in.

"Can his mother be in here?" I asked Lucas.

"Long as she doesn't coach him."

"She won't." I knew Willie would cooperate if she was with him.

Willie's mother walked in first, dressed in white with a name tag pinned on her massive breast. It read MRS. FAUST—LPN. Willie followed, head down. I introduced Mrs. Faust to Lucas, Dan, and Mitch.

"I know you," she said to Mitch. "From when we stay at Rat Row. You the college boy."

When I first met Mitch, he was living in a public housing project named Blount Homes. Everybody called it Rat Row. He grew up in inner-city Newark and said Rat Row felt like home. It was also cheap. He was in school on a government grant and once he left the dorm, it was all he could afford and still eat.

"Good to see you again," Mitch said.

Mrs. Faust cocked her head and squinted her eyes. "You sound different. Use to sound like Michael Jackson."

Mitch shrugged. "Grew up, I guess."

I suppose he didn't want to get into the pastime that he hadn't outgrown. He'd told me his imitations had helped him survive the mean streets of Newark. At five feet six, he would have been easy prey. Instead, he became a mascot to the gangs.

Lucas said to Willie, "We just want you to look through this book. Tell us if you see anybody you recognize."

"Now Willie, you look good," his mother said.

I glanced at Mitch, whose elbows were resting on the windowsill. "*My* mother," he mouthed and smiled.

Willie cast his splotched eyes on the pictures and turned the pages. I watched him and thought about the difference between him and his mother. She was clear-eyed with a bright face. Despite her girth, she was full of energy. Given half a chance, she could have been, should have been, running a hospital's nursing staff.

Willie, on the other hand, was wasted. Dull, dead eyes looked at the pages in front of him. This was a phenomenon I'd seen often. A young, male black client sitting in front of me looking half-alive, with his hardworking, distraught mother sitting next to him. I'd seen enough of them to know it wasn't genetics. Our society kills young, black males. Mitch was a rare exception.

As Willie turned the pages, he'd occasionally put a name to a face. Lucas had told him to identify anybody he knew. He knew a surprising number of the faces in the book. But he passed by Buddy Crowe.

After they left, we stood silently. "Well . . ." I said, but couldn't think of anything else to say.

Lucas said he was due to meet with the Patsboro chief of police and left.

"Y'all had lunch yet?" Dan asked.

Mitch and I said no.

"How about Helen's?" Dan suggested. We agreed.

I slapped the door as we left the room.

Chapter 14

Helen's Restaurant is a frame-built shotgun building on Alexander Street, surrounded by homes occupied by black families whose incomes are slightly above the necessary amount to qualify for public housing. It had been a white section that converted during the turtlelike progress of the last thirty years.

Helen's was a popular place for Catledge University students who wanted to demonstrate their social consciousness. I liked it because I could afford it and the food was just flat good.

"OK, what do we have?" Dan said loudly because of the noise from the window air conditioner above us. The cold air was a blessed relief after the walk from the police station that had left me dripping.

"We got zip," I said.

"Not true," Mitch said. He unbuttoned the vest he was wearing under his coat. "Willie and Bear aren't exactly visionaries. They see just what they see. They were looking at an old picture of Crowe—a picture of a man with long hair and a big ol' scar down his cheek. Wasn't the same guy they saw. Didn't look like it to them, anyway."

"What *about* the scar?" Dan asked. "Neither one of them saw a scar. Scar that big sort of sticks out."

"It's been four years," I said. "Buddy Crowe made a lot of

money smuggling for Jarvis. All cash. It wouldn't be hard to get a scar taken care of."

The waitress brought our food. My plate was heaped with turnip greens laced with pieces of ham hock, yams, and a large, crispy fried breast of chicken. On the side was a huge biscuit. Fat city. Why'd I order it? I'll just eat half of it, I thought.

Dan cut into his country-fried steak smothered in white gravy and took a bite. "Here's what we got. We got two people murdered and the police figure it's done by a black kid who makes a perfect suspect in this town. And we got an automobile wreck. The kid says a blond-haired guy named Buddy was involved in the killing. Another guy says a blond-haired guy named Buddy did the wrecking. Neither one recognizes Buddy Crowe."

My mind flashed to the rose. Just like Landry to be unable to admit sending something expensive when the response wasn't what he wanted. That's what I told myself, anyway. I was more concerned about the embarrassment that would result from talking about some man sending me a rose than the possibility that Buddy Crowe was involved. When I think about that now, I am dumbfounded by the power of ego.

Dan went on. "Maybe when we go to Atlanta tomorrow, that'll tell us something, but I'd like to know more."

Mitch put down his tea. "Yeah, like more about the Reeveses. If Bear didn't do the deed, somebody else did. Why? What's the motive? We ought to look a little closer at Dr. and Mrs. Reeves."

"You willing?" I asked hopefully. Bernard had agreed to help the society on a part-time basis. I didn't want to ask him for help that required a lot of time. And asking Landry was out of the question.

Mitch smiled broadly. "Oh, yeah. Be like old times. When we got Jarvis. Maybe be a reporter again. From . . . *Popular Genetics.* Doing a profile on the late, famous, Dr. Gary Reeves."

"I don't think it'd work. You're too well known around here now," I said.

"Disguise. Wait and see."

I didn't doubt him. I had another thought. "Mitch was right. Neither Willie nor Bear is likely to look past what's obvious. I wonder if we could get some kind of rendering of what Crowe'd look like with less hair and without a scar."

"Good idea," Dan said.

"I'll talk to Lucas this afternoon. See what we can do," I said.

We finished our meal. I cleaned my plate. What was wrong with me? Dan and I made arrangements to meet the next day to go to the Atlanta federal pen and meet with Jarvis.

On the way out, Helen herself approached us and said to Mitch, "Aren't you Mitch Griffith? The man selling stoves on the cable?"

Mitch spoke in a West Indian accent. "I'm sorry, madam. You've got the wrong bloke. I'm a reporter with a magazine. Called *Popular Genetics*."

"Never heard of it," she said and walked away.

"Piece of cake," Mitch said with glee as we headed into the heavy Georgia summer air.

The rest of the short afternoon was spent in my office on the phone dealing with Dillon's Financial. The company specialized in loaning poor folks money at an interest rate that ended up exceeding 60 percent. They'd get double their money back and still repossess the television set or sofa my clients had bought with the loan money. Then they'd loan them some more. It's a vicious cycle that's close to impossible to break. I spend a lot of time dealing with Dillon's and their ilk.

That night, I took a load of clothes to the Laundromat and watched young Catledge couples walk by snuggling and laughing. A bearded man, whose wedding ring mysteriously disappeared while moving clothes from the washers to a dryer, talked to me about the million-dollar real estate deal he was closing. I responded in monosyllables and tried to continue reading my Tony Hillerman novel, but he kept on anyway.

It was nine-thirty when I got home. After taking a bath, I stood in front of the mirror to see how much fat I'd put on from lunch, then put on my nightgown. I lay down and finished the novel and picked up another, but decided I was too sleepy to start a new one.

I turned off the light and pulled off the nightgown and panties. It was my nightly ritual. Girls raised in the Congregational Holiness Church didn't sleep naked, or even say the word. But the truth was that I found sleeping in anything to be constricting. I tried every night, but always ended up pulling and tugging until I couldn't stand it anymore. The best evidence of the long arm of Mama was my nightly ritual.

I fluffed the pillow and lay back again. Another rip-roaring evening, I thought.

The front door? Had I locked it? I knew I had. But better check. I got up and walked across the large room to the central hall. Light from the streetlamp outside filtered through the leaded glass above the front door. The knob was locked. Need to get Dan to install a dead bolt, I thought. He had spent a summer when he was a teacher working for a locksmith and I knew he'd do it for me. As I returned to my room, I thought about how quickly he had picked the office locks that night we had gone in to examine Jarvis's tax records. I tried not to look into the gloom of the rooms and uncovered windows on the other side of the house.

I locked the door to my room, got back into bed, and lay on my side. Shadows of the leaves from the water oaks danced on the white sheets covering the windows. Thunder rumbled in the distance. Good. We needed rain badly and maybe it'd cool things off for a while. I closed my eyes.

The image came immediately. I was standing in the Picayune Trucking parking lot in New Orleans. A Ford Ranger pickup truck with a rifle in a gun rack on the back window drove by. The driver was staring at me. The driver was Buddy Crowe.

I opened my eyes. Don't think about him now. Think about something else. He's not here. He's not that stupid. Just some weird coincidence. I closed my eyes again. He was gone. Good. Think about . . . Michael. Michael Hutcheson and Friday night. I put myself in an auditorium listening to the symphony. The roar of the air conditioner became the roar of the crowd at the end of a movement. I was drifting . . . drifting.

Something brought me back. I lay and listened. A noise. A

. . . scraping. It stopped, but started again. It was hard to hear over the air conditioner, but the sound was definitely there. Silence. *Scrape, scrape, scrape.* Silence.

Maybe branches were hitting the house. I opened my eyes. Yeah, that was it. The leaves were really moving now. I breathed deeply, trying to slow the galloping beat of my heart. Relax, Tammi, I thought. I was itching, all over. I turned on my back and scratched. I closed my eyes again.

Scrape, scrape, scrape. My eyes flew open. *Scrape, scrape, scrape.* It wasn't outside. It was inside.

Inside my house.

Inside my room.

I reached out from my protected cocoon under the sheet and grabbed for the tiny switch on the lamp. Where *was* that thing? Finally, I found the switch and pressed it.

Light, blessed light, filled the room. I looked around. Nothing but my furniture. A dresser, a rocker, and a chest of drawers Aunt Ouida had given me years ago. I focused on the closet door that stood between the chest and dresser.

In the closet? How? While I was gone?

I reached to the phone on the night table and picked up the receiver and held it. I put it down again.

I was being paranoid. The sound was gone. I heard it in the dark. Probably *was* something blowing outside. I sat up and looked at the closet.

Got to check, I thought. Just open the closet door and look inside. I got up and started to walk across the room. I stopped, picked up my nightgown, and put it on.

I approached the closet door, reached out to turn the knob and—

Scrape, scrape, scrape.

I whirled to my right.

"Damn you, Snickers!" I screamed.

The gerbil Dan's kids had given me jumped from the metal wheel he'd been running in and hid under his nest of cedar shavings. I stood, breathing hard, looking down at the Habitrail complex. I reached into the cage and twirled the wheel.

Scrape, scrape, scrape.

I walked across the room and sat on the bed. That gerbil had been running in that wheel for a year. Why hadn't I heard it before? Just never noticed. No reason to notice.

I sat and thought. Thought about how vulnerable I felt. First at Pine Lake Lodge and again tonight.

I do *not* want to feel that again, I thought. I looked at my clock. Only 10:15. Not too late. But I'd have to handle it right. I picked up the phone and dialed.

"Hello," I heard.

"Hey, Mama, it's me."

"Hey, baby," my mother said. "How's my big-shot attorney-at-law?"

"No big shot, Mama. Just barely making a living. How are you?"

"Had to go to Doc Singer today. Got these pains in my side that won't go away. He gave me some pills and said I needed to relax."

"What kind of medicine, Mama?"

"Nerve pills. Said I worry too much."

"Doc Singer's a general practitioner. If you're going to get those kinds of pills, you need to see a specialist."

"Doc brought you into this world, Tammi. You don't need to be runnin' him down."

"OK. Whatever you want."

"Guess who I saw today?"

Here it comes again. "Who?"

"Paul Starling, baby. He always asks about you, darlin'."

I didn't say anything. Mama didn't know about Paul and me in the back of his Trans Am, of course. But couldn't she see what he was? The woman who hadn't let me wear makeup wanted me to marry that jerk? I just could *not* understand. I still don't. Somehow my getting married and providing her with grandchildren superseded the Congregational Holiness.

"Baby, I worry about you. You're almost twenty-eight years old. Way past time to be gettin' on with your life."

"I'm getting on with my life. I'm an attorney and I help people who need it. I'm happy, Mama."

"Woman ain't never happy till she gives her Mama grandchildren."

"Someday I might get married, but it will never be to Paul Starling."

That got her off her favorite subject and she went on to tell me who all in Maytown was in the hospital, getting divorced, or having affairs. Finally, the time was right.

"Listen, the reason I called was to ask you to do me a favor."

"What's that?"

"Well, the truth is I *have* met a man I kind of like. His name's Bernard and he's a lawyer at the Legal Aid Society."

"Ooh, Tammi, tell me about him."

"Well, he likes to hunt and shoot. He said he'd teach me how to shoot a pistol. I was wondering if you could send me Daddy's pistol. Save me having to buy one."

"It's still in the box. I'll send it to you. Nice-lookin' girl like you needs protection, anyway."

It worked. Mama would've balked if I just said I wanted the gun. She never would have quit asking questions. But for a man, it worked.

"Now tell me about this man. What's he like?"

"Oh, he's real nice."

"Not married, is he, like last time."

"No. And I already told you a million times there really wasn't a last time."

"I know what you say, baby. He want children?"

I couldn't help myself. "I don't know. We haven't talked about it. To tell you the truth, I'm not sure he can."

"What you mean?"

"Just don't know. He's gonna be seventy-two next month. Hard to tell."

"*Tammi!*"

I said, "Good-bye, Mama," and hung up. The wilted rose still sat on my nightstand next to the phone.

Scrape, scrape, scrape.

I looked at Snickers in his cage. Tomorrow Dan and I would meet with Jarvis. Maybe he would make it clear that Crowe was elsewhere.

Maybe there *is* a Santa Claus.

Chapter 15

"That guy's trying to kill us!" I shouted to Dan over the whine of the Geo's engine and the blasting rain that was beating on the tiny car. I tried to concentrate on the road ahead, but kept glancing at the truck's grille that filled the rearview mirror.

Dan turned in his seat. "Just a typical Atlanta driver. Kicks it up a notch when it's raining."

I grunted a reply and turned on the defroster again. That cleared up the window but created a sauna, so I turned it off again. The wipers were slapping at full speed, but the road disappeared with every pass. A Volvo station wagon cut in front of us with only inches to spare. "These people are crazy," I said through gritted teeth.

We were on I-85 heading into Atlanta to see Jink Jarvis at the Atlanta federal prison. I hadn't seen him since his trial, when he was convicted of smuggling and racketeering. When he finished his time in Atlanta, he had an appointment at the Georgia State Prison in Reidsville for murder. I was nervous anyway, and driving in Atlanta's demolition derby in a gushing rain didn't do much to relieve the stress.

Great time for the drought to end. It had hardly rained since January, but this afternoon was making up for it. Last night's thundershowers were the leading edge of a front coming in, and they had ended at daybreak, but started again just as we left Patsboro at eleven o'clock.

I said, "You know, we should have come up here this morning. Would have missed all this."

"Didn't you have an appointment this morning?"

"Never showed. The lady said she had information about James Cleveland, but must have changed her mind."

The truck driver decided I wasn't going to be intimidated and blew his horn as he passed us on the left. I maintained a steady fifty-five and noticed a break in the traffic behind us. I tried to relax.

"Of course, that's not unusual. When something's in the paper, we always get phone calls that turn into zip. Thing is, this one sounded different."

"Mmm," Dan said and we fell into silence.

The morning hadn't been totally wasted. Yesterday afternoon Lucas Anderson had told me that the Patsboro police didn't have a police artist. He said when the need arose, they used one from the Georgia Bureau of Investigation or the Atlanta police. I had spent the morning on the phone arranging to meet one of Atlanta PD's artists after we were finished with Jarvis. I wanted to have James and Willie look at a picture of Crowe with short hair and no scar. I was ready to quit worrying about him.

In the light of day, last night's panic seemed foolish. What was I going to do with a gun, anyway? Shoot Snickers the next time he decided to get some exercise? I had tried to call Mama and tell her to forget it, but she didn't answer.

Somehow I negotiated the absurd intersection of I-85 and I-20 and headed east to the exit that led to the prison. The rains had stopped by the time I parked the car.

"Last time I saw this place was on television when it was burning," Dan said. That was when the Cuban prisoners had rioted and nearly destroyed it. We walked into the imposing main building. I told the man at the reception desk what I wanted and he told us to wait in an adjoining room. Another man entered wearing the uniform: brown pants, tan shirt, and a tie. I once again explained that I was an attorney defending a client, and that I needed to talk to Jarvis and see his visitors' roster. The man left and we sat again.

"Gonna check with the president," Dan said.

I said, "Should have called ahead."

A third man stepped into the room and motioned us to follow him into the hall.

"I'm Assistant Warden Jones. Doug Jones. Normal visiting time isn't until Sunday, but I can let you see Jarvis." He indicated me.

"How about letting Dr. Bushnell look at the list of his visitors? It would save us some time."

"That'd be fine. Be right back," he said and left us standing in the tiled hall.

"Are you going to be OK? Seeing him by yourself, I mean?" Dan asked.

"Sure," I said without conviction.

The last time I'd been with Jarvis alone was when he and Willie "Rambo" Williams kidnapped me. A few days before that, I'd been in his house when his wife tried to get me to perform with her for his video camera. I was not looking forward to seeing him again.

Warden Jones returned with a uniformed woman who accompanied Dan down the hall. I followed the warden through a maze of passageways. We entered a room filled with tables and chairs. Jones said Jarvis would be in shortly and left. I sat in a metal chair and waited.

A guard appeared across the room, followed by Jarvis, who was wearing a light blue jumpsuit. I watched the former Catledge University quarterback as he walked toward the table. He didn't look much different. In fact, he looked in better shape than before. Must have been working out with weights in here. Jarvis sat in the chair on the other side of the table and stared at me.

Suddenly it struck me that I didn't know what to say. "Good to see you" didn't exactly fit the occasion. Finally I just said, "Mr. Jarvis."

He didn't say anything.

I said, "Mr. Jarvis, I'm an attorney now and am defending a boy on murder charges. I think he's innocent. I could use your help."

Jarvis leaned forward. "I should have listened to Rambo. I was a fool." His voice was flat.

I could only guess what he meant. "I'm glad you didn't. You didn't hurt me when you had the chance."

He blinked slowly.

"I think you're basically a good man," I lied. "Just got caught up in something that spun out of control." I remembered the chest of pornography we'd found in his office. Was my nose growing?

"What do you want?" he asked coldly.

All right, I thought, forget all that. "I want to find Buddy Crowe."

A strange half-laugh emerged from Jarvis.

"I want to be sure he's not involved in the murder. A man fitting his description was seen. I thought you might know how to get in touch with him."

"Fitting his description?" The question wasn't for me. I suddenly realized how stupid this was. Did I really expect Jarvis to tell me anything?

On the other hand, I remembered what Dan had told me while we were trying to figure out what Jarvis was doing four years ago. Dan had said that when he was writing his dissertation he had gathered a lot of information, much of it seemingly irrelevant. Suddenly he'd run across something that made the rest of it make sense. The same was true with this situation. You just keep looking and hope something comes together.

"I guess you're not inclined to help me," I said.

He leaned forward, resting his elbows on the table. "To tell you the truth, I'd like to find him myself. I've got a little job I'd like him to do." He stared at me.

The anger I felt surprised me. Daddy taught me to bury anger. I was a teenager before I realized he buried his in sour mash. "Jink, you've got a long way to go. It might behoove you to think about adjusting your attitude."

He leaned back. "What we have heah is a failyuh to commu'-cate." He laughed.

Cool Hand Luke was Mama's favorite movie and I'd watched it on TV with her. Jarvis had taken the words from the movie to mock me. I said, "Good luck, Jink," stood, and left without looking back.

The woman corrections officer who had been sitting on the other side of the room took me to the waiting room. Dan wasn't there so I sat and thought. Jarvis hadn't changed an iota in four years. He was as arrogant as ever. I reviewed what little he had said. He said he'd like to find Crowe, too. Did he really not know where Crowe was? He had reacted to someone fitting Crowe's description being seen in Patsboro. Did that mean Buddy shouldn't have been there, or something else? Did it mean that Crowe didn't look like himself anymore? Crowe was an integral part of Jarvis's organization four years ago. They had stayed in touch, somehow. I was sure of it.

Dan stuck his head in the door. "You ready to go?"

"Yeah," I said and stood. "You find anything?"

"Unbelievable. Let's talk about it in the car."

The sky was cloudy, but not as dark as when we had arrived. Steam rose from the streets. You could swim in the atmosphere. Once again I was soaked. I drove the Geo toward the interstate.

"Jarvis tell you anything?" Dan asked.

"Not much." I recounted our conversation.

"About what I expected."

"Yeah. Would've been nice if he'd said Crowe's in Oregon and here's his phone number." We were on I-20 now, heading for downtown and the Atlanta PD. "What's unbelievable?"

Dan remained silent for a moment. "Jarvis hasn't had a lot of visitors. At least not recently. His wife came every Sunday for a while, but that tapered off. Only came a few times last year and only once since then. An occasional visit by his attorney. Radar Gilstrap a couple of times, once years ago, once a few months ago . . ."

"Gilstrap still trying to find Crowe?"

"Guess so. They say he always gets his man. That's why they call him Radar."

At one time Dan and I had suspected that Gilstrap was involved with Jarvis. When Dan and I were with Jarvis the night he was caught, he'd said to Rambo Williams, "They haven't talked to the police. Radar would've told us." The subsequent investigation indicated an innocent relationship. Jarvis was friends with all of Patsboro's honchos, including the mayor. Gilstrap had since left Teal County and joined the Georgia Bureau of Investigation.

Dan continued, "Happy Holcombe, Jarvis's football coach at Catledge, came once. It was a short list." He became quiet again.

"And?"

Out of the corner of my eye I saw him turn toward me. "One visitor came several times during the past year—at least once a month. He was here again day before yesterday."

"Who?"

"Detective Lucas Anderson."

"Lucas!" I cried, and the car swerved into the right lane. Luckily it was empty. I got back in the middle lane and glanced at Dan. "Lucas Anderson?" I said, trying to comprehend.

"Yep. Stayed at least an hour each time."

The Martin Luther King Drive exit was approaching and I had to concentrate on crossing two lanes of traffic to get to it. We looped around and I pulled to the side the first chance I had.

I looked at Dan. "What's Lucas doing talking to Jarvis?"

"Maybe doing what we were. Trying to find Crowe."

Relief flooded over me. Of course. That's it. But then I wondered, "Why didn't he tell us he's been talking to Jarvis? When the Buddy Crowe possibility first came up. I mean, why didn't he say something yesterday?"

"Maybe Jarvis didn't tell him anything and it didn't seem relevant." We sat silently. "But, the other thing is—"

"The other thing is, if Jarvis was uncooperative and Lucas didn't learn anything, why an hour at a time? Two hours a couple of times."

There was a tap on the window. I turned to see an Atlanta policeman standing beside my door. I rolled down my window.

"You folks need some help?"

I realized we weren't in a parking space. "We're trying to find the Atlanta Police Department."

"I can probably help you with that," he said through a smile. He told us to turn right at the next light. We would find the police station on the left. I thanked him and pulled away.

"There must be an explanation," I said. But something was wrong. "Lucas hasn't been too excited about the Buddy Crowe theory all along. I've had to push him to pursue it, or to allow me to pursue it. Even setting up this thing this afternoon with the police artist required some cajoling. I thought he figured Crowe'd be crazy to come back to Patsboro. You don't suppose . . ."

"I don't know what to suppose. Did Lucas know we were seeing Jarvis today?"

"I didn't say anything. It never came up."

"I didn't either." The police station appeared on the left and we were silent while I found a place to park. Before we got out of the car, Dan said, "It's nearly two o'clock now. Depending on how long this takes, we might be able to talk to Lucas this afternoon. I don't want to keep wondering about it. But I think we ought to be careful how we ask him."

"OK," I said, and we got out of the car. I looked at Dan across the roof. "There's got to be an explanation."

"Yeah," he said and hit his fist on the roof of the Geo.

Chapter 16

⊐ ⊐ ⊐ ⊐ ⊐ ⊐ ⊐ ⊐ ⊐ ⊐

I put the picture on the desk in front of me. Dan, Lucas, and I were in Lucas's tiny office in the same positions we had been in on Friday night. The picture was a computer-created rendering of Buddy Crowe with a crew cut and no scar. It even added four years to the image. It looked exactly like a photograph.

Lucas picked up the rendering. "Amazing what they can do now."

"I appreciate your making arrangements for me to get that," I said.

Lucas waved away the thanks.

"You know, I didn't feel like you were real excited about my doing this."

Lucas looked up from the picture. "Worth a shot, I guess. Just don't believe Crowe'd come back here." He put the picture down. "What next?"

"I'll call Willie Moon, or better yet, I'll call his mother, tonight. Can we set up another look for him and James tomorrow morning? Say about nine?"

"Shouldn't be a problem."

Dan was squatting next to me, leaning against the door. "Why're you so sure Crowe's not here?"

Lucas shrugged. "Not really sure. Just find it hard to believe he'd come back here, where he's wanted."

"The other night you said he was in Oregon. How'd you know that?"

"I said a sighting was reported in Oregon. We've had bulletins out on him for four years. Reports come in now and again. None have panned out yet."

"Who checks on them?" I asked.

"In the beginning, I did. Did more traveling during that time than when I was in the army. Time moves on, though. Department'll pay for only so many false reports. Now we let the locals do it."

Dan shifted in his position. "You ever talk to Jarvis about Crowe? Or anything else?"

A moment passed. "Nope. Word is Jarvis isn't gonna talk anyway. Seemed like it'd be a waste of time."

I wanted to look at Dan but kept my eyes on Lucas. He was flat lying.

"Might be worth a shot," Dan said.

"I suppose." Lucas stood. "I've got a meeting with Chief Bryant. See you tomorrow at nine?"

"Yeah," I said and stood, too.

"You sure do meet with the chief a lot, Lucas," Dan said. "Is that normal?"

We were moving out into the hall. Lucas said, "Didn't used to be. He's nervous about the consolidation vote. Wants to keep his job. All of a sudden he wants to know everything that's going on."

A referendum was being held to combine the governments of Patsboro and Teal County. Only one of the chiefs could remain head honcho. That made sense. Nothing else did.

Dan and I were standing on the sidewalk in front of the station. He'd parked his van in the lot across the street when we had met earlier today. "What do you think?" I asked.

"I think he's a terrible liar. Wouldn't look at us and wanted to leave immediately."

"This is depressing."

"I know."

"What do we do?" I held up my hand. "Wait, don't say it.

Keep looking. Meet with James and Willie in the morning and see if they recognize Crowe from the computer picture. Find out if Mitch learned anything about Dr. Reeves today. See if we can find another motive for the murder other than a project kid acting like he's brain damaged by leaving TVs and stereos and going for candlesticks. Keep looking and see what comes up and what comes together."

"That's what I'd say," Dan said.

"Thought so," I said, smiling.

It was past six o'clock as I approached my house. My mind was spinning with ideas, trying to explain Lucas Anderson's duplicity. I couldn't think of any that made sense, other than that he was involved with Jink Jarvis and Buddy Crowe.

I didn't notice the car in front of my house until I got out of the Geo. It was an old Cadillac, one with wings on the back, colored a hideous peach. There were bullhorns as a hood ornament and the words BIG JACK PELHAM on the side. I figured whoever owned it was visiting across the street. I walked between the magnolia trees and when I got to the porch steps, I was shocked by the voice.

"Well, it's about time, baby."

"Mama?" She was sitting in one of the rusty metal chairs on the veranda. "What are you doing here?"

"Fine way to greet your mama," she said, coming toward me with her arms open. I hugged her, and over her shoulder I saw a man come around the corner of the porch. He was huge. Fat, anyway. He must have weighed 350 pounds and didn't reach six feet. He had a white beard that fell below his chest and was wearing overalls and no shirt. I let go of my mother and backed up a step.

Mama followed my eyes. "Baby, I want you to meet my friend Jack. He volunteered to come with me up here to see you." Must be his Cadillac, I thought. Big Jack Pelham. The words didn't lie.

"Hey," he said in a raspy voice. "Viv talks 'bout you all the time. It's good to finally see you." He reached out his hand.

His meaty hand slid into mine and just sort of sat there. No grip at all. My eyes moved back to my mother.

"Now don't go lookin' at me that way. Last night you said you wanted your daddy's gun and I brought it to you. I wanted to talk to you anyway. But look, you look tuckered. Why don't you let us in the house so's you can freshen up and we can get settled?"

"Settled?"

"Well, baby, we need to stay the night. Long way back to Maytown."

"Oh, sure. Yeah . . . we?"

"Darlin', you told me about this big ol' house of yours. I figured you'd have enough room to put us both up. You do, don't you?"

"Oh, there's plenty of room. I just don't have much furniture."

"We'll make do, somehow. You know your grandma and grandpa never had much furniture, but we made do. Won't hurt for one night."

I sighed inwardly and unlocked the door.

Jack said he'd be right back with the luggage and moved down the walk.

"Who *is* he?" I asked when he'd left.

"Plenty of time for that," Mama said as she walked through the doorway. I followed her in and tried to think where they could stay. I'd fixed up my room and the kitchen, but the rest of the house was empty except for the dust. Didn't even have the windows covered in the rest of it.

"This is the biggest house I ever seen. Look at all these rooms." She had already gone through the empty rooms on the left, on through the kitchen and was heading up the stairs. There were rooms up there I hadn't gone in yet.

Mama was an inch taller than my five-eight and weighed twenty pounds less than I did. She never stopped moving. For as long as I can remember, I thought of Mama as moving. Her features were sharp and her face was creased with lines that came from years in the fields while she was growing up. The sun had withered her.

I sat down on the stairs and listened to her prattle. "Oh this'll be perfect. You got any extra sheets to put on the windows? 'Course, you don't really need any, this being upstairs and all. Somebody'd have to be trying real hard to look in. Who'd want to look at me, anyway? Don't worry about the sheets, darlin'. We won't need 'em. Oh, look, here's a bathroom. Needs some cleaning up, but that won't take long. You got any Pine Sol, honey?"

Big Jack came in the door carrying two huge suitcases, and a box under one arm. He was pushing a guitar case with a foot. "Where you want me to put these?" he asked.

"Upstairs, I guess. Mama says y'all are staying up there."

He was breathing hard from carrying the suitcases. He looked up at the stairs, put the luggage down, blew hard, and came toward me. "Think I need to rest 'fore I tote 'em up all those," he said, nodding at the stairs. He sat next to me.

He smelled of cigarettes and . . . what? Garlic. The man smelled like a garlic. Not just of garlic. Like a garlic. He slapped my thigh and said, "Yes ma'am, it sure is good to finally see you."

I stood reflexively. "Good to meet you too, Jack. Listen, I'm going into my room to change clothes. Be right back." I closed the door behind me and leaned against it. Lord help you, Randall, this is just what you need right now, I thought. That damn gun. That damn gerbil. I looked over at Snickers. He was on his haunches, looking back at me. I went over to the cage, bent down, and tapped the glass.

"Hey, it's not your fault. I'm just a scaredy-cat." I could hear Mama walking around upstairs. Oh well, might be good to have somebody else in the house right now. What were they going to sleep on, though? I sat on the bed and thought.

Dan. He had built a camper for his family's trip to California. He had showed it to me. It had some small mattresses in it. I called him and he said he'd be glad to bring them right over. I started to put on some shorts and a halter top, but thought of

Big Jack and changed my mind. Instead I put on some loose-fitting white pants and a light, full blouse.

When I came out of my room, Mama and Big Jack were coming down the stairs. I told her Dan was bringing over some camper mattresses.

"Dan," Mama mused. "He's the married man you was messin' around with, ain't he?"

"We *never* messed around. He was my boss and he's my friend. That's all. Oh, and don't tell Dan about the gun. OK?" I didn't want Dan to know about my spell last night.

"Why not? Afraid he'll be jealous of that old man?"

"Lord sakes, Mama. He's not gonna be jealous. 'Sides, Bernard and I just work together. Said he'd teach me to shoot." There was the Maytown accent coming back again. That always happened when I was around Mama, unless I paid attention.

"Sure do have lots of men friends. Wish you'd find one to be a little more than friends with. I mean one that's not married or 'bout to join the good Lord in the Promised Land."

I said slowly, "I am *not* going to talk about this. Is that clear?"

She grunted and asked for the Pine Sol. I gave her what I had. It wasn't Pine Sol, and she grunted again, then went upstairs.

Big Jack stood and looked at me, grinning. I suggested we go out on the veranda.

After we sat, I said, "So, Big Jack, what do you do?"

"*Re*tired. From the ring."

"You were a boxer?"

"Nah. Wrestler. Professional wrestler. Held the big belt for ten years."

Oh, Lord, I thought. "Mmmm," is what I said.

He began telling me the tales of his athletic, so to speak, history when I heard the banging of Dan's Volkswagen van coming down the street. Interrupting his monologue, I said, "That's Dan with the mattresses, Big Jack. I'll go out and help him." By the time I reached the street, Dan was pulling them from the back. He was wearing Umbros, a Hawaiian shirt, and flip-flops. Mama'll love that, I thought.

"You didn't tell me your mother was coming," Dan remarked.

"Didn't know until I got home." I had been sort of vague with Dan regarding my mother. Too late to explain now. Dan and I carried the mattresses into the house and up the stairs. Mama was coming out of the bathroom as we arrived on the landing.

"There, now," she said. "Looks good as new. Oh, you must be Dan."

"Yes, ma'am. Glad to meet you."

"Uh huh," she said and walked into the room next to the bathroom. "One of those'll go in here and the other'n in the room next door." Dan and I laid down the mattresses in their places while Mama tried to open the windows. They wouldn't budge. Dan banged the frames with his palms and with great effort got them to move a couple of inches. I suggested we join Big Jack on the porch.

There were only three metal chairs on the porch, so I brought out my rocker and sat in it. I introduced Dan to Big Jack.

Mama said, "Dan, you a churchgoin' man?"

Oh Lord, I thought.

"Yes, ma'am. We go to the Unitarian church in town."

"Unitarian?" Mama said. "Ain't that the church where you can believe anythin' you want?"

Dan pursed his lips. "Well, it's not that simple. But it is less, uh, doctrinaire than some others."

"Uh huh," Mama said.

"Now, Viv," Big Jack said. "You know Elena Haney goes to the Unitarian church over to Valdosta."

"Elena Haney's one of them weird women."

I glanced at Dan. He was smiling, thank goodness.

I wanted to change the subject. Get Mama started on the Congregational Holiness, and that'd be it for the evening. "You said you had something to tell me. What's the news?"

Mama looked at Dan. "I guess I can. Tammi, Big Jack and I gonna get married. We wanted you to be the first to know."

"Married?" I said. I looked at Big Jack. His discolored teeth showed through a grin on his hairy face. "When?"

"Next month, baby. Now listen, I know this is kind of sudden news for you, but the time's come. Your daddy's been away nearly ten years."

"I love your mother," Big Jack said. "I'll take good care of her."

I nodded my head and watched him reach over and slap Mama on the thigh. This man was gonna be my daddy?

"Be on the twenty-seventh, darlin'. We got the house up for sale, and I'm gonna move into Big Jack's double-wide."

"You're going to sell the house?"

"Big Jack's idea. Said we didn't need to be in that big old house. Just ramble around in it, is all."

I looked at Big Jack. He was grinning. "House isn't all that big," I said.

"I know that's the house you growed up in, but you and your brother don't never come home anymore and I just don't need it."

"It's not that . . ." I stopped. It's that Big Jack's going to get the only thing you got, I thought.

"Congratulations," Dan said and reached out to shake Big Jack's hand. He winked at me. The wink said, Relax.

"Well, Mama. You're a big girl. It's just . . . a shock, that's all."

Dan suddenly jerked and started scratching his right side. He looked pained. "You all right?" I asked.

"Yeah. Just had a flare-up of the shingles. Get them every once in a while."

Mama looked at Big Jack. "Shingles go all around your body, you die," she said knowingly.

Dan looked at me. I shrugged.

"Well, now that the big news is out, I best be gettin' upstairs and finish cleanin' up." She went inside.

Dan said he had to be going. I told him I'd walk him to his car. We left Big Jack sitting on the porch, grinning. When we reached the van, Dan said, "Your mother's an interesting person."

"Yeah."

He rounded the van. "See you at the police station in the morning. Nine o'clock." He stopped at his door. "Might be a little late, though. Got to go by Mayfield's Funeral Home in the morning."

I laughed. "Gonna make arrangements in case the shingles make it all the way around?"

Dan smiled. "No." His smile faded. "Got to go by to make arrangements for our staff to be honorary pallbearers. My principal called me when I got home to tell me our librarian died last night."

"Oh, I'm sorry, Dan. I didn't mean to—"

"Don't worry about it. It is a shame, though. She's been at the high school for thirty-six years."

"Had she been sick?"

"No. An accident. Weird one, too. You know the Piggly Wiggly at Idlewood Shopping Center?"

"Yeah."

"She was coming out last night about nine. She went by nearly every night to buy doughnuts for her breakfast. Anyway, a tractor trailer hit her in the parking lot. Apparently the driver didn't see her because he didn't stop."

"That's awful."

Dan sighed. "Yeah. School won't be the same without Minerva Hildegarde stomping around in it."

Electricity shot from my bowels to my head. "Oh God, Danny." The only other time I had called him Danny was in New Orleans.

"What is it?" Dan said as he came back to me.

"Minerva Hildegarde. That was the woman who was supposed to see me this morning. The woman who knew something about James Cleveland."

Chapter 17

The clock radio read 6:32. Another thirty minutes and it would go off. What woke me up? I felt like I hadn't slept at all.

It suddenly came back. My tossing and turning while thinking about Hildegarde. She called me in the morning saying she wanted to tell me about James Cleveland and the same night, she's dead. Run over by a truck that doesn't stop.

Buddy Crowe is a truck driver. Surely somebody at the Piggly Wiggly, or another store in the shopping center, could confirm a delivery. If none was made . . .

Have to ask Lucas what they found out.

Then Lucas came back.

It was automatic to think of asking Lucas. He'd helped us with the Jarvis case. In the year I'd been at Legal Aid, he'd shown the most concern among police officials about justice being done. Real justice. Constitutional justice. And yesterday he had lied. Said he hadn't seen Jarvis.

Why?

I sat up, threw off the sheet, and leaned on Aunt Ouida's headboard. That's when I noticed what had awakened me: the smell of bacon.

Then Mama came back. She was here, and Big Jack.

Why can't we wake up and remember everything all at once?

I heard the doorknob to my room rattle and dived under the sheet.

"Goooood mornin'. Time to rise and shine. You're sleepin' your youth away."

With the sheet pulled to my neck I said, " 'Morning, Mama."

"You always sleep this late, baby? That's not the way I reared you."

"Lord, it's not even seven o'clock."

"Watch your mouth, young lady. Don't use the Lord's name in vain."

"I'm not. I'm asking for His help."

She grunted and sat in the rocker. "Got breakfast ready for you. Need to get up before it gets old."

"I don't eat breakfast," I said while trying to look at her without raising my body. It was hard. "Makes me feel bloated all morning."

"Breakfast's the most important meal of the day. Read that in the *Star*."

"Right next to the baby born with two heads, I guess."

She ignored that and began rocking. "Big Jack and I were talkin' last night and decided we'd like to stay on a little longer. I don't ever get to see you anymore."

I closed my eyes and made a sound. "It's a real busy time, right now. I may not be around much."

"Oh, we don't mind. A little bit's better than nothin'. Anyways, I'd like to see Patsboro, too. Ain't never been up here."

"All right, Mama."

I was waiting for her to leave, but she just sat there.

"What's in your closet, honey?" she asked.

What kind of question was that? "Weird stuff . . . clothes, shoes. Things like that."

"I wondered why you had a big ol' lock on it."

I raised my head enough to glance at the closet door. She was talking about the dead bolt above the knob.

"That was there when I moved in. This was being used as a boardinghouse before the professor bought it. I guess one of the renters wanted some privacy."

She nodded her head knowingly and said, "Had drugs, I bet." She continued rocking. "Well, you just gonna lay 'round all day, or are you gonna get up?"

Oh, what the hell, I thought. I pulled off the sheet and stood.

"Tammi! Where's your pajamas?"

"I don't sleep in 'em. Can't stand 'em." Somehow it felt good to say it. Finally.

She rocked hard. "Only loose women sleep naked."

I lost it. As hard as I tried, I lost it.

I put my hands on my hips and said, "Mama, I'm twenty-seven years old. I've had sex exactly once, when I was seventeen in the backseat of Paul Starling's car. *Once!* You know how many twenty-seven-year-old women there are in the world who've had sex *once* in their lives? Hell, I deserve some kind of medal. Ought to call me Saint Tammi. But I'll tell you something, Mama. I'm thinking real hard about rectifying that!" I realized by the end that I was screaming.

"What's goin' on?"

I whirled to see Big Jack standing at the door and dived back into bed and pulled the sheet up.

" 'Scuse me," he said and left.

Mama got out of the rocker and walked across the room. She stopped and said, "I thought . . . I thought you didn't like Paul."

I enunciated slowly. "I was seventeen."

There wasn't a lot of conversation at the yard-sale kitchen table I'd bought the week before. I tried to eat some bacon and scrambled eggs, but most of it stayed on the plate. Big Jack just sat there and grinned. As I drank my coffee, I remembered somebody writing that a son wasn't a man until his daddy died. Was that true for a daughter and her mother? I didn't want to wait till Mama died to grow up.

Still, the guilt hung over me heavy as an anvil.

I entered the lobby of the Patsboro Police Station at quarter till nine and told the uniformed woman behind the counter that I wanted to see Detective Anderson. She talked into the telephone and told me he'd be out shortly. I leaned against the counter and waited.

A chubby black man with glasses and a graying beard was sitting in one of the chairs that lined the far wall. He stood and walked toward me. "Pardon me," he said in a high-pitched, hoarse voice. "Have you got the time?" He seemed familiar.

I looked at my watch and told him what it said. He thanked me and returned to his seat.

The swinging door to my left opened and Lucas Anderson emerged. "Come on back," he said, and turned to move back through the door.

As I bent to pick up my briefcase, I felt a tap on my shoulder. It was the chubby black man.

"Hi, Tammi," he said.

I gaped at him. "Mitch? Is that you?"

He bowed. "How do you like it?"

"I can't believe it. I guarantee nobody'll look at you and see the guy who sells appliances on TV. It's great."

"Thanks. Guess we better get in there." He gestured toward the door.

I started to turn, then stopped.

"Listen, Mitch, why don't you get out of that outfit? I'd rather you not go in there looking like that."

"Why not?"

"Tell you later. No time now."

"It'll take me a while."

"That's fine."

He went out and I walked down the hall to the same room we were in Monday. Lucas was in there with the mug book. We stood in awkward silence for a minute before Dan arrived. Willie Moon and his mother followed shortly.

We were in the same places as two days before, except for Mitch, who wasn't there. Willie flipped through the pages of the book quickly. "Still not here," he said.

I said, "Look again, Willie. Go a little slower this time." Lucas looked at me and shrugged.

Willie looked again, studying, or looking like he was studying, each picture. When he finished, he closed the book and shrugged.

I looked at his mother. "We appreciate your coming up here again, Mrs. Faust. This'll be the last time."

"Oh, don't worry 'bout that, honey. Don't mind at all. I want to tell you, too, that I talked with Essie Dillard yesterday. Won't be saying nothing else 'bout that man stealin' that car."

"I appreciate that, Mrs. Faust." And I really did. One less dodge for Cotton Land Consortium Insurance.

After they'd left Dan said, "Willie was about half-lit that night. I'm not sure he'd have recognized his mother."

"Maybe," Lucas said. He was leaning back in a chair at the end of the table. "Why are you so anxious that this guy be Buddy Crowe?"

"I'm not," Dan answered.

Dan looked at me. I looked back. What was the story?

James Cleveland was brought in. He sat ramrod straight as he turned the pages of pictures.

I counted down the pages as he approached the one with Crowe's picture. I realized my jaws were hurting from gritting my teeth.

When James got to the page with Crowe's picture he said, "That be him."

Chapter 18

"Which one, James?" I asked.

He pointed to Buddy Crowe. I looked at Lucas. He remained expressionless.

"OK," Lucas said and nodded to the guard, who took James out the door. Lucas looked at me. "One doesn't know him, one says he does."

"Bear wasn't drunk," Dan said.

"True," Lucas said. "Could score one for the defense. Except that picture is one of the few white men with short, light hair in the book. Maybe Bear's finally figured out he better start identifying somebody."

"He'd have thought about that before," I said. "Like Mitch said, he ain't dumb when it comes to getting out of trouble."

Lucas stood. "Well, we've had a wanted bulletin for Crowe for four years. I guess we can up the exposure some." He walked out the room.

I wanted to ask him about Minerva Hildegarde's accident, but didn't. Not being sure what was going on with him, I didn't want him to know we were interested in that.

"Mitch should be back soon," I said to Dan, and told him about Mitch's disguise. In the lobby we found Mitch coming in the station's front door. I suggested we go to my office.

We had just started out when Dan said, "Look at that."

He pointed toward the parking lot next to the police station. Lucas was getting in a brand-new Oldsmobile convertible.

"He got a new car," I said.

"At least it's not a Maserati," Dan said.

"Still . . ."

Mitch gave us a puzzled look.

"We'll tell you in the office," I said. On the way, I stopped at the Geo and got the box with Daddy's pistol from the trunk. I didn't tell Mitch and Dan what was in it.

Upstairs, Mrs. Thompson was leaning over her desk and reading the New Testament.

"Good morning," I said. "Any messages?"

It was important to ask. Mrs. Thompson rarely remembered to tell you of her own accord.

"No. It's been a slow morning." A crooked grin appeared on her thin face. "By the way, did you hear about Preacher Rothchild?"

I shook my head and motioned for Dan and Mitch to go into my office.

"Told the deacons the Lord called him to another church. Police may not be doing anything, but the people wouldn't stand for a preacher who's a chicken thief."

I suspected Mrs. Thompson's telephone campaign of the last two days probably had considerable influence on the Lord's decision. "I'm going to be in conference," I said and closed my office door behind me.

Mitch and Dan had already taken the chairs in front of my desk. I didn't notice the package on it until I sat in my chair. It was a box of Russell Stover candy with a small envelope on top.

The card inside was blank.

"What is it?" Dan asked.

Minerva Hildegarde's death had stripped away my fear of feeling foolish paranoia. I told them about the rose.

"I don't like it," Mitch said.

I got up, went to Mrs. Thompson, and asked her if she knew

anything about the candy. She said a little boy with freckles who she didn't know had brought it in. I told her I wanted to talk to the boy if she saw him again.

Back in my office, Dan and I told Mitch about Lucas Anderson's visits to Jarvis and his denying having seen him.

"I can't believe Lucas is involved with Jarvis . . . or Crowe," Mitch said.

Dan and I shook our heads in agreement.

"That's what your interest in his new car was all about."

"Lucas has been talking to Jarvis. A man and his wife are killed and Crowe might be involved. All of a sudden Lucas has a new car. Makes you wonder," I said.

We sat quietly. During the past year, I'd had a fair amount of contact with Lucas, but mostly on a professional level. On several occasions, though, we'd eaten lunch together during a court break, or when we happened to run into each other at Woolworth's lunch counter. Now, as I thought back on those occasions, it occurred to me that our conversations almost always centered on the Jarvis case. I mentioned that to Dan and Mitch.

"Hmm," Dan said. "Now that I think about it, the same thing happened to me. In fact, last November he was at school investigating some Halloween hijinks. After he interviewed some kids, we ended up in my office. It was late Friday afternoon, and we spent a couple of hours in my office rehashing Jarvis."

Mitch stood and leaned against my filing cabinet. He said, "And *Lucas* brought Jarvis up with me and asked a lot of questions."

Dan and I looked at him.

Mitch continued, "He came into the store to buy a refrigerator for his mother."

"He still lives with his mother," Dan said.

"The guys closed up while we talked. We stayed . . . a long time. I don't remember how long."

I leaned back in my chair. "Dan, you know him better than Mitch or I. What was he like in high school?"

"Introverted. That's what I remember mostly. Pretty much kept to himself. Good student. I required students to write a term paper in my senior Ag class. He turned in a dissertation. I remember that clearly because my Ag students tended to shy away from writing. His paper was unusual . . . and excellent."

Again we sat quietly, all thinking the same thing. How had Lucas got mixed up with Jarvis?

Dan broke the silence. "OK, let's get organized. Take the worst-case scenario. Crowe was with Bear and was in the car that ran into us. Sequence of events goes like this: Two weeks ago Crowe recruits Bear to go with him to the Reeves house."

"Crowe and another white man," I said.

"Right. Bear stays in the garage while Crowe kills Reeves and his wife with Bear's bat."

"Or the other white man does," Mitch said.

"Or that. Couple of weeks later, the police get a call saying Bear had done it. Fingerprints match, they get a warrant, find the bat, and arrest Bear. Somebody gives Bear your name right after he's arrested."

"Crowe," I said. I knew where Dan was going with this. I thought about the Mustang.

"The message says to call you immediately. Crowe knows where you live, what kind of car you drive, and the route you'd probably take to the police station. He's been going to Sable's and knows how to get hold of a car. He picks out a big one, a tank, waits for you, then rams you."

"But misses," Mitch said. "Sort of, anyway."

"Maybe that's all he wanted," Dan said. "He leaves a rose that night."

"Sends candy today," Mitch said.

Dan looked at me. "He wants to scare you. Enjoys it. But he's too smart to do it directly."

"Why me? You guys had as much to do with getting Jarvis as I did. Actually a lot more."

Dan leaned forward. "You know how I feel about you, Tammi. I'd want to help anyway. But I have to tell you when the notion that Crowe might be involved came up, my motivation increased a bunch." He looked at Mitch.

Mitch nodded. "Same here."

Dan turned his eyes to me again. "But you're a woman. Crowe's crazy, Tammi. I'm convinced of that. You picked up on it the first time we saw him at the high school construction site. You called him evil. Sometimes that can be another word for crazy. He's into the macho thing, too. Chewing on a toothpick, no coat on, and all of that. You remember how cold it was then? Can't stand that a woman ruined his golden opportunity."

"Way too convoluted," I said.

Mitch said, "He wouldn't have planned all that. It just came one step at a time. He's here, and thinks, Why not kill two birds with one stone?"

I could tell Mitch was sorry he had chosen those words.

I leaned forward and pulled my hair away from my neck. It was still damp from the walk to my office.

"This is all assuming the worst case," I said.

"True," Dan said. "Willie didn't recognize him."

"Still," Mitch said, "I don't like you being alone, Tammi."

"I'm not. My mother and Big Jack are staying with me."

"I thought they were leaving today," Dan said.

"I did, too. Mama said this morning they'd like to stay. I wasn't too wild about that, but I guess under the circumstances . . ."

"Right," Mitch said.

After a moment of silence, I said, "Suppose everything we just said is true. Why'd Crowe kill the Reeveses?"

"That's the question," Dan said.

"I started working on that yesterday," Mitch said.

"I thought you were going to Augusta." I said.

"I canceled the opening because of the storms. The 'grand' part anyway. So I stayed here and made some phone calls. Talked to a neighbor and talked to a woman who had been the Reeveses' housekeeper."

"What'd she say?" Dan asked. He had slid into his usual semireclining position.

"She said she'd been worried about Dr. Reeves. That she had liked working for him because he was a nice man, easygoing, always smiling. A few months ago he changed—quit smiling. Even fussed at her a couple of times. Spent most of his time in his office. She says his wife talked to her about it a little bit. Not too much. Can't get too close to the hired help, you know. Anyway, the wife was apparently worried, too."

I was trying to concentrate on what Mitch was saying, but I kept looking at the box of candy sitting on my desk. I picked it up and tossed it in the trash can.

I said, "So something happened that made him change. Wonder what it was?"

Mitch shrugged. "I called the Genetics Department at Catledge. Reeves and another professor, a Dr. Cutlip, had worked together. I've got an appointment with him this afternoon."

"As a reporter with *Popular Genetics*?" I asked.

"Nah. He might want to talk business and I'd be up the creek. Gonna be from the Georgia Bureau of Investigation. Same costume, though."

I laughed. "You should have seen him, Dan. No way you'd tell it was him. Looked like Hosea Williams."

"He was my model," Mitch said. "I'm going to keep a low profile when I drive, though." Hosea Williams was a politician and civil rights leader in Atlanta. Williams was known for his many arrests for traffic violations.

I heard the phone ring outside the door. I lunged for mine and got it before Mrs. Thompson did. Dan and Mitch looked at each other in puzzlement; they didn't know about Mrs. Thompson's problems with the phone system.

It was Michael. I unconsciously turned away from Mitch and Dan and lowered my voice. He said he had met with the governor about the airport. He said the governor had listened but hadn't provided much hope. The airlines were insistent on a northern site and weren't likely to change.

"Well, you tried anyway."

He mentioned how he had enjoyed our dinner Sunday night and was looking forward to Friday night. I told him I was looking forward to it too.

When I hung up, Mitch and Dan were looking at me. "Michael Hutcheson," I said.

"Nice guy," Mitch said. "Working on the airport?"

"Yeah. By the way, are you coming to the Atlanta Regional Commission meeting next Tuesday?"

"Plan to," Mitch said.

"I'd like to go, too," Dan said.

We sat there with them looking at me, both too polite to ask.

"We're going to Athens Friday night. The Atlanta Symphony's giving a concert."

"Like I said, seems like a nice guy," Mitch said.

"OK," I said, trying to hide my embarrassment, "Where were we?" I looked at Mitch. "Oh yeah, you're meeting with Reeves's colleague this afternoon."

Mitch nodded. "I'd like to see the Reeveses' coroner's report, too."

"Good idea," I said.

"Speaking of that," Dan said, "I got a report on Minerva Hildegarde's accident this morning." He pulled a sheet of paper from his back pocket. "Doesn't say much. Like I told you, Tammi, she got hit by the front tires of the trailer. Like he was turning and didn't see her."

"What about Minerva Hildegarde?" Mitch asked.

I told him about the phone call and Dan started to tell him more about Minerva.

Mitch interrupted him. "I knew her. She bought the audio-visual stuff for the school system. I sold her a bunch of TVs and VCRs. Hell of a haggler." He sat quietly. "Crowe again?"

"He's a truck driver," Dan said.

"How would he know about the phone call?" I asked. "And even if he did, how would he know about her buying doughnuts every night?"

"And, more important, what kind of connection does a school librarian have with a geneticist and a creep like Crowe?" asked Mitch.

"If there is one," I said. "It could have just been an accident." I took from my purse the second copy of Crowe's picture the Atlanta police had provided. "I'm going over to the shopping center this afternoon and show this around. See if anybody recognizes it."

"Good idea," Dan said. He sat up in his chair. "I'd like to take a look in her house, too. May be something there to tell us why she wanted to see you."

I looked at Mitch, who was looking at Dan.

I said, "Normally we could ask Lucas, but . . ."

"Yeah," Dan said.

Mitch said to Dan, "Kept up with your locksmith skills?"

"Get a lot of practice at school. Kids are constantly locking their keys in their cars. I think they do it on purpose now, just to watch."

"Tonight?" I asked.

"After dark," he said.

"It gets dark around nine," Mitch said. "Think around ten o'-clock?"

"Yeah," Dan said. "Meet at my house. Go in one car."

Dan and Mitch left, but not before telling me to be careful. They didn't have to do that.

I went next door to Bernard's office with the box containing the gun. He was in his work boots. I sat down by his desk.

"Bernard, I want to ask you something."

He leaned back and put his hands behind his head. "Shoot."

"Funny you'd say that." I opened the box and showed him the pistol.

He picked it up. "It is a Smith & Wesson, Model fifty-eight. Nice pistol, particularly if you want to blow somebody to smithereens. Evidence?"

"No. Belonged to my daddy. One of the few things he did with me was take me out to shoot. I guess he thought it wouldn't hurt if I knew how to use a gun. That was a long time ago, though."

Bernard nodded.

"I was wondering if you'd give me a refresher course. You've talked about going out to Jackson's shooting range."

"I would be pleased to oblige." He looked at his calendar. "How about tomorrow afternoon?"

"That'd be fine."

We sat for a moment. He raised his eyebrows questioningly.

"There's something else. I know you came down here to take it easy, but I've got a problem. The Cleveland case is becoming time-consuming and my other stuff's starting to back up. I was wondering . . ."

"Give me your files. The young man's charged with murder. You must concentrate on that."

"I would ask Landry, but—"

"You do not need to be beholden to Peter." That was the nice thing about Bernard. You rarely had to explain anything to him.

That taken care of, I retrieved my purse and headed to Idlewood Shopping Center. Part of me hoped somebody would recognize the photograph.

Another part prayed nobody would.

Chapter 19

The phone rang and Mama picked it up. She was sitting in my rocking chair. I was pulling off my blouse and skirt.

"It's for you," Mama said.

"No kidding," I answered. I turned off the water in the tub and went to get the phone from Mama.

"Some Chinese guy."

"Hi, Mitch," I said into the telephone.

"How'd you know it was me?"

"Lucky guess."

Mama got out of the chair and moved toward the door. "Never heard of no Chinese named Mitch," she mumbled.

"What's going on?" I asked.

"Dan and I've been talking. We decided to change plans some. We'll meet at your house. That way, we'll know that you got home."

"Mama and Big Jack are here," I reminded him.

"Still in all, we'd like to do it that way."

"Fine with me. Still about ten?"

"Right."

In the tub, I thought about how I had worried about fallout from what I'd said to Mama this morning. I don't know why. Basically I told my mother that I was as close to being a virgin as you can get without actually being one. Why did I feel guilty? Honor thy father and mother, and all that. That was part of it.

But mostly, I decided, I was angry.

No, not angry—hurt. Hurt that was tied into approval. I wanted my mother's approval. But how was I to get it? Near as I could tell, it'd be to marry Paul Starling and start having kids. Yuck. Not yuck to the kids part, necessarily. Don't want to get into that. It's too depressing to think about, biological clocks and all.

If marrying Paul Starling's what it takes, why do I keep worrying about it? That's out of the question. She might as well want me to flap my arms and fly.

It must be something primordial. I know that when I have represented kids who've been taken by Family and Children's Services, they always want to go back to their mothers. Even when their parents had beaten them, neglected them, sexually abused them. It didn't matter. They all wanted to be with Mommy and Daddy.

I'm no different, I guess.

I took the washcloth and soap and started scrubbing. Ought to be interesting tonight, I thought. It was going to be bad enough leaving the house at ten o'clock. Now, I'll be leaving with a married man and a black man.

I wondered if I remembered my CPR.

Mama cooked fried chicken, mashed potatoes with gravy, fried okra, corn on the cob, and biscuits. Mama and I each had a leg and Big Jack ate the rest. I had to admit I had missed Mama's cooking. Afterwards, we sat on the veranda and listened to Big Jack's wrestling tales. They turned out to be pretty interesting. I was surprised. I was also surprised at how well he played the guitar and sang. The biggest surprise of all, though, was when Mama didn't say anything when I told her I was going out so late. I went to my room to dress for the occasion.

Mama and Big Jack were in the kitchen eating the pecan pie she'd bought at the store. Mama had a piece, Big Jack had the rest. I entered wearing black trousers, black socks and tennis shoes. I had on a black, long-sleeved top.

"You belong to one of them covens?" Mama asked.

I got a broom from the corner, turned, and, with wide eyes, whispered, "Yesssss, Mama. Gonna put a spell on all parents tonight. They'll never be able to ask a question again. They'll only be able to make statements. Statements like 'My, what a lovely daughter I have,' or 'I'm so proud of you, darlin'.' "

Mama just harrumphed, but Big Jack laughed. Bits of pecan pie spit out as he said, "Oooweee, Tammi, you sure are a hoot."

I heard a knock, hurried down the hall, and went outside. "Come on," I said, and headed down the steps. We got in my car.

"You in a hurry?" Dan asked.

"Just getting the hell out of Dodge."

I started the car, pulled into the street, then stopped. "I don't know where she lived."

Dan said, "I looked in our school directory today. Eleven-fifty-eight Partridge Drive."

"Partridge Drive? Isn't that a little ritzy for a school librarian?" Partridge Drive is near Catledge University and is known for its large houses and beautifully manicured lawns. The Who's Who of Patsboro lived there.

Dan shrugged. "What it said. I was surprised too."

"Ought to be great weather for breaking and entering," Mitch said.

"No breaking, Mitch. Only entering," Dan said.

"Anyway, we're under a severe thunderstorm watch. The storms are already in Atlanta. Should be here soon."

"Great," I said.

"Doesn't matter," Dan said. "This is an indoor activity."

He reached into the bag he'd been carrying and pulled out three pairs of surgical gloves. He threw a pair to Mitch in the backseat and put a pair next to me.

"Your wife's sister still work for a proctologist?" Mitch asked. Looking in my rearview mirror, I could see Mitch holding them up with two fingers.

"Straight out of the box, Mitch."

"You and your sister-in-law get along pretty well?" Mitch asked.

"Straight from the box," Dan repeated.

Ten minutes later I was driving slowly down Partridge Drive. Dan was looking at house numbers on mailboxes and I was thinking about "entering." This would be the second time I had done this. Four years ago we had gone into Jarvis's office to look at his tax returns. Tonight we were going into a dead woman's house to look for . . . something. Not stealing anything. Doing it for a good cause.

I was beginning to drift into thoughts of situational ethics when Dan said, "There it is."

I pulled to the side of the road. A mailbox with the number 1158 sat next to a graveled driveway winding between two large houses. Hedges surrounded the driveway.

"I understand now," Dan said. "She lives in what used to be servants' quarters, behind the big houses. Saw one last year during the Tour of Homes."

"Where do I park?" I didn't want to draw attention to us.

"Look up there," Dan said. Around the curve ahead, cars lined both sides of the street. "Somebody's having a party. We'll park there."

I drove the hundred yards to the curve and pulled behind a Seville. A man dressed in a tux was opening the passenger-side door, and a woman in a flowing formal emerged.

"Wait a minute," I said. "We're not dressed for the occasion."

After waiting until the couple was well away, we headed toward the Hildegarde house. We were each carrying flashlights that Dan had provided. We crunched up the gravel driveway and I whispered, "Wish we could walk quieter." The hedges prevented us from moving off the granite chips.

Finally, a small house with a steep roof appeared in front of us. It was dark, and well away from the former master's house. We walked to the small alcove and Dan took the packet of picks given to him by Mr. Bailey, of Teal Lock and Key, after the summer Dan worked for him. He tackled the knob lock first, and turned it. It opened. The dead bolt wasn't locked.

Hot air hit us as we went in. Another death house, I thought. At least she hadn't died here. Dan flipped on his flashlight and went over to the window on the right. "Pull down the shades, but still use the flashlights, just in case." We each went to a window and lowered the shades.

There was a small living room with a fireplace, a kitchen in back of the living room, and a good-sized bedroom on the right side. Mitch came from inspecting the kitchen. "There're some stairs behind a door in here. Must go to the attic."

We stood in the living room in a small circle, waving our flashlights around. A sofa with a floral print sat in front of the fireplace. A thirteen-inch TV was in one corner. Next to it the wall was lined with bookshelves from the floor to the ceiling. A small desk sat between the windows facing the front. Above it, the wall held a shelf full of books.

"This is a small place," Dan said. "Shouldn't take long. Better start looking."

I could hear thunder in the distance as I watched Mitch go to the bedroom. Dan moved toward the floor-to-ceiling bookshelves. I looked around and decided to check out the desk.

I started with the drawers. One was filled with stubs from bills. There weren't many, and they went back at least three years. Mainly utility, telephone, that kind of thing. The only credit-card bill was from Macy's, and that was paid in full every month. One drawer contained letters. Mostly from someone who appeared to be her cousin in Missouri. The others yielded nothing of interest.

Dan was examining the bookshelf. He whispered from across the room, "Quite a collection."

I sat back in the chair and waved my flashlight around the room. There simply wasn't anything else that would have anything in it. I turned back to the desk and looked at the shelf above it. I saw mostly reference books: a dictionary, a thesaurus, an almanac. In the middle was a book with nothing written on the spine. I pulled it out and opened it up.

"Dan," I whispered.

He moved next to me.

"Her journal," I said. The book had fine binding, and contained lined pages. About half was filled with writing, the last dated three days ago.

Mitch returned from the bedroom. "Nothing in there. Chest of drawers and a small closet."

"Come here," Dan said.

Mitch stood on the other side of my chair and looked over my shoulder. All three flashlights focused on the journal.

I was afraid it would come to this. Back when the boys first came to me, I knew I should have told them to go to the police. I knew it. But I could not. I thought I was getting old. Old and no husband. No man. How little I knew then.

I could not resist the boys. They trusted me. Tackle told me what they had done. He confided in me. It felt good to have his trust. Actually, I violated that trust. I told him to keep quiet. It would pass. Nobody would really care. Nobody who counted, anyway. I was convinced I was helping the boys. Now, I know that I was lying to myself.

Times change. I changed. Experience does that. I know now how wrong I was, and am amazed how I thought what they had done was so insignificant.

Bait came to see me. He said he wanted to be rid of it. He said Fish said no. I do not know what Tackle thinks. I worry about him the most. Fish has always been strong. He'll survive. Maybe he shouldn't.

Bait knew where the evidence is. The others don't know. Bait would not tell them. He wanted the evidence to be there when he was ready. He said he just had to get that last thing done. I wonder if he did that before he was murdered? I pray he did.

I cannot believe what happened, but frightened people do frightening things. And Bear is being

blamed. Bear did not do it. I know that. I must tell
someone.
Maybe then, I can sleep in peace. It was a long
time coming. This awakening—to the truth.
God Bless Earl Warren.

"God bless Earl Warren?" I said. That was the last line in the journal. "What the hell did she mean by that?" I sure am using expletives a lot lately, I thought. Why'd I think of that now?

"Former chief justice of the Supreme Court," Dan said.

I started to say I know, but I knew he knew I knew. He was talking to himself.

"Obviously, Reeves was Bait," Mitch said.

"Yeah," I said. "So who are Fish and Tackle?" I slammed my hand on the journal. "Why did she have to use *nicknames?*"

"Wonder what they did? Back then, I mean," Dan said, pointing to the journal.

"It must've been a biggie, considering the results," Mitch said.

I picked up the journal. "I'm going to take this."

"Means more than entering," Mitch said. "Means burglary."

"TV lawyers do it all the time and get away with it."

Dan moved his flashlight off the journal, which was still open. "What're you going to do with it?"

"It's evidence, of some kind."

"Police ought to have it," Mitch said.

I said, "If we give it to the police, Lucas sees it. All you have is the opinion of an elderly school librarian that Bear's innocent. Unless somebody investigates, her babbling about Fish, Bait, and Tackle won't matter much. Not enough to cause a shadow of a doubt, anyway, considering the bat, the prints, and the blood work. No, I just want to keep it. Read the rest of it."

Dan was flipping though it as I talked. "Don't see anything else about this in here. Wonder how long she's been keeping these?"

Mitch said, "If we could find more, they might cause a

shadow of a doubt." He paused. "I know there aren't any in the bedroom."

"Not on the bookshelf, either," Dan said.

Maybe upstairs, I thought and told them that.

In the kitchen, Mitch indicated the door to the stairs. There was another door next to it. "What's in there?" I asked.

"Water heater, ironing board, stuff like that," Mitch said.

"Come on," Dan said, as he went through the door to the stairs.

The stairs were steep. Another door at the top led into the attic. The three of us could stand in the middle, but the roof sloped sharply on both sides. The space was filled with boxes. Dozens of boxes.

The flashlights brightened the enclosed room. I looked at Dan and Mitch. I knew what they were thinking. How could we look in all these boxes? Yet the other journals could hold the key. They could tell us who to look for. Lucas's involvement with Jarvis notwithstanding, this called for a search warrant. We'd never be able to look through all these boxes surreptitiously. It might be worth a shot to get official permission, though, even if Lucas knew.

I sighed and said, "I'm going back downstairs."

Mitch and Dan followed. "How old was Reeves?" Dan asked.

"Forty-three," I answered.

"He was in high school during the late sixties. Hildegarde has every yearbook from when she started teaching." He went to the living-room bookshelves, pulled out several, and brought them to Mitch and me. "Look through these. Focus on the candids. See if you see Reeves."

"Why?" Mitch asked.

I knew what Dan was thinking. "Assuming Reeves was Bait, we need to find Fish and Tackle. If they were friends, they might be together in a candid picture." I flipped through the yearbook on my lap. "I wonder if Reeves changed much since high school. I saw him around town some, and saw his picture in the paper, but people change."

Mitch said, "Let's find him in the class pages. Then we'll know what to look for."

I looked at my watch. It was only 10:20. It seemed like we'd been in there for hours. We sat on the couch, holding our flashlights and turning pages.

"Here it is," Dan said. We looked at Dr. Reeves's senior picture.

We went through the book looking for candid shots. Mitch said, "Hot-toe-willy!" and pointed to a picture. Reeves was plainly visible. He had signed *Bait* across his face. The other two students in the picture were picking him up, but their faces were obscured by his legs. They were signed *Tackle* and *Fish.* That was the only picture we found.

"I'll ask around," Dan said. "Maybe somebody remembers the nicknames. Check on classmates, too. We have annuals at the high school. I'll—"

The sound of breaking glass stopped him in midsentence.

Someone else was breaking and entering.

Chapter 20

━ ━ ━ ━ ━ ━ ━ ━ ━ ━

We looked at one another.

"What?" Mitch whispered.

The sound of a window sliding open came from the bedroom. Dan stood and motioned us to follow him. I didn't argue. I grabbed the journal and followed them into the kitchen. Dan turned the knob on the door that led to the backyard. It wouldn't open. The door had a dead bolt that opened with a key, but the key wasn't there. Dan pulled out his picks as the sound of footsteps came from the living room. A light was switched on, and Dan turned away from the back door. Mitch and I followed him as he headed for the door to the attic.

I didn't want to go up there. There were boxes but nothing else. Whoever was in here might look up there. I grabbed Dan's shoulders and indicated the door that led to the water heater.

The space was small, but all three of us could get in it. We were beside the water heater. The ironing board was in front of us. Anybody opening the door wouldn't likely see past the ironing board in the dark closet. I was next to the wall and leaned on it, trying to breathe. I felt as if I couldn't get any air, but I was afraid to try harder for fear of making noise. Dan put his hands on my shoulders and squeezed.

Light flashed in the tiny space. I tensed and looked up. A vent with wooden slats was on the wall right above my head. Beams of light showed through them. I stood on my tiptoes and peered through the slats.

Oh Jesus, God!

All I could see was the top of a head. Just the top covered with short, blond hair, not more than six inches from my eyes. I strangled a cry, went flat-footed, and bent my head, squeezing my eyes. Was it Crowe?

I felt a tap on my shoulder and looked up. Dan was looking at me.

"Crowe?" I mouthed, and tried to make my face look like a question.

He didn't react. Just looked at me.

I stood, leaning on the wall, waiting for the door to open and to see Crowe looking in. Somehow, I knew if it was Crowe, he'd see us. I heard his footsteps, first in one direction, then another. There was the sound of a door opening. He walked up the stairs next to us.

"Can we get out?" I whispered.

Mitch shook his head.

Dan too.

Stupid question. How do we know he's alone?

His footsteps moved from one side of the attic to the other. Thank God we hadn't gone up there.

He was coming back down the stairs. More movement in the kitchen, then a banging. Or scraping. The scraping of metal against metal.

What's he doing?

The sounds stopped.

I looked at Dan and he shrugged.

We waited. Finally, I got up on tiptoes again and looked. The room appeared to be empty, but I smelled something.

What was it?

Gas! I smelled gas. Seconds later it permeated the closet.

"Gas," Dan said. "We gotta get out of here. To hell with him."

When Mitch opened the door, the smell of gas hit us in the face. The room was filled with it, and the gas, rushing out, sounded like a hurricane. Gasping, we headed for the door. Dan tried the knob again, to no effect. He kicked the door, but it was solid. Mitch stood on the small table under the window next to the door. He put his foot through the window. The sound of shattering wood and glass filled the room. He kicked more until there was a space big enough for us to crawl out. I kept expecting Buddy Crowe to run in from the living room. He didn't. Dan and Mitch pulled me up and pushed me through the window. Soon all three of us were outside.

"Run!" Dan said as he pulled on me. Mitch was on the other side. We dived under hedges at the rear of the yard. I looked back at the house.

A hundred years of history blew into the inky sky.

Heat surged over us. Flames shot through what had been the attic and roof. Pieces of flaming wood were falling all around us.

"Come on," Dan urged.

I followed him and Mitch along the hedge, behind the adjoining house. We felt our way through the dark to the street. People were coming from everywhere and running toward the towering flames.

It was then that I realized it was raining. A bolt of lightning brightened the sky as we walked toward my car. I wanted to run, but Dan kept saying, "Walk, walk. Look natural." I don't think it really mattered. Nobody was paying a bit of attention to us.

When we got to the car, Dan asked, "Want me to drive?"

"No. I'll drive," I said. "Gas just got to me." We got in the Geo and I pulled away.

I drove without thinking where I was going. "Shouldn't we go to the police?"

Mitch said, "What are we going to tell them? That a house on Partridge Drive was just nuked?"

"Reasonable chance they're already aware of that fact," Dan said.

"Yeah, but," I said, "it could have been Crowe."

"Did you see him?" Dan asked.

"Just his hair," I admitted.

"If it was Crowe, he couldn't be any more wanted than he already is," Dan said. "They've been looking for him for four years. Still are. He's wanted for murder. What's the point? And at what price?"

Dan was right. I could be disbarred, Dan could lose his job, and Mitch his business. All to tell them Buddy Crowe *might* have done something in addition to committing murder. This time he just torched a house.

Along with the evidence, I thought. The journals. I looked at the book next to me. We still had that. That was something.

"What do we do now?" I asked.

"Go home," Dan said. "Before we get killed by this storm."

The rain was beating on the Geo. Lightning flashed continuously and the trees were flying from the wind. Normally, I'd have been scared to death in this chaos in a car. Einstein was right. Everything is relative.

The storm hadn't let up when I parked behind Big Jack's Cadillac. Mitch and Dan insisted on going in with me and checking out the house. I reminded them that Mama and Big Jack were there and pointed to their lights on upstairs. They still wanted to check. We dashed through the rain and wind and went inside. They walked with me into the bedroom. Everything was as I had left it.

When we walked back to the hall, Mama was standing at the foot of the stairs. "You all right, baby? I was worried 'bout you in this storm and all."

"I'm fine, Mama."

She was staring at Mitch.

"This is Mitch."

"Hidy, ma'am," Mitch said with a slight wave of his hand.

Mama gave Mitch a hard look and arched her eyebrows. She focused on me and sighed. "Well, I'm goin' to bed now, Tammi."

"Good night, Mrs. Randall," Dan said.

" 'Night," Mama said without turning around.

After she had closed her door, I looked at Dan and Mitch and said, "So?"

"So tomorrow I see if I can find out who Fish and Tackle are." Dan paused. "We need some time to process all this. How about coming to my house for dinner tomorrow night?"

I looked up the stairs.

"No problem. Bring them along." He said he'd call tomorrow to confirm the time. He and Mitch left.

I went in the bedroom and locked the door. I pulled off my clothes and lay on my bed. Naked. Right on top. One nice thing about what had happened that morning was I'd never have to wrestle with that issue again.

Mama knew.

There was no way I was going to sleep anytime soon. I was about to reach for my Tony Hillerman novel when the air was filled with a crack, followed by an incredibly loud boom. The lights brightened for a split second. Darkness followed.

Noooo . . . not now!

I was lying in pitch black. No streetlights were filtering through the sheets hanging on the window. I was wide awake. I *needed* light. *Had* to have it.

Candles. In the kitchen. In the drawer next to the sink. I got out of bed and groped around for my clothes. Where were they?

Oh, the hell with it, I thought, nobody can see me, anyway, and I needed light.

I felt my way to the bedroom door, turned right in the hall, passed the stairs, and moved into the kitchen. The rain was beating on the aluminum awning covering a small patio off the back door. I bumped into a chair that shouldn't have been there. Mama and Big Jack had moved it. The window in here had no sheets and the lightning provided some occasional light. I moved toward the sink and opened the drawer with the candles.

"Ahhhhhhhh!" I screamed, as a body bumped into me and a hand squeezed my breast.

Through my scream, I could hear another one. I crossed my arms in front of me as I heard chairs being knocked over.

"Lordy, Tammi, I'm sorry. I didn't know you were down here."

"Big Jack?" I said.

"Came down to see if you had a flashlight in here."

I took a deep breath. It was absolutely black except for occasional quick flashes of light. Big Jack was standing in the corner on the far side of the room.

"Don't have a flashlight. But I'm putting a couple of candles on the table. Wait till I leave, then take them upstairs. Just be careful."

"Sure will." A flash of lightning revealed him on the other side of the table, grinning.

I took a candle, some matches, and a plate. I felt my way back to my bedroom and closed the door. I lit the candle and dripped wax on the plate until there was enough to hold the candle. I put the plate on the nightstand next to my bed. Lying in bed, I could feel my heart beating a hundred miles a minute.

As I lay there, the events of the evening washed over me.

No, not just that evening. The whole thing. The wreck. The dumb thing with Snickers. The rose and the candy. Big Jack. The repressed fear that had become constant. I twisted my neck. Pain shot from the continually tight muscles. I can't take this anymore, I thought as the room became blurry through tears. No. Don't cry.

You're not a crier, Tammi, I told myself.

I wiped my eyes and looked around the room, now dimly lit by the flickering candle. Twenty-seven years old. Living in a room with sheets on the windows . . . alone.

All alone.

The tears came again. Tears from fear and loneliness. I'd never felt so alone.

Wouldn't Friday ever come?

Chapter 21

"I presume your goal is to become familiar with this," Bernard said. "You are not interested in shooting three bottles in the air in one throw, or anything like that, are you?"

He was holding Daddy's pistol. We had been sitting in the lobby of Jackson's Indoor Firing Range for an hour. Bernard had insisted that the pistol be serviced before we shot it.

While we waited, he had explained that the Smith & Wesson Model 58 hadn't been manufactured for at least ten years. "How old were you when your father showed you how to shoot?" he had asked.

I shrugged. "I don't know. Maybe fifteen."

"What do you remember about it?"

"Oh, it was fun. We shot at cans."

"You were not shooting that pistol," he said while nodding his head toward the man at the desk behind the counter.

"How do you know?" I asked.

"The Model fifty-eight is a forty-one-magnum with a four-inch barrel. You will see in a little while, but if you had shot it, you would remember more than shooting cans."

Now we were standing in front of a concrete-sided firing lane and he was holding the six-shot revolver. He pulled back the hammer. "Much better," he commented.

"It's been sitting around a long time."

He handed me the pistol and showed me how to break it down and load it, and gave me a lecture on gun safety. After that, Bernard said, "This pistol is quite a beast. You need to stay relaxed, but be ready for it to want to come back to you. Do not jerk the trigger. Squeeze it gently." He gave me a pair of ear mufflers. "Please put these on. This weapon is quite noisy." He attached a target to a clip on a wire and flipped a switch that moved the target about twenty feet away. "Keep both eyes open, and squeeze the trigger, gently."

I put both hands on the grip as Bernard had shown me, pointed the gun, and squeezed. Despite his warnings, I was not ready for the result. The gun flew back and the noise was incredible, even through the mufflers. I looked back at Bernard, who was laughing heartily. "Has somewhat of a kick, does it not?"

I shot for an hour and it got easier—I even hit the target a couple of times. When we were through, I bought a small cleaning kit and he showed me how to use it.

When we were in his Land Rover heading back to the office he said, "If you are going to keep this pistol, you should practice regularly for a while. I will meet with you weekly and you practice in between."

"I'd appreciate that."

He looked at me briefly. I had the feeling he wanted to say something. "Yes?" I asked.

He glanced at me again. "I have been debating whether I ought to mention this to you or not." He hesitated.

"What?"

He cleared his throat. "I received a call from Mayor Darnton today." He hesitated again.

I didn't say anything.

"It seems Chief Bryant's concerned about the Cleveland case."

"Aren't we all."

"This is all thirdhand, you understand. Mayor Darnton's concerned because Detective Anderson says you are pursuing a theory that some fellow involved in the Jarvis case came back to town and committed the murder." He glanced at me again.

Where's this going? "Maybe. Either him or another white guy

James Cleveland says was with him." My puzzlement was turning to anger. "Anyway, where does the mayor come off getting involved—"

Bernard lifted his right hand. "Let me finish. The mayor talked about the consolidation vote coming up, and how he was planning to run for office in the new government. He is concerned about the Reeveses' murders being drug out and him being blamed. This is a high-profile case." Bernard stopped talking while he moved across three lanes of the Atlanta Highway so he could turn left. He continued, "The mayor pointed out how much evidence they had, and he understood that our job was to protect our client's rights . . ."

"Uh huh," I said sarcastically.

". . . but that the evidence was overwhelming in this case. He indicated his displeasure at our becoming, in his words, 'some kind of publicly funded ACLU.' "

I was fuming. "So he's threatening our funding." I looked at Bernard. "What'd you tell him?"

He sighed. "You know, Tammi, through my years in the courtroom I learned there's a time for subtlety and a time for being straightforward."

"And?"

"I told the mayor to go to hell. I told him that if a conversation like the one we were having ever occurred again, I would ensure he had as much chance of winning an election in Teal County as Saddam Hussein."

"Good for you," I said. But I was thinking, What are you doing, Lucas? Why?

"The conversation was not even worth mentioning. That is why I said nothing until now." He glanced at me again. "But I hear that, and connect the man Detective Anderson is talking about with what you have told me, and I must assume he is talking about Raven—"

"Crowe. Buddy Crowe."

"Oh, yes. I knew it was some kind of blackbird. Anyway, I think about that and suddenly you want to learn how to use a pistol. It gives me pause."

I shifted in my seat so I could look at him. "One's not necessarily connected to the other."

He stared straight ahead. "Yes, well. What I read in the papers this morning also gives me pause. If you remember, I was in your office the other day when you received a phone call. I did not mean to listen. So impolite. However, I was sitting there and could hardly help . . ."

"No problem."

"Yes. In any event, I could not help but hear the name Hildegarde. Rather unusual name. I read of the unfortunate accident that befell her. Now this morning I read that her house met a rather spectacular demise last night."

"I read that, too."

I hadn't involved Bernard in the investigation because I didn't want to infringe on his retirement. I'd already asked him to take my cases. That was enough.

Now I couldn't involve him because of last night. No matter what my rationalizations were, going into Minerva Hildegarde's house was clearly illegal. I would not allow Bernard to become implicated in that.

I said, "The fire chief blamed the explosion on a gas leak. Empty house, so nobody noticed. A pilot light or any tiny spark, maybe something from the lightning, could have set it off. Just a coincidence."

He pursed his lips and nodded.

I continued, "And on the other thing, the guy James Cleveland saw sort of looked like Crowe. I'm just checking out his story, the way I should."

Bernard didn't look satisfied.

"And like I told you, Daddy used to take me out shooting. That's one of the only things he ever did with me. I felt good when we were out there together. Just re-creating a memory, I think."

We were at a stoplight. "Well, I am here if you need me."

"Thanks."

After that, we rode in silence.

Chapter 22

⌐ ⌐ ⌐ ⌐ ⌐ ⌐ ⌐ ⌐ ⌐ ⌐

I was in the backseat of the Cadillac. Mama was driving and Big Jack sat beside her. Right beside her, in the middle of the seat.

I leaned forward and asked, "Why are you driving, Mama?"

"Oh, Big Jack likes to play around sometimes."

Likes to play around? Is this my mother? Suddenly an *ahoooga* blasted from the front of the Cadillac.

"Land sakes, Big Jack," Mama said, "Give me some warnin'."

Big Jack reared his head, howled, and reached under the glove compartment, and the *ahoooga* sounded again. I slid down in my seat when people started pointing.

We were on our way to Dan's house. He'd left a message with Mrs. Thompson that we were to come at seven o'clock, and by some miracle I had got the message. Mama didn't want to go when I told her about the invitation. She's not comfortable with strangers. That was fine with me, but Big Jack wanted to go, and he talked her into it.

Mama stopped behind Mitch's Mercedes in the circular driveway in front of Dan's house. Kristen and Megan ran out of the house yelling, "They're here! They're here!" Megan was ten and looked like her mother. Seven-year-old Kristen favored Dan. After hugging me, they ran to the front of the car to look at the bullhorns on the hood.

Big Jack was still in the car, and he blew his horn. The girls jumped back and giggled. He laughed as he got out of the car. "How you like that?" He picked up Kristen in his massive hands and tossed her in the air.

"Be careful," I called to him. Big Jack tossed her again and Kristen laughed wildly.

"Looks like Kristen's made a friend," I heard from behind me. Meg was standing behind the railing on the porch of the brick house.

"Looks like it." I motioned Mama to follow me. We stepped onto the porch and I introduced her to Meg.

Mama said hello. She looked at me. I knew what she was thinking: This is the woman whose husband you was messin' with.

I shook my head at her.

"Come on, you guys," I called to Big Jack and the girls.

He carried Kristen and held Megan by the hand and followed us into the house. Mitch and Dan were in the living room, and introductions were made to those who hadn't met yet.

"Where's Samantha?" I asked. I wanted to tell her about how Snickers had scared me the other night. But the fourteen-year-old was spending the week with a friend and her family at their mountain cottage in Highlands, North Carolina.

We ate on the deck that extended off the dining room. The front that brought the storms had passed, leaving a blue sky and cooler temperatures behind. The pork chops Dan barbecued almost melted in my mouth. I ate way too much of Meg's sweet potato casserole and fried squash. I passed on dessert, but Big Jack ate three helpings of the black-bottom pie. I had forgotten to warn Dan about Big Jack's appetite. He had provided only a couple of pork chops per person.

Dan and Mitch cleared the table and Mama, Meg, and I cleaned up in the kitchen. Mama and Meg found a common interest in the crafts Meg made. They went to Meg's workshop in the basement. In the living room, Big Jack was telling Kristen and Megan about how he had beaten the Avenging Assassin. I joined Mitch and Dan, who were sitting at the table on the deck.

"Read the paper today?" Dan asked.

Mitch and I nodded.

"Looks like Crowe's gotten away with it. If it was him."

"I'm tired of saying that," I said. " 'If,' I mean."

"Well, Bear confirmed it, but Willie Moon didn't. Be nice if somebody else saw him," Dan said.

"Nobody at Idlewood Shopping Center did," I said. "None that I could find, anyway."

"Are the police looking into Hildegarde's death?" Mitch asked.

Dan took a sip of iced tea. "Would think so. Of course, with Lucas there . . ."

"Yeah," Mitch said sadly. "But listen, if you're through with Crowe's picture, Tammi, I'd like to use it. Thought I might go over to Sable's bar. Ask around there. Willie may not remember, but others might."

"Are you sure you want to go there?"

"Hey. Be like old times in Newark. Drink, drink, laugh, laugh, bang, bang." He held his hands in the shape of a gun as he said it.

"So tell us about Dr. Cutlip," Dan said.

Mitch crossed his legs at the knees and said in a soft voice, "Dr. Cutlip very much regrets the passing of his dear friend and colleague, Dr. Gary Reeves."

Despite what we were talking about, I couldn't help but laugh. That had to be Cutlip, exactly.

Mitch continued in his own voice. "Basically, Dr. Cutlip was pretty disgusted with Dr. Reeves. For years they'd worked together on genetic research. Mostly dealing with the nature of abnormalities that exist in closed societies. Isolated peoples, ethnic groups . . . things like that. I didn't understand it all, but their theory was that therein lay the key to a variety of other ailments. Multiple sclerosis, for example."

"So, why was he disgusted?" I asked.

"He says Reeves went bonkers. He didn't say that exactly, but that's what he meant. He said a few months ago Reeves came up with something he called 'sociogenetics.' Wanted to study the relationship between a person's genetics and his environment."

"Why bonkers?" Dan asked.

"Cutlip equated it with a research physician studying the techniques of a medicine man. From what I could gather, which wasn't easy, Cutlip believes all things stem from a genetic predisposition. Not only physical stuff, but behavior, too. Said Reeves was with him on that for years, but suddenly decided maybe it wasn't so."

"Did he say what Reeves was doing to pursue the theory?" I asked. Maybe some idea of his activities would give us a motive for his murder.

"He didn't know. They quit working together. He said Reeves became moody, quiet. Wouldn't talk much. But he was working on something. Some kind of article, he thought."

Dan leaned forward in his chair. "First his housekeeper and now his colleague say Reeves changed. Sure would like to know what he was doing." He was silent for a moment. "Maybe we ought to look in his study again."

"For more than one reason," I said. "I got the coroner's report today and talked to the pathologist. It appears the wife was killed first. Maybe a good while earlier. Not hours, but earlier, anyway. Not at the same time."

"Like maybe somebody was trying to get something from him," Mitch said.

"Like information," I added. "Hildegarde's journal indicated Reeves knew where some kind of evidence was. The other two wanted to know, too."

Mitch said, "One thing I know for sure, James Cleveland didn't interrogate them. If he killed them, he would have gotten the man first. And . . . the thing is . . . if somebody was looking for something, the place should have been torn up. It wasn't."

"Might have been careful," Dan said. "Remember, this was supposed to look like Bear was there to steal stuff. Might have looked funny to leave the room a mess."

"Maybe," Mitch said. "But guys just tear things up for the hell of it sometimes."

"That's true too," Dan said.

"Da*ah*dy," Dan's ten-year-old daughter, Megan, said from

the sliding glass door, "Kristen won't give me that slimy hand thing."

"That slimy hand thing?"

"Yeah. She says she won't give it to me unless I let her be a dog. I don't want her to be a dog."

Mitch and I looked at each other and tried not to laugh.

"Look," Dan said. "If Kristen wants to be a dog, she can be a dog. If you want the 'slimy hand thing,' whatever that is, I'd suggest you approve. Anything else?"

"But I don't want her to be a dog."

"Way life is, darling. Sometimes you just got to give a little." Dan looked at us. "Both these children have been identified as gifted. Sometimes, it's hard to fathom."

Dan's daughter laughed and turned to leave.

I said, "Megan, where's Big Jack?"

"He's watching wrestling on the TV in the playroom." She looked at Dan. "Daddy, is it true that watching too close to the TV will ruin your eyes?"

"That's what I've always heard, but I don't know if it's true or not. Why?"

Megan turned and said as she went through the door, "Got to tell Uncle Big Jack."

I rolled my eyes. "My future daddy." I thought about that for a moment. "Anyway, I'd like to look through Reeves's study again."

"Another covert entry?" Mitch asked.

"Not this time," I answered. "This is the crime scene. If we get caught, it'd not only mean we're in trouble, it'd mess up the case. Can't do that to James."

"Means we got to deal with Lucas," Dan said.

Quiet followed. They were probably thinking what I was. None of us could believe that Lucas was involved with Jarvis.

"Then we'll just have to," I said. Looking at Dan, I asked, "Find anything on Fish or Tackle?"

"Nothing. But I did find something interesting. Went by school today and talked to Chris Mize. He's running the summer school, so I figured he'd be there. Started as a teacher thirty-five years ago and is a vice-principal now. Figured if anybody'd know something like that, he would."

"But he didn't?" Mitch asked.

"Nope. Never heard of Fish, Bait, or Tackle. He did say something about Minerva Hildegarde, though." Dan had been in his usual reclining position in the plastic chair. Now he sat straight up. "Said about twenty years ago she was called into the principal's office. Mize was a teacher then so he didn't know the details, but the rumor was she was told she was getting too close to the students. Especially boys."

"Twenty years ago," Mitch said. "About when Reeves was in school. Principal might know who the boys were."

"Thought of that. I checked, and he's dead. He was about to retire at the time. Same with the superintendent. I got Mize to let me look at Hildegarde's file. The one the principal keeps. Nothing in there about it, either."

"Nuts," I said.

"I'm still checking. So far everybody I've talked to who was around at the time only heard the rumor. Nothing else."

"Is that what was interesting?" I asked.

"No, something else." Dan put both elbows on the table and looked at Mitch and me. "Figured one of Reeves's classmates might know Fish, Bait, or Tackle. Or at least who Reeves hung around with. The library has all the yearbooks. Didn't have much time to look at them last night at Minerva's."

"Got that right," Mitch said.

"Plenty of time today. I copied their names. Classmates, I mean. It struck me that they'd have had their twenty-year reunion recently."

"That means somebody has their addresses," I said.

"I found out who organized the reunion. She still lives in Patsboro. I talked to her today and she said I could get the list tomorrow."

"That *is* interesting," I said.

"No, that's still not it," Dan said.

"Damn it, what the hell's so interesting?" Mitch asked. He echoed my sentiments.

Dan looked at both of us again. "Guess who was a classmate of Dr. Reeves?"

"Come on, Dan," I said.

"How about Lawrence K. Gilstrap?"

"Radar?" I said.

"None other."

I stood up and moved to the railing around the deck. "You said Radar visited Jarvis."

"Twice," Dan said. "Once a long time ago and once a few months ago."

Something connected when he said that. What was it?

"Radar was cleared of any involvement with Jarvis. Even got a better job afterwards," I said.

"Georgia Bureau of Investigation," Mitch said.

"Who wants to talk to Radar?" Dan asked. "See if he wants to say why he was seeing Jarvis."

"I will," I said. "Tomorrow."

We sat silently. Apparently that was it.

Mitch stood. "Well, I think I might pop over to Sable's. You got Crowe's picture, Tammi?"

I took it from my purse and gave it to him. "We need to be getting home. Didn't get much sleep last night."

"I can't imagine," Dan said. "Thought you'd sleep like a baby. Wish you didn't have to go back to that big old house."

"Hey, Big Jack'll be there. After the Avenging Assassin, Buddy Crowe's a piece of cake."

Everybody gathered to say good-bye. I had to drag Big Jack away from the girls. He'd been playing his guitar and singing. Mama had a couple of ribbon bows Meg had taught her how to make. It was obvious that Mama had taken to her. Standing on the porch, Dan said, "Have fun with Michael tomorrow night."

Meg said, "Michael?"

"Michael Hutcheson. Tammi's moving into prime-time Patsboro society."

"Shut up, Dan," I said. I noticed a funny look on Meg's face. She smiled and said how much she enjoyed having us over.

"Who's this Michael?" Mama asked as we walked toward Big Jack's car.

I was in the tub again. The water was as hot as I could stand it. I thought it might loosen the muscles that had stayed tight for days. And the bath did help, along with the passage of time from last night's scare with Big Jack. Knowing Daddy's pistol was under my pillow helped, too. I have never liked guns, but . . .

I didn't want to think about that.

Michael came to mind. Why had Meg looked so strange when she heard his name? It was obvious there was something she wanted to say, but didn't. I'd call her tomorrow . . . as if I was calling for something else, like thanking her for the dinner, and get her into a conversation.

I didn't want to think about that, either.

I began washing and when I got to my legs, I noticed they were getting stubbly. Shaving legs seems real stupid to me, and I envy European women, who I've read don't do it.

But I was going out tomorrow night. I decided to shave with a razor blade tonight, to give the inevitable cuts time to heal. Nothing like going out with blood oozing down your legs. I'd touch them up with my electric razor tomorrow.

I ran the water in the tub and sat on the toilet lid with my left leg propped on the tub's side. As I was working on the inside of my upper thigh, a fly landed on my forehead and I jerked my head to get it off.

There was Big Jack.

"What are you doing!" I yelled over the sound of the running water.

He was standing in the doorway.

I yelled, "Get out!"

He grinned. "I'm sorry. I used your bathroom this morning to brush my teeth. Just came to get the brush."

I had doubled up and didn't want to move. My towel was on the floor at the far end of the tub.

"Get *out!*" I yelled again.

"Sorry, Tammi." Big Jack went to the sink and got his toothbrush.

As he went out my door, I heard Mama saying, "What's goin' on?"

I put the towel around me and hollered, "Mama!"

That was enough. Last night was no accident. How long had he been standing there? And the other morning, too.

"Mama, come in here!"

"What's goin' on?" she repeated.

"Listen. I've enjoyed you and Big Jack being here and all and it sure has been nice visiting, but y'all have to leave."

"But Tammi, baby . . ."

"Tomorrow," I said firmly.

She turned on her heels and marched out. "Just don't want me 'round so that Michael feller can come over here."

"I wish," I said quietly and shut the door. I threw off the towel, turned off the lights, and crawled into bed. Time to get some sleep, finally.

Time. I thought back to Dan's deck. What had Dan said? Radar had visited Jarvis. Once a long time ago and once a few months ago. Something happened a long time ago. Something happened a short time ago. That's what Minerva Hildegarde wrote. Something bad back then, something bad now.

Reeves had changed—within the last year. Detective Lucas Anderson had seen Jarvis many times—within the last year. GBI agent Radar Gilstrap had seen Jarvis—within the last year.

Something had happened within the last year.

What was it?

Chapter 23

Ellie Sampson had passed away during the night, and Mrs. Thompson was in top form that Friday morning. She was on the phone, busily spreading the word. From my office, I heard her cluck-clucking, hanging up, and quickly dialing again.

I rubbed my arm that was sore from an early morning session at Jackson's Indoor Shooting Range and reread the message she had left on my desk. *Gone to Athens for the late ceremony. Stables was a success.* Beneath that, Mrs. Thompson had written, *Miss Randall, considering all the troubles they cause us, you should be careful with those Arabs.*

I was impressed. Mrs. Thompson wasn't too far off this time. I suspected the message was, Gone to Augusta for the delayed grand opening and somebody at Sable's had recognized Buddy Crowe's picture. Mitch must have used his Middle Eastern accent. As with the others, it was superb.

I leaned back in my chair. Buddy Crowe *was* here. Willie Moon either didn't remember or didn't want to remember. Two, maybe more, confirmations, though. Mama and Big Jack were packing when I left this morning. Big Jack hadn't said a word to me. Mama hadn't said that much. I'd be alone again.

Big Jack or Buddy Crowe. Some choice. Or find somewhere else to stay. I thought about being in that house alone. I thought about Big Jack again.

So he liked to look. Somehow confirming Buddy Crowe's presence put that in a different light. Except one time he didn't just look. He had copped a feel.

But it had been dark. Maybe . . .

I picked up the phone and dialed my number. No answer. They were gone.

Good, I thought. I don't want Big Jack around. I felt my arm throbbing again. That was something. May not get much sleep, but I was hitting the target. Not necessarily bull's-eyes, but with that gun it wouldn't take much to discourage anyone if I had to.

I shook my head. Enough of that.

After dialing information for the GBI's number in Atlanta, I worked through a couple of bureaucratic layers and finally was talking to Radar Gilstrap's secretary.

"He's out of town until Monday," she said.

"I'm an attorney in Patsboro. I need to talk to him about a client I'm defending. You know how to get in touch with him?"

"You can't. He's with Jerry Moreau in his cabin in Rabun County. They're fishing. There aren't any telephones. Like I said, he'll be back Monday."

The name was familiar, but I couldn't place it. "Jerry Moreau," I said, hoping she'd add to that.

She did. "Head of Pardons and Paroles."

Of course. I'd written a couple of letters for relatives of clients who were coming before the board. They'd been addressed to him. "Do they go fishing often?"

"Not since I've been here. But I haven't been here all that long. About a year."

When we were trying to figure out what Jarvis was doing four years ago, it was seemingly insignificant information that eventually led to his downfall. I thought about that and extended the conversation.

"How's Radar doing? I haven't seen him in years."

She laughed. "How long has he been called Radar? That's what we call him, but not to his face."

"At least four years. That's when I knew him."

"I guess he's doing OK. Keeps busy."

She was a talker. She described some cases he'd closed out and said he always got the tough ones. I kept her going. I moved the conversation to her past, and she told me how she ended up in Atlanta from Tupelo, Mississippi. Soon I pretty much had her life story, including some intimate details. I guess with Radar gone, she didn't have much to do.

"How do you like working for Radar?"

She said he could be pretty hard, but was usually fair. She paused. "Except maybe for one thing. I don't think he likes blacks too much. Here in the office, when we're alone, he calls them 'niggeroes.' Not Negroes or niggers, but niggeroes. I guess he figures with me being from Tupelo, it doesn't matter. But to tell you the truth, I don't like to hear him say that." With a hint of apology in her voice, she said, "I mean, I had some black friends in school, you know?"

I told her I'd recently seen a mutual friend who said he'd changed in the last few months. Had she noticed anything?

"Now that you mention it, he has become a little different. Quieter, or something. It's hard to tell, though. He never says a whole lot anyway. Maybe distracted is more the word." She paused, "Yeah. Kind of distracted. That's why I thought this fishing trip was a good idea. Maybe he needs to relax. He stays awful busy."

We talked a while longer and she said we should get together for lunch if I was ever in Atlanta. I said that'd be nice and hung up.

Radar Gilstrap had been quieter than usual and went to see Jarvis in the last few months. I thought about Lucas. What was the connection between Lucas Anderson and Radar four years ago? Lucas had been a deputy in the Teal County Sheriff's Department and Radar had been a detective. They didn't work together too much. At least it didn't appear that way. But still, they were in the same department and both played a part in getting Jarvis's organization.

I was facing the window behind my desk while I was thinking about all that, so I didn't know that Landry had come in until I heard him clear his throat.

When I turned he said, "Heavy-duty stuff?"

"Just thinking about this case. James Cleveland, I mean."

Landry didn't want to talk about the Cleveland case. Getting the kid off would mean that Patsboro's voters, those who counted anyway, would be ticked off. He wanted no part of it. Instead he whispered, "This Sampson lady must've been somebody pretty important."

"What makes you think that?"

"Alva. She's on one of those highs she always gets when somebody important dies. Especially when she's the one who gets to spread the word. I swear, I think she's gonna bust."

I shrugged. "Never heard of her."

"Anyway, Bernard asked me to tell you he talked to the mayor again. He said he—the mayor, I mean—backed way off. Bernard wanted me to be sure and tell you he said 'way off.' "

"Good."

Landry stood there waiting. He couldn't stand not knowing what the mayor was backing off of. I didn't enlighten him. Finally, he asked the question that had become ritual. "Doing anything tonight?"

"Yeah."

He stood looking at me.

"I have a date with Michael Hutcheson."

It sounded funny saying that. Why, for God's sake? I was twenty-seven years old. That's probably why, I thought. Landry stood there, looking hurt.

"Landry, I sure wish Victoria's Secret had a store here in Patsboro. I'd love to buy something special for tonight."

"I gotta go," he said and left.

I picked up the phone and started to dial Dan's number. No, I decided. I'd rather talk to his wife face-to-face.

Which is what I did later that afternoon. Meg was in the yard planting azaleas when I pulled into the driveway. She was in shorts and on her knees. We exchanged greetings and she said Dan wasn't home.

"Actually, I wanted to talk to you," I said. "I wanted to thank you for having us over last night."

She finished patting dirt around an azalea, then stood. "I enjoyed it. Your mother is quite a person."

"Yes, she is."

"Kind of surprised me, though. You and her seem quite, uh . . ."

"Different."

"Yeah," she agreed.

"I'm not sure how that came to be. Sometime around seventh grade, I decided to speak standard English. Mrs. Hanners, my English teacher, worked with me. Somehow, speaking standard English sort of led me in other directions. I can't really explain it."

Meg nodded her head and waved toward the porch. "Want to sit a while?"

We sat on two plastic chairs. "You're doing wonders with your yard."

"I gave up trying to plant grass. With all the oaks, that was a mistake. Azaleas and liriope grow fine, though. Works a lot better." Meg went on to outline what she planned to do to complete the landscaping.

After that we talked about the kids, who were all at various activities at the moment. It was after a pause that I said, "Meg, when Dan mentioned Michael Hutcheson's name last night, you looked kind of . . . funny. Or something. Do you know him?"

Meg shrugged. "No. Never met him. Really, I don't know much. . . ." She looked uncomfortable.

"Well, I don't know him well. He came to one of the anti-airport meetings and he's gotten involved in that." I looked at her. "I do kind of like him, though."

She looked at me. The image of Dan and me in the hotel in New Orleans flashed in my mind. Stop that, I thought.

"I just happen to know somebody. I really don't know anything."

"Somebody who knows Michael?"

"Yes. It's his ex-wife. I don't know her all that well. Her children go to school with mine. We've worked together on some things for the parent-teacher group."

I knew Michael had been married, but that had been long ago and I hadn't heard anything about children. She explained that.

"She remarried. She and Michael didn't have any." We sat in silence. Finally, Meg said, "We worked a booth together at the Fall Festival last year. It was the early shift and there wasn't much business. We got to talking. Of course, we had spoken before so we weren't strangers. Anyway, she talked about Michael."

I nodded my head. What? What? was what I was thinking.

She shifted in her chair toward me. "Look, I don't like to gossip. I hate it. And most of what she said was good. He was nice, considerate . . . loving." She hesitated again. "But she said he went through periods of . . ." She stopped again.

"Yes?"

"Moodiness. Depression. He'd be fine for a while, then go into a funk. He was hospitalized a couple of times."

"That's what caused the divorce?"

"No. She said it wasn't easy when he was going through one of those times, but he never did anything to her or anything like that. The thing that she couldn't take, though, was his mother."

"His mother?"

"Yeah. She said he couldn't let go of his mother and his mother . . . well, controlled him. She felt like she was living with a little boy. She said she didn't know, but thought that was what caused his depression. Some kind of conflict between trying to grow up and still be Mommy's boy. Anyway, she said she wasn't going through life playing second fiddle to his mother. Those were her words."

I thought about his reaction at Pine Lake Lodge when I mentioned his father.

"But look. That was twenty years ago. Things may have changed. It may not have been that bad, anyway. It's amazing how little it takes for somebody to decide to get divorced these days." Her sentence was punctuated with banging and popping from the street. She laughed, "There's Dan. I sure wish he'd do something with that van."

Dan's VW pulled in the driveway and he stopped behind my Geo. He walked to the porch and kissed Meg on the cheek.

"I wondered who was here. Keep forgetting about your car. What's going on with that, anyway?"

"We'll Insure Anybody insurance company finally decided they were responsible. An adjuster looked at it yesterday and it's in the shop."

Meg stood. "Well, I guess you two want to talk." She went inside.

"Have you told her what you're helping me with?" I asked.

Dan sat in Meg's chair. "Sure. Basically we tell each other everything."

I asked him if he had talked to any of Reeves's classmates.

"That's where I was. I got the list of phone numbers of Reeves's classmates this morning and went to my office at school to do some calling. Trying to talk on this phone's impossible. Even when the kids aren't here, the phone rings constantly. We've got call-waiting for survival, but the constant beeping drives me nuts." He leaned forward and put his elbows on his knees. "Anyway, nobody I talked to had heard of Bait, Tackle, or Fish, or knew anything about Miss Hildegarde and some boys."

"I'm not surprised. You remember what her journal said. The nicknames may have been used by just her and the guys."

Dan leaned back and reclined in his chair. "Could be."

"I got a message, of sorts, from Mitch. Seemed to indicate he found some folks at Sable's who recognized Crowe's picture."

Dan sat straight. "Damn. He *is* here."

"Evidence seems to point in that direction."

"I know Lucas may be a problem, but I think we need to talk to somebody about this. Somebody higher up."

"Who?" I told him about Bernard's conversation with the mayor and about my talk with Radar's secretary. I ended with, "At this point, I don't know who to trust. Besides myself, I've got James to think about. Crowe may be the only chance we've got to prove that James is innocent. Somehow, we've got to find something that links him to the murders before he disappears again."

Dan reclined again. "Guess you're right. Have you arranged for us to look at Reeves's office again?"

It was my turn to sit straight. "I forgot about that!" I banged my fist on the arm of the chair. "I knew there was something else." I said I'd call Lucas when I got home.

And I did. He said we'd have to do it tomorrow, because after that, they were turning the house over to the Reeves children. I didn't want to have to ask their permission, seeing how I was defending their parents' accused murderer.

Lucas said he'd arrange it and have someone call with the time. He said he couldn't be there, that he had to go to Atlanta. This time I asked the detective what he was going to do there.

"Meeting with an old friend," he said.

Chapter 24

🗗 🗗 🗗 🗗 🗗 🗗 🗗 🗗 🗗

Tonight Michael and I were going to the symphony.

When I graduated from law school, I went into hock to buy a black satin cocktail dress with spaghetti straps for the traditional reception given by Catledge's president. I wore that now along with a black lace shawl, black pumps, and a black satin evening bag. I pinned my hair in a bun, and added long, silver earrings with a single pearl at the end. I had bought the earrings at an estate auction. I looked in the mirror and wondered if my memories of *Seventeen* magazine were correct. Black hides weight.

The concert was to begin at nine o'clock. Because Athens was forty-five minutes from Patsboro, and dinner reservations were for seven-thirty, Michael picked me up at six-thirty. The weather had turned hot and muggy again, but with the top down on the Porsche and a strong stream of air flowing from the air-conditioner vent in front of me, it felt fine. I was glad I'd pinned my hair. The sun was low to our back and created sharp shadows as we traversed the narrow serpentine road to Athens. As we drove past stands of woods and pastures with cows chewing lazily in the early evening, Michael and I talked of what this place would be like after the airport was built.

But that wasn't all. Talking to Michael was easy. Throughout dinner, I talked about my father and growing up in Maytown. Of the travails of high school and the highs of winning swim meets at Georgia Southern University. Of law school and my aspirations for the future. I told him I didn't drink because my father was an alcoholic and I'd read about alcoholism possibly having a genetic origin.

Michael listened attentively. He told some stories, too. He talked about playing football for Harve Bennett, the renowned, now retired coach who perennially led the Jeff Davis Academy Tigers to the state play-offs. Jess Davis Academy was a private school in nearby Park County. Michael had a keen sense of humor and told stories well.

He told of the time he was a senior and Coach Bennett took the team to Jekyll Island for football camp. The coach was a hard case. After one of his camps, Michael said, Parris Island was a snap. He told of a player who sneaked away during the night. Hitchhiked home. The next morning at the 5:30 devotional, Coach Bennett told the players what had happened. Two hours later, during one of the twice-daily practices, a shotgun blasted in the woods adjacent to the practice field. The team's quarterback said, "Well, Coach got him."

Michael didn't speak of depression, and he said nothing about his father. The time slid by. I watched him as he talked with the waiter who brought the check. His medium-length blond hair reflected the light of the chandelier above us. His face emanated strength—strong cheekbones and a chin with a slight dimple. His only flaw was a slight bulge above the hips. For age forty-two, it was a truly slight bulge.

I'd always thought a symphony concert would be boring. It wasn't. I was enthralled. I'd never heard a live symphony orchestra, and the difference from recordings was astounding. When bands at the rock concerts I'd gone to played stuff I hadn't heard, I took the opportunity to visit the ladies' room. If I hadn't heard something a zillion times on the radio, the music had no meaning. I recognized only a couple of these pieces, but it didn't matter. The music was beautiful.

After the concert, Michael took me to a place called the Flamingo Room, a dessert café, where I had cherries Jubilee and he chose Derby pie à la mode. Our arms were around each other when we walked back to his car.

He pulled in front of my house at midnight. As we were walking up the stairs to my door, I stopped short. Sitting in front of the door were a dozen red roses.

Michael pulled me up the stairs. He picked up the envelope that was with the flowers and handed it to me.

"Why don't you go ahead and open it?" he said.

"Michael, I don't want to. I don't know who's sending these and I don't want to know."

"Oh, go on. Open it. I'd like to see what my competition has to say."

This card was not blank. *Hope you had a good time tonight.* Michael had signed it.

I looked up at him and he was smiling. Tears came. I guess in relief and in gratitude that the flowers were from him. I put my arms around him and looked up. He wiped a tear from my cheek. I reached up, pulled down his head, and kissed him.

"Why don't you come inside?" I said.

I apologized for my pathetic collection of accumulated goods, and he waved it away. After making a pot of herb tea, I sat in my rocker and he sat on the bed.

Now I talked not just of professional goals, but also of personal doubts. I talked about my fear of making a commitment, which probably stemmed from growing up with my father. I talked about things I'd only said to myself before.

Michael sat on my bed, leaning against the headboard with his legs crossed. His intense, gray eyes stayed on me. Not in an intimidating kind of stare. It was the soft look of caring. I looked at my clock on the nightstand next to him.

At 2:13 I made a decision.

My shoes were already off. I went to the end of the bed, crawled up it, and lay next to him. He put his arm around me and I put my head on his chest. He had taken off his coat. I loosened his tie and took it off. He brought my face to his and we kissed again.

He was gentle and took his time. Nothing of the harried grabbing of Paul Starling's backseat. Nothing of the guilt of being in a hotel room with another woman's husband.

We kissed, caressed, and laughed. He didn't mind my safety precautions. He made them a part of the process. I had a terrible time getting the condom on him; first, because I couldn't figure out how to do it, then because I was laughing so hard I couldn't see what I was doing.

Finally, he was on top of me. When he filled me, I locked my arms and pulled him to me. Nothing . . . nothing, ever, had felt like this. He placed his hand between us and caressed me. For the first time I knew what an orgasm was.

I was totally drained. More than I would have ever dreamed. He lay on top of me, not moving. I kissed him behind his ear and he moved again.

It happened again.

I gently pushed him with my hands and said, "I can't stand any more."

When I turned on my side, he reached over to turn off the light, slid over next to me, and wrapped his arm around my waist. It felt so good to have his warm body next to mine.

No wonder people get married, I thought.

That was my last thought until I suddenly awakened. I'd been dreaming. Something significant. What was it?

Fishing. In my dream, Radar Gilstrap was fishing.

My sleepy mind began to stir.

Fish and Bait and Tackle.

Gilstrap. Gill.

My eyes opened wide.

Fish have gills!

Yes! *Gilstrap* is Fish.

It was the *name!*

I moved Michael's arm from my waist and got out of bed. The clock on the nightstand said 4:42. Stupid time, but I had to do it. I got the phone, pulled it as far away from the bed as I could, and called Dan's number.

He answered almost immediately.

"You awake?" I said. "No, never mind, dumb question. Look, I'm sorry, Dan, but I've got to tell you something." I told him about Gilstrap and gills and fish.

Dan sounded alert. "Makes sense. But what about Reeves?"

"Bait. Some kind of bait."

"What's Reeves's name? His whole name."

"First name was Gary. The middle one was weird. Some kind of family name, I think."

"You remember it?"

I closed my eyes and tried to picture the reports. Suddenly it came clearly. "Yeah. Rapalla. Gary Rapalla Reeves. Does that help?"

"I'm not sure of your pronunciation. How do you spell it?"

I told him.

"Confirms Gilstrap," Dan said in a surprisingly calm voice. "Rapala is a company that makes fishing lures. Spelled with one *l*. Dad swears by 'em." He paused. "Fish and Bait. Now who's Tackle and what the hell happened?"

"Lucas? No, Lucas was one of your students. He's way too young."

"He would have had Hildegarde, before she became a librarian. Maybe that's the connection. Or he's connected to Jarvis. That's just so hard to believe."

I sat cross-legged. "Jarvis got connected through Gilstrap and Lucas. Hence Buddy Crowe."

"I'll check Reeves's class again tomorrow. Concentrate on the names."

"OK."

"How you doing?"

"Other than dealing with this case, I'm doing wonderful. Just wonderful."

I turned to put the phone on the nightstand and flinched. Michael was lying with his arm resting in his hand, propped up by an elbow. His gray eyes reflected light from the streetlamp that was filtering through the sheets on my window.

"I'm sorry. Did I wake you?" I asked.

"That's no problem. What was that all about?"

I replaced the phone and crawled over him to my side of the bed. Funny. Already, that was my side of the bed.

"Case I'm working on. I guess all the physical release freed my mind. Thought of something and wanted to share it. Kind of dumb timing, though."

I turned again and felt his hand on my head. He slid it down to my neck and squeezed.

"You're all tense again," he said. He began applying gentle pressure to the back of my neck and shoulders.

"That feels wonderful," I said, and added to my suddenly burgeoning experience.

Chapter 25

The ringing phone pulled me into consciousness. When I finally realized what it was, I turned to answer it and was startled when I bumped into Michael. Twenty-seven years of waking up alone hadn't prepared me for this. Michael grunted and turned over.

I got out on my side and walked around the bed to answer the phone. As soon as I did, I wished I'd put on a nightgown, or something. I felt funny standing there naked with Michael a couple of feet away. I thought about what we'd done just a couple of hours earlier and smiled at my discomfort.

And it had been just a couple of hours. The clock said 7:58. Officer McDaniel was on the phone, the giant policeman who'd handled my wreck with Essie Dillard and Willie Moon.

"Sorry to call you so early, but I thought I should."

I told him not to worry about that.

He said he'd be at the Reeves place at noon. "There's something else I've got to tell you, though. James Cleveland's in the hospital. Teal General. He tried to hang himself last night."

"No!" I exclaimed. I'd been so busy trying to prove his innocence, I'd hardly seen him. "Is he . . ."

"Physically, he's fine. He tied some sheets to the plumbing in the cell. A guard happened along just as he stepped off the toilet. Got him on the fourth floor, though."

The fourth floor of Teal General held the psychiatric wing. I thanked him for calling and said we'd be at the Reeveses' at noon. After wrestling with how to sign it and finally deciding on plain *Tammi*, I left a note for Michael and headed to the hospital.

On the way to the hospital, I thought about the night before. Did I feel guilty? Sort of. I could hardly help it. At the same time that I had decided to speak standard English, I had also decided to quit going to church. I'd had enough of listening to the preacher screaming about the sins of women and how my period, which had just started, was a curse put on me by God. But while I rejected the Congregational Holiness, I couldn't shed my upbringing, of which guilt was a major factor.

The question was, *Should* I feel guilty? Dan had said in New Orleans that he didn't think an omniscient God would really care about our sex lives. What he did care about was love and caring, not hurting people. And sex without commitment invariably resulted in hurt.

But I didn't know if that was true, either. Maybe I wasn't feeling guilty. Maybe I was feeling scared. What would we do now? Michael and I, I mean. Could I just have a fun night and let it go? That's what a lot of people at school had done. Or so it seemed. Could I do that?

I shook my head. Think about James Cleveland lying in the hospital. I should have paid more attention to him. Guilt, again. I slapped my hand on the steering wheel.

Guilt! Guilt! Guilt!

Damn you, Mama.

McDaniel had called the ward nurse and told her I was coming. She let me in through a door that buzzed when it unlocked, then showed me to James's room. He was lying in bed, staring at a small television set that wasn't on. As I walked toward him, I wished Dan was here. He'd dealt with this kind of thing before. I hadn't. What do you say?

I said something insipid. "How you doing, James?"

He moved his head and stared at me.

I pulled over a plastic chair and sat next to the bed. "Listen, I should have talked to you more. I think you're innocent and think I can prove it. That's what I've been doing."

He blinked.

"Why'd you do it?"

He looked back at the television. In an almost inaudible voice he said, "I be scared."

"Look, James. Even in the worst case, if you get convicted, found guilty of killing those people, you wouldn't be . . . in . . . for long. Considering your age."

Actually, that was not necessarily true. Several juveniles around the country had been sentenced to death recently. But that was rare and I wanted to give him some hope.

"And I don't think you'll be convicted." Not necessarily true, either.

James kept staring ahead. "Don't wanna go to no prison."

"I know you don't. But I say again, if you have to go, it'd probably only be for a little while."

"Man come," he whispered.

"What?" I said and leaned closer.

"Man come. Say what gonna happen to me in prison. Say they make me act like a girl. He say if I say I did it, I might not go to no prison."

"What man?" He shrugged. "What'd he look like?"

He shrugged again. "White man. Say I be better off dead than goin' there."

"Was he the man you saw at the Reeveses'?"

James shook his head.

"Not Detective Anderson?"

"No."

"Did he have dark hair? Light hair? Big man? Little man?"

"Big man. That's all." He turned on his side, away from me.

I took a deep breath and let it out. "Look, James, I'm going to find the man who killed the Reeveses. I don't want you doing anything like . . . this again. You understand?" I stood and he stared again at the television. "You want me to turn that on?"

"No."

Big man, I thought when I was back in the Geo. Lots of big men around. Lucas and Crowe were big, tall anyway, but James knows them both and said it wasn't either of them. I hadn't seen Radar in a while, but four years ago he was big. Not tall, but stocky, muscular. Hell, even the mayor was a big man.

And so was Officer McDaniel. A real big man. And he had been there when Buddy Crowe ran into me.

Come to think of it, he'd been there real fast.

Chapter 26

Mitch, Dan, and I were back in Dr. Reeves's study.

When I arrived home from the hospital, Michael was gone. He'd left a note saying he'd call me. Nothing else. I called Dan but he wasn't home. Meg said he'd gone to the high school, but she'd tell him to be at the Reeves's at noon. I called Mitch. He confirmed that several patrons at Sable's had recognized Crowe's picture.

Officer McDaniel, Mitch, and Dan were waiting when I arrived. I'd gone by Bernard's house to borrow his Polaroid camera and stopped to buy some film. As McDaniel led us to the study, Dan asked what the camera was for. Just in case we missed something, I said. What it was for was to get a picture of McDaniel to show James.

I asked McDaniel if he could find out who visited James the night before. He said he'd check and left the room. I told Dan and Mitch about James.

"And you think McDaniel might be the man?" Mitch asked.

"I don't know. He's big. Awful big. And he was at the accident scene right after it happened. Just makes me wonder."

"Didn't Lucas say he was new to the department?" Dan asked.

"Just said he wasn't around four years ago," I said. "Listen, it's probably a long shot. We need to find out what happened that resulted in the Reeveses being killed." I looked at the floor.

The markings were gone, but I remembered where they had been. "Knowing who Tackle is would help."

Dan leaned on Reeves's large desk. "Might. But knowing who Bait and Fish are hasn't particularly helped. By the way, none of the names in the yearbook provided a clue."

"None? Seems hard to believe there wouldn't be one that would be some kind of fishing tackle."

"Patsboro High, as it was called then, was a small school in the late sixties. Only a couple of hundred students, total. None fit."

I walked around the room. "The answer must be here. Somewhere. Hildegarde's journal said Reeves had some kind of evidence the other two wanted. Of course, it could be in his office at the university."

"Don't think so," Mitch said. "Dr. Cutlip let me look in it. There wasn't much in there. Cutlip said when Reeves started working on his sociogenetics, he took most of his stuff home."

I looked at the large desk, filing cabinets, and bookshelves. "We need to look through everything. Carefully. It's going to take a while."

And we did. McDaniel came back and said there was no record of visitors to James Cleveland the night before, but he added there wouldn't necessarily be. Especially if the visitor was a police official. While he was there, I started taking pictures and got him in a shot. He said he had to go, but if we'd call the station, they'd call him on the radio and he'd come back to lock up. His comment about police officials made me feel better about him. The fact is, I decided, I was getting paranoid about policemen.

Dan searched the desk. "Didn't Dr. Cutlip say Reeves was working on an article?"

Mitch said he had.

"Entry in his appointment book says *Article due*. Written on a date two days after he died." His eyes returned to the book. "Why would he be going to Elysian Fields?"

Elysian Fields was a hundred acres of land filled by old trailers and dilapidated houses in the northern portion of the county.

"Redneck city," Mitch said.

"Entry for this coming Monday says *K: Elysian Fields*—9:00. It's followed by a question mark."

I was at the bookshelves, opening every book and shaking each out. I wondered again about the civil rights collection, then remembered the sociogenetics thing. Maybe it was a part of his research. But the books looked like they'd been there a while. Some had yellowed pages with what appeared to be notes in Reeves's handwriting. Could just be old books. I bought most of mine at yard sales. I looked around the room. I didn't really think Reeves frequented yard sales.

Mitch was looking through the file cabinets, folder by folder. He was finished with one cabinet and starting on the other by the time I had looked at every book on the shelves. I looked around the room and noticed the paintings on the walls.

I took each down and removed the backing. Reeves was good, I thought, as I examined them. I looked again at the abstract that was so out of character compared to the realistic beaver-pond scenes. Splotches of paint with random markings here and there. Wonder what he was trying to get across, I thought. The paintings were another waste of time. They contained nothing.

I was sitting in the chair behind the desk and Dan was going through professional journals of the Society of Genetics Research when Mitch said, "Here's the sociogenetics stuff. Several folders." He pulled them out and we each took a couple and sat on the floor to go through them.

"This folder's mostly on the Klan," Mitch said.

"Same here," I said.

Dan said the same for his. There was a general history, but most of the notes were on activity within the past few months.

"Lots of firsthand research, interviews, of sorts," Dan said.

"Of sorts?" I asked.

"Looks like he was acting like he was one of them," Dan replied.

"Maybe he was one of them," Mitch said.

"I don't think so," I said. "The Klan's a secretive organization. They can even wear masks again and some do. I don't think a member'd be taking notes for an article."

"I thought they always wore masks," Mitch said. " 'Course we didn't have too many in my neighborhood in New Jersey."

I said, "Georgia passed a law in the fifties outlawing masks. It stood until a superior court declared it unconstitutional recently."

Thirty minutes later all of the folders had been examined.

"Find anything? Any names you recognize?" I asked.

Mitch and Dan said they hadn't.

"Let's look again till we've all seen each folder. Maybe one of us'll recognize something the others missed."

Another hour passed. Still nothing.

We were on the floor with the folders between us. "Something happened a long time ago, and something happened in the last few months," Mitch mused.

"Something with the Klan?" I asked.

Dan stood and stretched. "Nothing I can remember. Of significance, anyway. In early April we had a fight at school that turned into a black-white thing. Started over something silly. A volleyball game in PE. Anyway, a couple of days later the Klan rallied on the square and marched to the high school."

"I didn't hear about that," Mitch said. "And I tends to notice when the Klux be 'round."

"Didn't make the papers. Probably because the march consisted of a grand total of two. Two guys in white sheets surrounded by fifteen deputies and the state patrol. Stayed in front of the school for a half an hour and said they'd be back in force. Never showed again."

I picked up the folders and replaced them in the filing cabinet. "Well, that's it."

"Yeah," Dan said. "Guess this was a waste of time."

"So what now?" Mitch asked.

"I'll take McDaniel's picture to Bear. Probably be a waste of time too, though." I picked up the phone. "Might as well call McDaniel. Tell him we're finished."

I made the call and we sat on the front porch to wait. Mitch said, "Maybe they found what they were looking for and killed 'em anyway."

"Could be," I said. "Just covering their tracks now."

"Minerva Hildegarde and her house," Dan added.

"And me," I said, then wished I hadn't.

I felt Dan's and Mitch's eyes on me. Dan said, "Which is something else I want to talk to you about. You shouldn't be in that house alone. I worried about you last night."

"Wasn't exactly alone last night."

"Oh," Dan said.

From behind me I heard, in a perfectly pitched soprano, "I hear the whippoorwill singing above. . . ."

"That's enough."

He continued singing anyway. "Tammi, Tammi, Tammi's in love."

"That *is* enough, Mitch."

"What about tonight?" Dan asked.

"I don't know."

"Well, look. If something doesn't, uh, work out, call me. You can stay with us."

"How long am I supposed to do that?" I said angrily.

Dan responded calmly, "Till it's over."

"Till it's over."

"That be him."

"*What?*" I said, too loudly.

I was convinced that my suspicions of McDaniel were the product of a hyperimagination resulting from the shocks that kept coming at me. This was just an exercise in covering all the bases. Now James Cleveland said, "That be him."

"The man who tell me that. That be him." He was looking at the Polaroid.

"You sure, James?"

He nodded.

I was going through it again as I headed home in the Geo. What was going on? Three policemen. Lucas, Radar, and now McDaniel. I felt certain Radar was connected to Reeves because of Hildegarde's journal and the names, but what about the other two? Lucas was fifteen years too young and McDaniel wasn't even from here. Lucas *was* connected to Jarvis, who had to be involved somehow, because Crowe was. Jarvis had been a quarterback for Catledge. Was McDaniel connected to Jarvis through football? McDaniel was big enough. But he had gotten here too soon for whatever happened in the last few months and too late for a long time ago. It didn't make sense.

And whom do you go to when every time you turn around another officer of the law is involved?

I parked in front of my house and waved to Mrs. Stancil, who lived next door. Out of the corner of my eye I could see her watching me through the bushes as I walked up the veranda. Had she seen Michael come out this morning? I felt myself blushing.

I put the key in the door but didn't turn it. This was the first time the house had been empty all day since Mama and Big Jack left. I looked back toward the street at the sunlight filtering through the oaks, dogwoods, and magnolias that filled the yard. Still plenty of daylight, I thought.

I opened the front door and went straight to my room and locked the bedroom door. After checking under the double bed and in the closet, I sat on the bed and looked at the telephone. I'll call Michael, I thought. Just see what happens. I realized I didn't know his home phone number. I looked in the phone book and found Michael Hutcheson, Sr., on Partridge Circle. His dad. His mother must have never changed it. Michael Jr. was not in the book. It must be unlisted. Did his plant operate on Saturday? Probably. Would they give me his home phone number? Doubtful.

I dialed his mother's number. I'd ask someone there. A woman with a stately, deep voice answered. I told her what I wanted. She said Michael lived there. He wasn't home. She asked if she could take a message. I told her to ask him to call me and hung up.

He lived with his mother? The conversation with Meg came back. Momma's boy. I shook my head. Sure doesn't seem like a momma's boy.

I looked across the room through the open bathroom door to

the pile of clothes in the basket next to the tub. I'd gone to the Laundromat earlier that week, but Saturday was my usual wash day and I didn't have enough clothes to let it pass by. Could do it tomorrow, I thought. On the other hand, why wait around here? I had my answering machine and there was plenty of daylight left. I took off the jeans and shirt I was wearing and added them to the pile in the basket and put on some shorts and a tank top.

A little over an hour later I was back at my front door. This time I didn't hesitate to unlock it.

I wish I had.

Oh God in heaven, I wish I had.

Chapter 27

On the way back from the Laundromat, I'd stopped at the Majic Market and bought a newspaper and some milk for coffee. After putting the milk in the refrigerator, I realized I was hungry. The last thing I'd eaten was a honey bun out of a vending machine at the hospital that morning. I managed to find a piece of chicken Big Jack had somehow missed, along with a little bit of leftover mashed potatoes and slaw. Better than Kentucky Fried Chicken, I thought, as I sat eating Mama's food and reading the early edition of the Sunday *Atlanta Journal/Constitution*.

When the chicken was gone, I was still hungry and examined the refrigerator again. There was a slice of Edwards apple pie. I lifted my blouse and looked down. I shrugged, retrieved the pie, and topped it with vanilla ice cream.

Nuts, I thought. Should have checked the machine when I came in. I looked at my watch. It was 7:34. I needed to figure out what I was going to do tonight before it got dark. I picked up the pie and ice cream and went to my room.

The odor hit me as soon as I opened the door. It was the smell I'd noticed the night Michael and I went to Pine Lake Lodge. Maybe Snickers's cage needed cleaning.

I put the plate next to the answering machine. The light wasn't flashing. Michael hadn't called.

"What you doing over there?" I said to the gerbil, as I went toward the Habitrail complex. Snickers was in the tube that led to his penthouse atop it. "You stuck, baby?" Strange how I talked to this gerbil the way my mother talked to me. I took off the penthouse and looked at the tube.

Snickers's mouth was wide open. A piece of metal was stuck through his head and was wedged on either side of the tube. He was hanging by the metal.

The room whirled. I tried to get a breath, but couldn't. I was in a dream trying to make a sound. I wanted to scream, but nothing would come.

Wake up! Wake up!

Finally a sound emerged. I shrieked as I backed away from the hideous sight. My scream was cut short.

A hand was over my mouth. A horrid smell, an overwhelming smell, emanated from that hand. I couldn't breathe. A voice was saying something behind me. Saying something over and over but I couldn't understand it. Something sharp pricked my side.

The pain brought me back. The blurry image in front of me suddenly focused. I got a quick breath. The prick deepened. I reacted instinctively. Both arms flew out as I bowed my back and the hand flew away from my mouth. Years of swimming had built muscles that hadn't totally atrophied. I turned and there he was.

Buddy Crowe.

Crew cut. No scar. Just like the picture. He was on the floor, pushing himself up by his elbows. He grinned and said something. I still couldn't hear through the rushing in my ears.

Got to get *out!* Oh God, *scream!*

I did. Crowe jumped up between me and the door. The windows were closed. The window air conditioner was on. Who could hear me?

No time!

I ran for the closet, slammed the door, and twisted the dead bolt. Crowe started pounding. The closet was black. No light anywhere. Not even at the bottom of the door. Crowe pounded. This was an old house—good solid doors. But how long would it take for him to break it? Suddenly the pounding stopped.

I pushed my clothes to one side and started feeling the walls. Plaster on either side, but the back was paneling. I remembered that now. Never thought about it before. Why paneling? I remembered the room on the other side of the wall, off the kitchen. I'd only glanced in there once. I pictured it now. Windows to the left. Door straight ahead. No windows on that wall. Door to the right. Closet door.

That's it!

Must have been a walk-through closet a long time ago. Got paneled in the conversion to a boardinghouse. The pounding started again.

I put my back to the door, lifted a foot, and timed the booms. When he hit the door, I kicked the paneling. The veneer splintered. Another kick and my foot broke through. The pounding stopped. Did he hear me? I stood quietly, listening. The sound of metal on metal. It was on the side of the door. The hinges. He was trying to loosen the pins on the hinges.

I felt the paneling in front of me, grabbed a piece, and pulled. The wood cracked. The pinging from the hinges stopped. I pulled on the paneling again. This time a large piece broke. I could feel paneling on the other side. I braced myself again and pushed with my foot. The paneling popped free. I moved forward and squeezed through the small open space into another closet. I felt for the door and opened it slightly. The room was empty.

I eased into the light and looked to my left. The door to the kitchen was open a crack, but I couldn't see anything through it. I went to one of the windows and pulled on the handles on the bottom frame. Nothing. I pulled harder. It didn't budge. I tried the other one. Same thing. No telling how long it had been since these windows had been opened. They were stuck fast. I looked at the door to the kitchen. The house's back door was in the kitchen to the right, but where was Crowe? I stuck my head back in the closet. No sound.

The other door. I turned to the far side of the room, the one with no windows. I walked to the door and it opened easily. A set of stairs was there, rising to the left. I walked up the stairs to a landing that led to another door. It was locked. To the right was a ladder attached to the wall. Dim light from below illuminated the lower portion of the ladder, but the upper portion was hard to see. Must lead to the attic. Maybe there was some way to escape up there. I started climbing. The first rung cracked and I quickly jumped to the next. The third one broke in two.

Pain!

Something stuck into my hand as I slid down the ladder. I caught myself and reached for the next rung. It felt solid. And the next and the next. At the top was an opening covered by a piece of plywood. I pushed on it and it gave way.

Noise. I bent down and looked down the stairs.

Crowe! Looking up the stairway.

I grabbed the side of the opening and pulled up. I put the plywood back on the opening and stood on it. It cracked. I quickly jumped off and lay across it. I felt around. Nothing. I shifted and kept searching the attic floor. The plywood underneath me pushed up and went down again. I tried to find something to hold on to, to get some leverage. There was nothing. The steeply pitched roof was too far away. I kept feeling around. The plywood bumped up again.

I felt something! What was it? I pulled it closer. It was a two-by-four about three feet long. I rubbed my hand along it. Another stab. What was that? A nail. Sticking out a couple of inches. I grabbed the other side of the board, making sure the nail was sticking out the right way.

The plywood under me pushed up, not just bumped this time. I was rising and couldn't stop it. I rolled to my right and the plywood flew up. I turned on my knees just as Crowe's head appeared, and swung the two-by-four at him. Light was coming through the opening now. He saw the board and backed away, but not in time. He screamed as the nail ripped into his face.

I stood, pulled back the board, and swung it again. Crowe grabbed it. I saw his right hand reach for my leg and I tried to jump, but he seized my ankle and pulled it. I fell hard on my back.

No air! I tried to breathe, but nothing would come. I wanted to kick, but couldn't. All my energy went into trying to get air into my lungs. Finally, with a gasp, I felt it rush in.

But Buddy Crowe was on me. His knees were on my shoulders and he held a large knife to my neck. He pulled on my hair and put his face in mine. Blood dripped off his jaw. The nail had ripped his cheek where his scar had been. This time I heard his words clearly.

"That's it, bitch," he said quietly as he pulled on my hair again. He dug his knife into my flesh. "Do you understand?"

I nodded.

"Now we're going back down. Together." He paused between each word when he said, "You make any kind of move and your guts will be spread all over this house."

I nodded again.

He turned me over and put the knife to my side. I was pulled back to the opening. He went down the ladder first and pulled on me to follow. When we were on the stairs, he grabbed my hair, pulled back my head, and pushed the knife into my back.

"Down," he whispered.

He pushed me down the stairs, through the empty room, the kitchen, and into my bedroom. He stopped me and turned to lock my bedroom door. He moved me into the bathroom and forced me to lie facedown. He put his boot on the side of my face as he looked in the mirror.

"You goddamned bitch. Cost me thousands to get that fixed," he growled. I heard water running. It stopped immediately. "Shit!"

He took his foot off my face and got on his knees. The knife was digging into me again. He grabbed my hair and pulled up my head, putting his bleeding wound directly in front of me.

"Lick it off."

Oh God, no. No! My tears blinded me. "No," I pleaded. "Oh, please, no!"

"Do it!"

I screamed, "Noooooo!" and cried hysterically. I felt a slap. And then another. The knife dug deeper. I tried to stop screaming. I didn't want to be hurt.

He put his face next to mine and said slowly, "Lick it. Clean it like a dog." He twisted the knife.

I leaned forward. As I neared his face, I could see the torn flesh hanging where the nail had ripped him open. The smell of fresh blood mixed with his unwashed stench. My stomach contracted and I threw up.

He jumped up, still holding my hair, and jerked my head toward him. He threw the knife in the sink and screamed, "God-*damn* you!" He forced me down again and washed his face. When he was done, he grabbed my hair, pulled me up, pushed me into the room and onto the bed. "Take 'em off."

I was on my back. I pulled away from him until I hit the head-board. "Why are you doing this?"

"Why?" he said and laughed. He crawled onto the bed. The knife was in his right hand as he moved toward me. He whispered, "Because you and that nigger and that doctor ruined everything. All my life, I had nothing. Nothing! I finally had something and you took it away."

"Why'd you come back? Why'd you kill Reeves?"

Crowe's eyes widened. "They *needed* me. Like Jonah in the belly of the whale." Crowe was kneeling between my feet. Suddenly he moved his hand and sliced the knife under my right big toe.

I screamed at the pain and Crowe was on top of me. His hand was across my mouth. He put the knife to my side. He smelled of vomit and rot.

"Shut *up*," he whispered.

I nodded and he removed his hand. I gulped air and started to heave again, but didn't.

His eyebrows arched. "Any more questions?"

I shook my head.

Crowe backed away and was on his knees again. "Now take 'em off."

My foot was throbbing where he'd cut it. I didn't want him to cut me again, somewhere even worse. I pulled off the tank top and unhooked my bra. He reached out and pulled down my shorts and panties. I tried to cover myself with my arms.

"Nuh uh," he said with a sneer. "Let me see it. Been waiting for this moment for years, baby." He grabbed my right ankle with his left hand and pulled me toward the edge of the bed. "Don't move." With the knife still in his right hand, he unbuckled his belt, tugged on his zipper, and pulled down his pants. He crawled on his knees toward me with his pants dragging behind.

I squeezed my eyes shut.

"Oh no. No way, babe. Keep 'em open." He pricked the inside of my thighs with the knife. I spread my legs to avoid the pain. He moved between them.

The phone rang. He looked at it. After three rings, my recording started. When it was over Michael's voice filled the room. "Tammi, this is Michael. Call me when you get a chance."

"Michael!" At my first move toward the phone, Crowe's knife was against my thigh again.

He leaned down onto me and expelled putrid breath when he said in a high-pitched voice, "Michael, Michael. Oh Michael." The knife went to the side of my neck, the point sticking into me. He raised his body slightly and entered me.

I felt as if I were being ripped apart. As he pushed into me, his knife jabbed against my neck with every thrust. I bit my lip and tasted my own blood. In an effort to get away from him, I brought my arms above my head. He moved the knife from the side of my neck to my throat. My right hand went under the pillow and I felt steel.

The gun! Under the pillow.

My eyes focused. The room became clear. The pain diminished. I grabbed the butt of the gun, moved my thumb to the hammer, and cocked it.

Crowe was thrusting and grunting. One tiny flick of his wrist was all it would take for the razor-sharp knife to slice into my throat. I knew what I had to do. I waited. . . .

He rammed down one more time and stopped. He slumped on me and the knife dropped from my throat.

I moved the gun from under the pillow, put it under his left armpit, and pulled the trigger.

His back exploded in front of me. Searing heat hit above my right breast. Still holding the gun, I pushed him off me and rolled off the bed.

I crawled to the wall and screamed.

Chapter 28

I don't know how long I sat naked on the floor staring at the bed. Time stopped once the screaming stopped. The pain returned first—the throbbing under the toe where Crowe had cut me, the burning on my breast and aches all over my body. With the return of pain, my mind began working again.

Suddenly, it seemed, I found myself holding the gun with two hands, like Bernard had shown me, and like I had practiced at the firing range. My elbows were on my knees to steady my aim, and I was looking over the bed. I was waiting for Crowe to get up.

I moved from my sitting position and squatted. When I did, fluid dripped down my leg.

Got to get that out. *Out!*

I stood and moved to the bed and lay on it. My arms were extended, a finger on the trigger. Slowly, I inched my way across the bed. Part of Crowe came into view. A hand. I moved closer. The arm was extended and I followed it as I moved. He was lying on his back. The wound in his side was away from me. One more move.

I jumped when I saw his face. He was glaring at me, his eyes wide open, his mouth twisted. On my knees again I looked for signs of breathing. He lay still. Blood spread on the hardwood floor under him.

I *had* to get to the bathroom. Clean myself. I could smell him. The stench of unwashed human. No, not human. The stench of unwashed evil. But I couldn't leave him. Couldn't take a chance. I looked at the clock by my bed. The red numbers said 8:17. My eyes shifted to the telephone. Keeping the gun pointed at Crowe, I moved to the phone, pulled my left hand off the pistol, and dialed.

Meg answered.

"Meg," I said.

"Yes," I heard.

I couldn't say anything. I didn't know what to say. Tears came.

"Yes?" Meg said. This time it was a question.

The sound that came out was "Maaah."

"Who is this?"

I took a deep breath and blew out air. "Meg, it's Tammi."

"What's wrong?"

"Oh *God,* Meg," I whispered.

"What, Tammi? What's wrong?"

"It's Crowe. I think I killed him."

"You killed him?"

"Shot him. Blood. All over. Don't know if he's dead. Looks like it."

"Where are you?"

"My house. On my bed."

"Where is he?"

"On the floor. Bleeding. Blood. Rape."

The sound of the word. Rape. The image flashed before me. Buddy Crowe between my legs. Touching him. "He *raped* me!" I exclaimed. And cried.

Meg waited. When the crying slowed she said, "Don't clean up. That's very important. Remember? Stay where you are. We'll call the police and Dan and I will be there soon."

I looked at Crowe. What if he's not dead? What if he's alive? Have a trial. He goes to jail. He gets out. I pointed the gun at his head, five feet away. Just pull the trigger, Tammi. Make sure.

"Tammi, are you there? *Tammi!*"

I shook my head. "Yeah. Don't clean up. That's hard, Meg."

"I know it is. We'll be there. Hold on."

"Don't call the police now. Come here first. *Please.*"

"OK, Tammi. We'll be there. Just a few minutes."

I stared at Crowe, looking for some movement. Any sign of life so I could blow him away. Make sure. He just lay staring.

"Damn you!" I screamed. *"Move!"*

I looked at the tub through the open bathroom door. Got to get him out of me. Off of me. I pulled up a pillow and bit it. Hard. I started breathing fast. Too fast. The room spun. I squeezed my eyes, pushed my head back, and made myself take a deep breath and hold it. I let it out slowly. Another one, I thought. Another deep breath. As the air began to come in, my stomach retched. Nothing came out.

"Come on, Meg," I whispered. "Oh please, God, *hurry up!*" I screamed.

Time stretched, but when I heard the doorknob to my room turn, the clock said twelve minutes had passed. There was a knock and I heard Dan call my name. I'd forgotten the door was locked. Keeping the gun on Crowe, I skirted his body and let Dan in. Meg was behind him.

"Tammi," he said, then stopped.

I realized I was still naked, but I didn't want to take the gun off of Crowe. Dan followed my gaze, walked to Crowe, and felt his neck. A gaping wound was visible from this side.

"He's dead, Tammi. Real dead."

I lowered the gun. Meg had found my housecoat hanging in the bathroom and brought it to me. She put her arms around me and I cried again.

Dan was on the phone calling the police. I felt another set of hands on my shoulder. They belonged to Bernard Fuchs.

"We called him," Meg said.

Bernard squeezed my neck gently. "As soon as the police arrive, we must go to the hospital." He pointed to Crowe. "It appears that you shot him. We must establish medically that you were raped and that he did it. The police will have a dead man and the person who killed him. They will have to investigate. It must be established that you acted in self-defense and that it was indeed that fellow who assaulted you."

Bernard was right. I had to start thinking straight.

The sound of sirens came from the street. "Better let me have that," Bernard said, pointing to the Smith & Wesson. I gave it to him.

Two uniformed policemen came in the room followed by a man and a woman dressed in white jumpsuits. Bernard led me to the rocking chair, where I watched the EMTs check out Crowe.

"Jesus," the man said, "This guy's nearly cut in half."

His partner glanced at me and said, "Shut up, Leonard."

One of the policemen told Bernard he'd take the gun. Kevin Spurlock, the detective who'd jumped on James Cleveland, came into the room. He looked at me and said, "What happened?"

"He attacked me and I shot him."

"I'll need the details."

Bernard stepped from behind the rocker. "My client needs medical attention immediately. Questions can be asked after that."

Spurlock looked at him. "She looks healthy enough to me."

Bernard cocked his head. "Could you please, sir, synopsize your credentials as a physician?"

Spurlock pursed his lips. "OK. I'll follow you to Teal General." He told the uniforms to stay there and wait for the lab men. He followed Dan, Meg, Bernard, and me out the door.

Bernard drove his court car, a new Ford Crown Victoria. I was in the backseat with Dan and Meg on either side of me. Each was holding one of my hands.

"Who's taking care of the kids?" I asked.

Dan answered, "Mitch is coming over. We left Kristen and Megan with a neighbor till he arrives. Samantha's still in Highlands."

I nodded.

Meg squeezed my hand and said, "This should be over soon."

I nodded again and looked out the window at the brilliant pink sky illuminated by the setting sun.

Chapter 29

A short, rotund nurse appeared from behind a swinging door. She looked at the file folder she was holding and announced my name. I rose and went to her. "Can my friend Meg come too?"

The nurse patted my arm. "Sure, honey. That'd be fine."

Meg and I followed the nurse through the door into a hall-like room with examining tables separated by curtains to the left. After weighing me, she led us to the last space and told me to sit on the paper-covered table and get into the hospital gown she gave me. There was a chair in the corner, which Meg took.

The nurse said her name was Rosalind. "I'll be getting your vital signs, sweetheart. Doctor will be here shortly. The Saturday night madness hasn't started yet, so it shouldn't be too long."

She was wrong. The madness had started an hour ago.

Rosalind took my temperature, pulse, and blood pressure and measured my respiration. After that, she looked at my toe.

"Nice clean cut. Not too deep. Don't believe you'll need stitches." She swabbed it with antiseptic. "Were you hurt anywhere else?"

"I wasn't cut anywhere else." I put my hand on my right breast. "I think I got burned here."

She loosened the gown and examined me. She grunted and cleaned the area. I winced when she did.

"I know, baby. This'll sting a little bit."

Just as she finished, the curtains flew open and a man in a white coat charged into the room. I covered my breasts with my arm until I could pull up the gown. He went to a storage cabinet and began rummaging through it. Rosalind said, "May I help you, Dr. Bates?"

"You could make sure each area is stocked fully. I've got an idiot who sliced himself with a chain saw and there's not a single ampoule of Lidocaine in there. I'm going to need at least fifteen for this deal."

"We had a memo last week. They've been moved to the cabinet that's on the right side of the sink. I believe you'll find an adequate supply there."

He looked at the nurse. "In the future, make sure I see those memos."

"You wrote it, but I surely will try to do better."

"Uh huh." He closed the cabinet door and said, "Do you own a chain saw?"

"Nope," the nurse said.

"If you ever do, make sure you keep the chain sharpened. That way when you cut yourself, it won't make such a mess."

Rosalind said, "I always take note of your helpful hints, Dr. Bates," but he was gone before she finished. "Besides," she mumbled to herself, "a chain saw injury should be sent to the OR."

"Is he going to be my doctor?" I asked.

"No, darling, thank God. Dr. Humphries will be here shortly. She's wonderful."

I was relieved. I'd been examined by male doctors often, but tonight I didn't want to be.

A few minutes later Dr. Humphries appeared. She stood by the table and took my hand. "I'm sorry I was delayed. How are you doing?"

"All right, I guess."

She squeezed my hand gently. "There are several things I need to do. I'll tell you as we go, but if you have any questions at any time, you ask them. OK?"

I nodded.

"Good. Now, first things first." After looking at my toe and repeating what Rosalind had said, she asked me to lower my gown. "Powder burns," she mused. "Not too bad, though. The worst is over. I don't think there will be any scarring."

She began the pelvic exam. "I'm looking for samples of semen." A moment later, she said, "You've got a couple of small places where the lining is torn."

I had been lying with my eyes closed. Now I opened them and looked at her.

"I have to tell you that the torn lining means there's a higher risk of transmission of HIV if your assailant was infected."

I closed my eyes again.

"His body will be checked. If he's positive, there's some chance you've been infected. If he's negative, you could be OK, or he may not have had the virus long enough for the tests to detect it. In any event, you'll need to be checked periodically. If you remain negative for a year, you are probably OK."

"Probably?"

"Almost certainly. Nothing is guaranteed. But the odds are in your favor. The vast majority of people are as yet not infected."

I didn't say anything.

"While we're on the subject of risks, when was your last period?"

"Last week."

"That's good. Probably still a week away from your greatest vulnerability for pregnancy."

Pregnancy. I can't imagine why, but that thought hadn't crossed my mind. Buddy Crowe's child in me. Oh God, no! Meg took my hand.

I felt Dr. Humphries combing my pubic hair. "I'm sorry, but I need some samples of your hair. I have to pluck twelve from your head and twelve from your pubic area."

I hadn't dealt with a rape case in my practice, but I'd read enough to know why she needed the hairs. Despite that, I didn't stop her from explaining.

"I combed for samples of his pubic hair. I have to establish they're not yours. Plucking yours by the roots guarantees we're not finding samples of his hair to compare." Twenty-four sharp pulls later, Dr. Humphries was through.

As soon as she left, Rosalind cleaned me. Afterwards, I clasped her hands in mine. Before I could say anything she said, "I know, honey. I know."

When we walked back into the waiting room, Michael was there. He stood and came to me. We hugged and I began to cry again. He stroked my hair and said, "It's all right. It's all right."

"I'm glad you came. How'd you know?"

"I was worried when you didn't answer the phone. I went over to your house and found policemen there. They told me what happened. I'm so sorry."

I squeezed him hard. "Oh, God, Michael, it was horrible."

He stroked my hair again.

Spurlock was beside us. "Miss Randall, we gotta get to the station and take your statement."

My head was on Michael's chest. I looked up at him. "I'm going to stay with Dan and Meg tonight. I'll call you tomorrow."

"I'll call you. Is their number in the book?"

"Yeah. His name is Bushnell. Spelled like it sounds."

Michael bent to kiss my cheek.

My vision blurred with tears when I turned away before he could.

Chapter 30

We were in the same room where Dan and I had talked to James Cleveland that Friday night that seemed so long ago. Bernard, Dan, and I had ridden with Spurlock to the police station. Meg had driven Bernard's car to my house to pick up some clothes. She had brought some jeans, the T-shirt I'd worn to the Pine Lake Lodge with Michael, and some tennis shoes.

I was sitting at one side of the scarred table and Spurlock was sitting at the other. Bernard was at the end. Meg had gone home to relieve Mitch, but Dan stayed and was in a chair behind me.

Spurlock took off his coat and sat with his tie loosened and sleeves rolled up. An air conditioner was running in one of the windows, but it couldn't beat the residual heat from another scorching day. The sweat burned the wound on my breast.

A tape recorder sat on the table, and Spurlock told me to describe what happened. I started with my finding Snickers and soon fell into a detached reverie as I told the story. When I got to the part when Crowe told me to lick his face, Dan stood and moved to the window. I saw a tear fall down his cheek. That was the only time I felt anything during the recitation.

When I was done, Spurlock said, "You knew Crowe from before." It was a statement, but I answered as if he had asked a question.

"Yes. He was involved in a situation we—Dan and I, that is—dealt with four years ago."

"Jarvis," Spurlock said.

"Right."

Spurlock turned off the tape recorder. "Been looking for Crowe since. Why would he come back to Patsboro after all these years? Seems stupid."

Dan turned from the window. "Could be for something else. We—"

The look I gave him stopped him in midsentence. James Cleveland was still my client and three policemen appeared to be involved in this deal, somehow. I wasn't real wild about talking freely with another one about the case. I looked at Bernard, who nodded his approval.

Spurlock turned toward Dan. "What?"

Dan bent down and worked on a shoelace, to delay, I imagined. "He probably hasn't been happy about how things turned out with Jarvis. Four years is a long time. Probably figured it was safe to get a little revenge."

Good job, Dan, I thought.

Spurlock grunted. "Suppose so." He turned back to me and started the tape recorder again. "Tell me about the gun, Miss Randall. Is it registered?"

I looked at Bernard and questioned him by raising my eyebrows. I had no idea. I hadn't thought about registration. Bernard shrugged, then nodded. Just tell the truth, was the message.

"I don't know. It belonged to my father. I suppose it was, but that would have been in Maytown."

"Why'd you have it?"

I considered the question. How much did I want to tell Spurlock? To get into my fear would mean explaining the James Cleveland case.

"Single woman alone. Decided I wanted some protection. Bernard's been teaching me how to use it."

Spurlock looked at Bernard, who nodded. The detective seemed satisfied with that. He turned off the recorder again and leaned back, chewing on the eraser of a pencil. He took it out of his mouth and said, "Assuming everything's copacetic with the physical exam, and I'm sure it will be, my recommendation to the district attorney's going to be self-defense, pure and simple. May even give you an award for getting rid of the bastard."

I wasn't relieved. I never thought I'd be charged with anything, anyway. But something else was on my mind. "What about the newspapers?"

Spurlock looked at me.

"I mean, they don't identify rape victims. I know that. But when the rapist is killed by the victim, does that make a difference?"

Spurlock shrugged. "Your name's on the paperwork and that's public information. Whether they report or not's up to them."

Bernard said, "I will talk to them. If you are not charged, there should not be a reason for them to change their policy."

Dan was back in his seat behind me. "Except Crowe is connected to Jarvis, and he was big news four years ago. Eventually the Atlanta papers will pick it up and might not be able to resist."

I sat back in my chair and twirled a lock of hair on a finger. I didn't know all the ramifications, but I knew I didn't want to have to deal with my mother about this.

Bernard said, without conviction, I thought, that if the local paper didn't headline it, nobody else'd notice. He reiterated that he'd talk to them.

Spurlock picked up the tape recorder and the pad he'd been writing on. "Gonna get Marsha to transcribe this and you need to sign it. It'll take a few minutes."

Bernard stood, saying he had to make some phone calls, and followed the detective out of the room. Dan sat in the chair next to me.

"How are you doing?" he asked gently.

I considered the question. The truth was, I was doing amazingly well. What had happened seemed like a dream. I'd been raped and I had killed a man, and I felt nothing.

"I'm all right."

That changed when the door opened.

A voice said, "I just heard . . ."

It was Lucas Anderson.

When I saw him, I thought, You *goddamned* son of a bitch.

Chapter 31

━ ━ ━ ━ ━ ━ ━ ━ ━ ━

As Lucas entered the room, I stiffened and turned away from him. I didn't want to believe that he had anything to do with Crowe, but I *knew* Lucas had lied about seeing Jarvis and I *knew* Crowe was connected to Jarvis.

When Lucas touched my shoulder, tears rolled down my cheeks. As he moved around my chair, I turned again. In a puzzled voice, he asked, "What's going on?"

Dan said, "Lucas, you have some explaining to do."

"What do I have to explain?"

"Lies," I said.

He put his hands on his hips. "What lies?"

Dan leaned on the table with both hands and glared at Lucas. "You said you haven't talked to Jarvis. Tammi and I saw him. Saw his list of visitors. The fact is you *have* talked to him. Not just once—a bunch. For as long as two hours at a time."

"You saw him two days before you lied about it," I added.

Lucas took a deep breath. "Oh," he said and sat in a chair.

"And there are other things," I said. "Like you see Jarvis, and after that, Crowe shows up. You kept denying it was him. Kept discouraging us from looking. You talk to the chief every time we see you. The chief talks to the mayor, who tries to call us off the Crowe idea."

"What?"

Dan said, "All of a sudden you have a new car. Convertible—not cheap. Sudden money."

"Jesus," Lucas said and bent his head back as he slid down the chair. "I really screwed up."

"Screwed *up!*" I jumped up. "Screwed *up?*"

Dan put his hand on my arm and pulled me down into my chair.

"I've got to show you something," Lucas said as he stood and headed for the door.

"Wait a minute," Dan said.

Lucas stopped. "I'll leave the door open. Just going to my office. Nowhere else." He walked out of the room and down the hall.

I looked at Dan. He shrugged.

A minute later Lucas was walking back down the hall. He had something in his hand. He closed the door behind him and threw a spiral-bound book on the table. It slid across and stopped in front of Dan. Dan placed it between him and me.

The cover was stiff, blue stock and was blank. Dan opened it. The front page had this written on it:

TRIPLE THREAT
The Story Of a True Crime
by
Lucas Anderson
About 85,000 words

Dan flipped through the pages It was about three hundred pages of double-spaced typewritten material.

"What's this?" Dan asked.

Lucas was back in his chair. "A book. The story of Gerald 'Jink' Jarvis and how three unlikely people, an employee of a school system and his two student secretaries, solved a mystery. True story."

I was still trying to figure it out. "You wrote a book?"

He pointed to the book in front of us. "First draft. That's my working copy."

"A book about Jarvis?" Dan asked.

"For as long as I can remember, I liked to write. I took some courses while I was in the army. Submitted a few things, but always got rejected. True crime got hot, at least that's what the magazines said. The Jarvis story was a natural. It had all the right elements. I wrote and submitted sample chapters.

"A totally amazing thing happened. An agent liked the chapters and the synopsis and got a publisher interested. Got an advance. It wasn't much, but enough for a down payment on a car I always wanted. Still making payments, but not enough to kill me."

"So you saw Jarvis . . ." I said.

"To see if he'd talk about his side. I knew the basic details from the investigation. I talked to you two and Mitch, too."

Dan and I looked at each other, remembering the conversation in my office.

"I didn't think Jarvis would talk to me, but he liked the idea. Still into glory, I guess, even if it's not exactly favorable."

"Why didn't you tell us about the book?" Dan asked.

"I planned to. The thing is that . . . I was embarrassed. I mean, everybody's writing a book, or, at least, talking about writing a book. I didn't want to say anything to you until I knew without doubt it would be published. Of course, now I've got to finish it. If I don't, I have to return the advance and the repo man gets the convertible. I've got another six weeks. I planned to give you the final copy and let you make corrections or add anything you wanted to. Also planned to dedicate the book to you."

He stood and put a foot on the chair, resting an elbow on his knee. "When you asked the other day, I didn't want to have to explain why I was seeing Jarvis. Not yet, anyway. It wasn't easy lying about that, but I didn't think it would matter."

"Oh, Lucas," I said. "The things I thought."

"I don't blame you. Knowing what you knew, I'd have thought the same thing in your place.

"As for resisting the idea of Crowe being here, I really didn't think he would come back. Seemed like a waste of time and I didn't want you to worry. Obviously, I was wrong. Boy, was I wrong!"

"It wasn't your fault."

"I could have done something. But when Willie Moon didn't recognize Crowe, I figured that was it."

I glanced at Dan. "We've got some things to tell you. Willie didn't ID him, but he was pretty ripped that night. Mitch found some others at Sable's who confirmed it was Crowe."

"When?" Lucas asked.

"Last week."

Lucas took his foot off the chair. "Why didn't you tell—" He stopped. "You didn't trust me. Thought I was in on this."

"Sit down," Dan said. "We've got a lot to tell you."

When I told Lucas of Minerva Hildegarde's phone call, he said, "My God!"

"What?"

Lucas shook his head. "We think we found the truck today, abandoned at a truck stop outside of Winder on Three-sixteen. It matched the description a witness at Idlewood Shopping Center gave. The truck turned up on the sheet as stolen. Till then, we figured the driver never knew what he'd done. We've been trying to figure out what was going on."

I digested that. "Did anybody at the truck stop see the driver?"

"Guy who pumps gas had a vague memory. Said the trucker was wearing a cowboy hat and boots."

"Nothing else?" Dan said.

"Not much. Except he said he wondered what the trucker was doing because he left in a vintage Mustang."

My head dropped. "It had to be him," I said.

"What?" Dan and Lucas said simultaneously.

I looked up. "Crowe. It *had* to be Crowe." I told them about the Mustang I'd seen the night of the wreck.

Just as I finished, Spurlock brought in my statement to be signed. Bernard was with him. I thanked Bernard and told him I'd call tomorrow.

After they left we told Lucas the rest. He said, "Radar Gilstrap. Wouldn't be surprised. But McDaniel—that does surprise me."

Dan and I looked at each other, then back at Lucas. "We were surprised by both," I said.

"I never liked Radar. Oh, he's good. He nearly always gets his man. But there was another side. Particularly with blacks. A couple of times when I was working with him, I had to stop him from going too far in interrogations."

I said, "That confirms what his secretary said."

"And you think Radar was connected to Reeves?" Lucas asked.

"Fish and Bait."

"And Reeves was killed in an attempt to get some kind of evidence of something that Minerva Hildegarde alluded to in her journal," Lucas said.

Dan shrugged. "I have no doubt about Crowe being involved in the Reeveses' murders. After Gilstrap sees Jarvis, Crowe shows up. Of course, it could be coincidence. Radar could be writing a book."

"I seriously doubt it," Lucas said. "He hates writing reports, much less a book."

I said, "The thing is, whatever happened when they were in high school was twenty years ago. All of a sudden it becomes important again. Something happened within the last few months to cause that."

"You figure Dr. Reeves's shift in philosophy and his interest in the Klan has something to do with that."

Dan and I both shrugged. Dan said, "Don't know what to think."

"I can tell you this," Lucas said. "The case on James Cleveland is solid. The fact that Buddy Crowe was in town and Bear picked him out of a book doesn't mean much. Nobody else saw him at the Reeveses' and there's no physical evidence of his presence. Like you said, the chief and the mayor are anxious to get this one settled. The only way to prevent Cleveland from getting convicted is to find out what happened and why." He looked at me.

"Be tough for any lawyer to create a shadow of a doubt, given the evidence."

"That's the premise on which we've been operating," I said.

Lucas stood and went to the window. I saw his reflection in the glass. It was black outside. He tapped his fingers on the sill. Still looking out the window, he said, "Assuming Crowe was driving Essie's car, he went after you and almost got you. He was pissed off about four years ago." Lucas turned and continued, "A week later he comes after you again. Maybe, just maybe, he was told to stop you. You asked Jarvis about Crowe, and Mitch asked about Crowe at Sable's."

"I had the distinct impression that Mitch and Dan were next when he was through with me."

"Why?" Lucas asked. "What did he say?"

"He talked about the doctor and the nigger and me."

Lucas tapped his fingers and stared out the window again.

"He said some weird stuff. About Jonah in the belly of the whale." I shuddered from forcing the repugnant vision of Crowe back into my mind.

Dan said, "Sounds like schizoid ramblings."

"You're the key, Tammi," Lucas said. "It's your job to defend Bear." He walked back to the chair he'd been sitting in and reclaimed it. He put both elbows on the table and intertwined his fingers. "You're not going to like what I'm going to suggest."

"What?" I asked warily.

"I've told the chief what you suspected but haven't told anybody else, as per his direction. He didn't want it to get out that there was any doubt we got the killer. Not until the vote on the consolidated government. He told the district attorney to expedite the case and told me not to write anything about Crowe in my reports." Lucas paused. "To my shame, I didn't."

"You're not responsible for what happened to me."

Lucas shook his head. "Anyway, Radar Gilstrap has access to our paperwork, and if McDaniel's involved, that'd make it even easier because Radar wouldn't have to make it known he was interested. He would notice my not mentioning Crowe. That means you're the only danger to Bear not taking the fall."

"And after tonight, that's still the case," Dan said.

My stomach fell. "Oh, my God."

Dan put his hand on my shoulder.

Lucas stared at me, his eyes intense. "Two—no, make that three—things can happen." He held up his left hand and slapped one finger. "One: we quit and Bear's convicted."

"That's unacceptable," I said.

He slapped another finger. "Two: from what you've said, I don't think Crowe and the other man with him found what they were looking for in Reeves's study. If they had, Crowe wouldn't have come after you again. I suspect Crowe got carried away. Killed Dr. Reeves and his wife before he told them anything. But with the doctor dead, and Crowe dead, the evidence may not matter. If they quit worrying about it, Bear's up shit creek."

"And three?"

He hit the third finger. "Three: I continue to insist Bear's the one. Even intensify that. Make sure they know you're the only threat. You keep looking. Act like you've found more than you have. They still have to come after you."

"Draw them out."

"No!" Dan said sharply and slapped his hand on the table. "*No* way!" He pointed to Lucas, "*You* make it clear Gilstrap's a suspect. Get it in the papers. Make sure Tammi's no longer a threat." He stood, leaned on the table, and said with quiet vehemence, "My *God,* Lucas. You know what she's been through tonight. You must be out of your *mind.*"

"Do I get my gun back?"

"*Tammi!*"

Lucas was looking at me. "I talked briefly with Spurlock before coming in here. No doubt about your not being charged. You should be able to get it back tomorrow."

Dan put his hand on my arm. "You're still in shock. You've got a tough row to hoe still."

Anger surfaced. "I *know* it's not over," I said and breathed deeply.

Dan put his hand on my shoulder.

"I'm just beginning to realize how much is in there that I'm not even feeling yet. But that doesn't take away from the responsibility I have to James." Dan started to protest, but I held up my hand to stop him. "It's more than that, though. I'm not ethically mandated to put myself . . . well, to do that to defend a client. The thing is, those *bastards* sicced Crowe on me. I'm convinced he'd have never come back if it hadn't been for them. I *want* them, Dan. I want to see them over the barrel of a Smith and Wesson Model fifty-eight, forty-one-magnum."

That ended the debate.

I asked Lucas, "Have you heard about any Klan activity scheduled for Monday night at Elysian Fields?"

"Yeah. Big rally. Supposed to have folks from all over the country."

"I thought that was supposed to be in Newnan." Dan said. Newnan is on the west side of Atlanta.

"It was scheduled for Newnan, but they decided it was too much trouble after people started protesting. Nobody in Elysian Fields's gonna complain."

Dan said, "Reeves knew that might happen three weeks ago. Even the location." Dan looked at me. "Remember the question mark?"

"They wearing masks yet?"

"More and more since the court decision," Lucas said. "Why?"

"We need to know what Reeves was up to."

Chapter 32

Lucas drove Dan and me to my house. I told them what I needed to spend the night at Dan's. I didn't want to go in there until it had been cleaned up. Lucas said he'd take care of that.

When we arrived at Dan's, Mitch was still there. It was one of the few times since I've known him that he had no voices or jokes. He simply hugged me when I got out of the car. He just said he was sorry. He did look askance at Lucas.

"Explain it to him," Lucas said before he left.

First I took a bath. I rubbed myself raw, except for my tender breast. In the mirror, I saw an oblong area of red where the powder had burned me. It still seemed unreal.

Afterward we told Mitch about Lucas and everything else. We were sitting on Dan's deck in the dark drinking sweetened iced tea. Mitch didn't argue much about my remaining a target. He'd grown up a target and was used to the idea. He did have a problem with my other notion.

"You want *me* to go to a Klan meeting?" he said in disbelief.

"You'll be covered by a robe and mask," I said.

He held up his hands. "Gloves part of the uniform?"

"I've got an idea for that."

"I can hear it now." He continued in deep redneck, "Hey, boys, I *know* I smell a niggah somewhere 'round heah."

"What about you, Tammi?" Dan asked. "Sheets aren't likely

to hide your sex. Klansmen put women about a half step above blacks. That's all."

"I don't need a robe. I'll just be there. If Tackle's part of the Klan, it'd be good for him to see me. For plan three, anyway."

"I still don't like—"

"That's enough," I said, and yawned. Suddenly I was exhausted. I said good night and went to Samantha's room.

I lay in the dark looking at the fluorescent stickers of stars and moons Samantha had stuck on the ceiling. Every time I closed my eyes, I saw Crowe's bleeding face in front of me.

Turn off the tape, I thought. Turn it off.

I looked at Samantha's clock. It was just past eleven. I picked up the phone she had by her bed and dialed Michael's number. When I heard his voice, the tears came again. Slowly this time.

We talked for an hour. He was kind and sensitive. He suggested a trip to the mountains tomorrow. Get away from Patsboro.

I agreed. After hanging up, I forced myself to imagine riding along mountain roads with the top down. Far away from here and Fish and Tackle. Far away from the memories of today.

I fell into a dreamless sleep.

The pain woke me up. Pain on my breast and between my legs, aches as I moved to find comfort. Suddenly Buddy Crowe was on top of me again.

Startled, I sat up quickly. Posters of Paula Abdul and R.E.M. on the walls reminded me that I was safe. I lay back on the pillow once again and stared at the ceiling. My vision blurred as tears eased into my eyes.

AIDS . . . pregnancy . . . horror. Those were my thoughts.

The door opened slowly and a head appeared through the crack. I wiped my eyes and saw it was Meg.

"I was walking by and thought I heard some stirring in here," she said after slipping through the door and closing it again. She walked to my side. "How you doing?"

I looked up at her and tried to hold the tears inside. I closed my eyes and took a deep breath.

Meg sat on the side of the bed. "It's OK, Tammi." She stroked the top of my head. "It's OK to cry."

Foreign sounds forced themselves out of the center of my being. Meg lay down and wrapped her arms around me. Images flashed through my mind—Buddy Crowe, my mother, my father, Michael, Buddy Crowe—like a high-speed slide show.

Meg squeezed me in her arms. "I know. I know."

Slowly the crying stopped, the visions faded. Meg let go and sat again on the side of the bed. I exhaled hard. "It was just the shock—of remembering."

Meg stood and said, "It would be good to talk to somebody. Dan knows some people who are good."

"I know. I will," I said, but thought, Not now.

Meg left the room, promising breakfast. I showered, scrubbing hard again, and put on the clothes I'd worn the night before.

The kitchen table held the remnants of the family breakfast. After Meg put a plate of scrambled eggs, smoked sausage, grits, and toast in front of me, she left, saying she needed to dress for church. I wasn't hungry, but sat down anyway. The Sunday edition of the *Patsboro Free Press* sat on the other side of the table. I hesitated, then retrieved it and spread it in front of me. Nothing on the front page. Maybe it had happened too late last night. No, I thought, surely not. It wasn't that late. I flipped pages until I came to the police report.

Its headline read, MAN KILLED DURING ASSAULT. The two-paragraph story reported the details, leaving out my name, saying the victim of the assault was not being charged. The name Buddy Crowe wasn't mentioned. He was identified as Melvin Kroanel.

I'd forgotten. That was his real name. In the initial stories about Jarvis four years ago, the papers had used that name parenthetically, but soon dropped it. I doubted that Atlanta reporters who searched outlying papers for leads would remember that.

"Bernard did good."

I looked up to find Dan pouring a cup of coffee.

"He usually does."

Dan was dressed in casual slacks and a short-sleeved shirt. "We're going to church. Wanna come?"

I shook my head. "I talked to Michael last night. We're going to the mountains today."

Dan sat across the table. "Good idea. Be good to get away from here."

I ate a couple of bites of toast, to be polite, but that was all I could manage.

Dan broke the silence. "Lucas called this morning. Said he'd have the house cleaned up by this evening."

"That's nice."

"I also called Johnny Little this morning."

"Johnny Little?"

"Lucas suggested it. You remember him."

"Yeah. Just wondered why you'd call him."

Little was been a construction contractor who had given up the business because he could never underbid Jarvis. It turned out that Jarvis was cheating a bit. When Jarvis went to jail, Little went back into the business.

"Used to be big in the Klan. He renounced his ties a couple of years ago. According to Lucas, his daughter married a black man. Instead of killing them both, he converted."

"A miracle."

Dan sipped his coffee. "Yeah. Anyway, Lucas had talked with him and laid the groundwork. I called and Little said he could supply some outfits for us. For the meeting tomorrow night. I'll pick 'em up today."

"Mitch'll be thrilled."

Dan laughed. "Tickles me just to think about it."

I cleaned up the kitchen over Meg's protests. Dan's family left and I got ready for Michael. It didn't take long. I don't wear much makeup anyway, but that day I didn't use any. I couldn't. Michael arrived at exactly nine o'clock, when he said he would.

The day was already hot, but the humidity was down. We headed north, *sans* top on the Porsche. He drove to Gainesville, where we joined the highway to Dahlonega. The landscape changed gradually from rolling hills to mountainous terrain, and the temperature cooled as the altitude gradually increased. Just before Dahlonega, a rocky stream appeared, paralleling the road. Michael stopped and we walked to the flowing water.

At the stream's edge, I took off my shoes and rolled up my pant legs. The water was cold as I waded carefully on the slippery stones. Michael sat on a boulder, watching me. We had said little in the car on the way up, but now Michael asked, "You doing OK?"

I looked at him. He was wearing white shorts with a yellow knit shirt. His hair was blowing slightly in the light breeze.

"Better," I said.

Back in the convertible, Michael drove through Dahlonega, the small town that gold had built over a century ago. The court-house in the square held a gold museum, and I told Michael I wanted to see it.

We looked at the artifacts and read the history of the gold rush that spawned the phrase, "There's gold in them thar hills." Michael paused in front of a map showing a shaded area running in a diagonal line across the mountains. "That's the Dahlonega belt," he pointed out. He stared at the map. "Did you know the Hall County belt runs adjacent to Teal?"

I shook my head, but he wasn't looking at me, so I said, "No."

"It runs from north Atlanta, through a portion of Gwinnett County and on to the northeast. There were hundreds of mines in Hall County. Around where Lake Lanier is now."

I nodded again.

"Even had a couple of mines in Teal County."

"I've never heard of any."

Michael moved away from the map, stopping in front of a display showing pictures of people in front of their small mines. "They tapped out years ago." He looked at me. "Actually, I've been trying to track them down."

"Why? I mean, if there's no more gold in them."

Michael shrugged and pursed his lips. "New technology might make a difference." He shrugged again. "Just something to do. Some people hunt. Fish. Play golf—"

"And you try to find old gold mines."

Michael nodded.

Another exhibit depicted the process used to pan for gold. I said, "Isn't there a record of where they are? I would think claims would be filed."

"They were." Michael looked at me again. "You've heard of the Fourth of July fire?"

"Yeah." As in any small town, disasters in Patsboro were named and the history passed down. In the late forties an errant Fourth of July firework had caused a blaze that destroyed much of downtown Patsboro.

"The records were lost in the fire."

We'd seen all there was to see. On the way to the car I said, "There ought to be people who remember. Where the mines are, I mean."

Michael's eyes were hidden behind his sunglasses. "Like I said, there were only a couple, and that's only rumor. They haven't been worked for a century." We got in the car. "People die and things are forgotten."

"Yes," I said.

Michael followed a looping route that eventually led to Helen. Thirty years ago, the town had been dying. In an effort to save it, the local citizens got together and decided to spruce it up. They picked an alpine village theme and began a slow process that resulted in a major north Georgia tourist attraction. Michael and I walked hand-in-hand among the dense crowd of fellow tourists, visiting the shops, which were manned mostly by young people in lederhosen. We watched glassblowers and candymakers though windows from the street.

The mountain air was cool. Aromas drifted from the multitude of eating establishments. Suddenly, I was starved. The previous day's consumption had been dumped on Buddy Crowe, and I had managed only two bites of breakfast that morning.

I ate two buns filled with bratwurst, sauerkraut, relish, and onions. I didn't even think about the calories.

After lunch, Michael suggested visiting Anna Ruby Falls. The twin falls are located near Unicoi State Park, just outside of Helen. We parked the car and took the long walk up an asphalt trail to the bottom of the falling water. We sat on a bench, where a fine spray of mist drifted across us. Again, we talked little. Just sat, holding hands, watching the cascading water. After a half hour on the bench, Michael pulled me up and led me to the side of the falls.

A sign said NO TRESPASSING BEYOND THIS POINT and in small letters revealed that fourteen people had died falling from there. The 14 had been recently painted.

"Want to climb?" Michael asked.

I looked up. A well-worn path wound between the rocks above us. I glanced again at the sign, then at Michael.

"We're not teenagers. We'll be careful."

I nodded and Michael led the way. After reaching the top, we sat on a large boulder overlooking the gentle stream that turned into the explosive show below. I was glad for the rest. My toe was beginning to ache.

"It must have been terrible," Michael said.

I looked at him. "Yes. It was."

"Did you know him?"

"Not really. Met him briefly years ago."

I wondered if Michael knew about the Jarvis episode. It'd been big news in Patsboro, but my name had figured in it only obscurely. No reason anyone should remember it.

"I'm glad you . . . got him."

"Yeah," I said while absently touching the tender spot on my breast. I stood and moved to the edge of the falls; a lake was visible in the distance through the trees. "Michael, there's one thing we need to talk about." I hesitated. "About the other night. We can't do that again for a while."

He didn't say anything.

"I've got to wait to be sure . . . about AIDS."

"We can be careful."

"No. I can't. You need to know that. I just can't."

I heard him move behind me. I felt his hands on my back.

"You still want to see me?" I asked.

Michael's hands moved up and gripped my shoulders. I looked down to the bottom of the falls. The people looked tiny. I became dizzy. His grip on the top of my shoulders tightened.

Suddenly, I was falling.

Chapter 33

I dropped to my knees.

Michael was on top of me. He rolled over and I crawled back to the boulder and lay on it with my eyes closed. When I opened them again, the dizziness had passed and Michael was standing in front of me. His cheeks were wet with tears. "I'm so sorry," he said.

I sat up and pulled him to me, wrapping my arms around him and laying my face on his chest. "You're such a good man."

He tensed when I said that, then stroked my hair. "Let's go back down."

Back in the car, we drove south through Cleveland and stopped at Xavier Roberts's Babyland General Hospital, where Cabbage Patch Kids are born. The conversation at the top of the falls had returned the funk, but it dissipated as I watched tourists' children delight in the pseudohospital. When we returned to the sporty car, my spirits had lightened.

As we were approaching Patsboro I said, "You live on Partridge Drive, don't you?"

"Yes."

"I understand you had some excitement over there the other night."

He glanced at me. "Sure did. Minerva Hildegarde's cottage was destroyed. Huge explosion. Gas, I understand."

"You live with your mother?"

He downshifted and passed a semi struggling up a hill. "Yes."

"I'd like to meet her."

"Why?"

"Oh, I don't know. Guess I want to know more about you, is all. I'd like to see your house, too. Those homes are so beautiful."

He didn't respond. Finally I said, "Could you give me a tour today?"

He looked at me, smiled, and agreed. His smile seemed forced.

It was just after five when he turned into the circular driveway in front of his house. Or his mother's house, to be accurate. It was set well back from the road. A creek wound through the front yard. Two footbridges with white railings crossed the creek. The house was Elizabethan, the bottom half of red brick, the top half some sort of masonry supported by beams painted red. A small turret was on the left side.

"I've always admired this house," I said as we climbed out of the car. "Never thought I'd get to see it."

Michael put the top up on the Porsche and led me to the front door. When we entered, a black woman approached.

"Good afternoon, Michael," she said in a deep, dignified voice. "I hope you had a pleasant trip." She was tall and thin and wore a white uniform.

"Very nice, Barbara," Michael said. "This is Tammi Randall."

"Pleased to meet you, Miss Randall." She bowed her head slightly.

Before I could respond, Michael asked where his mother was.

"She's in the garden room. Reading." Barbara reached into a pocket and pulled out a piece of paper. "A phone call for you. The gentleman left a message."

After glancing at the note, Michael led me through a large living room and through french doors to an area filled with plants of all kinds. The walls were windows that provided a view of a wooded backyard that featured graveled paths and steps surrounded by a wide variety of azaleas. Michael's mother was sitting in a bamboo chair with her feet propped on a bamboo hassock. She put down her book as we entered.

Michael introduced us. She was a big-boned woman with a slight roll of fat around her middle. Her hair was white and cut short. She wore glasses, but they didn't hide her strong face.

"Michael has mentioned you." Her voice was rich and powerful.

Michael appeared fidgety. He excused himself to go and return the phone call from the message Barbara had given him.

I went to the windows. "You have a beautiful yard, Mrs. Hutcheson."

She put both hands on the arms of the chair and pushed herself up. She walked to me with a slight limp. "Call me Boots, sugar. Everybody else does. Would you like to see it up close?"

I said I would, and she led me back through the living room, under an arched opening that led to a dining room and into the kitchen. We went through a pantry that had a door to the outside.

"Sorry for the roundabout trip. I left this here." She picked up a cane. "Damned hip. Fell last year and broke it. They replaced it with plastic. The doctor said it'd be just like new. Hell, it's been over a year and it still hurts."

I mumbled something sympathetic and started to follow her out the door.

Boots stumbled and I grabbed her. "Damn that boy," she said as she bent over and picked up a pair of muddy boots. "I've told him a thousand times not to leave these here."

Was she talking about Michael? A servant, perhaps. She was old South.

She stopped and turned. "His newest hobby. Gold mines, or some such nonsense. Always comes back with muddy boots. He's gonna kill me someday, leaving 'em here."

She *was* talking about Michael.

We walked through a small green area covered by fescue and up some steps formed by railroad ties. Soon we were surrounded by the azaleas.

"This must be incredible in the spring. When they're blooming."

"It is pretty," she said. "Michael's daddy did all this. By himself." She seemed proud that he hadn't hired it out. We walked through a labyrinth of trails to a sitting area that featured a small fish pond. She sat on a bench next to the pond and I joined her.

"Tell me about yourself," she said. It was almost a command.

I told her I was an attorney and worked for Legal Aid.

"An attorney. That surprises me. You are a beautiful woman."

She saw my embarrassed look and apparently misunderstood it for feminist indignity.

"Oh, don't get me wrong. I think it's wonderful. It's just that I've found that so many women with that attribute depend on it. Use that instead of their heads. It's sad. Too quickly the day comes when it's gone. And what do they have left? Nothing, is what." She chuckled. "So they dye their hair blue, or do something just as silly, to keep getting attention."

I nodded.

"I've always thought it must be difficult to be an attractive woman. I imagine people tend not to take you seriously."

I did not know what to say.

"Oh now, Tammi. Don't be modest. The fact is you are a very good looking woman. Don't deny that. Use it without depending on it. It could be a real advantage in front of a jury." She paused. "Yes, you should always try to pack the jury. With men."

Conversation with her was easy. I asked her about her husband. She told me how they met when she went to her cousin's promenade through Patsboro fifty years ago. Michael's father was there, and they were married within six months. He was in Europe two months later fighting the Germans. When he returned, he worked in chicken houses by day, and at night started his own business with one machine in the basement of a house they rented. Michael was her only child, she told me.

That gave me an opening to ask about him.

"The Lord blessed us with Michael," she said. "Always been a good boy. Never been a bit of trouble."

Meg said he'd been hospitalized. I guess a mother doesn't want to talk about that. Besides, that was a long time ago. From everything I'd been able to find out, he was a competent businessman and ran Hutcheson Mills successfully.

She went on to tell me that they had tried to have a child for ten years without success. "One day I went to Madam Zima on the Atlanta Highway. She looked at my palm and said Michael would be conceived at two A.M. the following Tuesday. When the time came, I woke his father. Nine months later, Michael Junior was born."

As Bernard would say, that gave me pause.

She went on to tell stories about Michael. "Oh, I don't mean to say he's perfect. He still can lose his temper with me. Did so just the other day."

"He did?"

"I was in his room. Looking for this." She indicated the cane. "I thought I might have left it up there the night before. I found an envelope ready for mailing, so I took it downstairs. However, I had a visitor and forgot about it. He found it when he came home and became very angry that I'd been in his room. Well, I don't really blame him. Everyone needs some privacy. Anyway, that's one of the few times I've seen him really angry."

Confusion reigned. I had found Michael to be sensitive and caring, but also manly. Athletic, strong, running a large business. It was hard to reconcile that with a forty-two-year-old man arguing with his mother about her going into his room.

And what about Boots? Same sort of dissonance. Very bright, perceptive, and aware. She also went to a palm reader to find out when to have sex.

My musings were interrupted by Michael, who was walking up the trail. "There you are. Wondered where you'd gotten off to."

"Your mother was telling me all of your secrets."

He looked at his mother, then at me.

"Said you get angry sometimes. Other than that you're perfect."

He smiled. "Moms tend to exaggerate." He paused. "Tammi, I've got to meet someone. Business. That phone call."

I stood, and so did Boots. We walked along the gravel pathway to the house and on to the car. As we approached it, Boots said, "Where did you say you were from?"

I hadn't, but I answered, "Maytown. It's in south Georgia."

Would I be investigated? I wondered. Big Jack passed through my mind.

When we got to my house, Michael insisted on going in with me to check it out before he left. The front door had a new addition, a dead bolt. Dan, I thought. Inside everything was as it had been before the attack except that the Habitrail was gone. Lucas had left a note on my bed.

Michael hugged me, kissed me on the cheek, and left.

I was alone again. For the first time since last night. I turned the dead bolt and went to the bedroom. I felt a moment of panic; then I picked up Lucas's note. I sat on the bed and read.

He wrote that police cars would be patrolling the area with increased frequency. He didn't want to scare off Gilstrap and whoever was with him, because all we had was their fear that I knew more than I did. Lucas hoped that somehow they'd show themselves. At the same time, I had to be protected as much as possible. That was tricky, he wrote, and he'd understand if I wanted to call the whole thing off. He also said the gun was in my top dresser drawer.

I went to the dresser and opened the drawer. The Model 58 was there. I broke it down and found that somebody had cleaned it. Lucas, I supposed. Georgia's gun laws are among the most liberal of the states, but a tiny effort is necessary to obtain a permit to carry a concealed weapon. I put the gun in my purse. Some things supersede codes of law. Like survival.

I took a bath and rubbed myself raw. Thoughts of Michael and his mother kept running through my mind. Better than thinking about Buddy Crowe.

I called Dan. He had gotten the Klan outfits. In fact, he had one on when I called. I could hear Meg laughing in the background. I thanked him for the dead bolt. He said I was welcome to stay another night with them. I said I'd have to stay alone sometime, might as well be now.

I read till my eyes wouldn't stay open. I lay with the light on and didn't take off my nightgown—I wanted to be covered. I was drifting when a shock ran through me. I sat up and looked around, breathing hard.

"Shit," I said to myself. Watch your language, I thought. *What's happening to me?*

I reached across the bed to the nightstand, got my purse, and pulled out the Smith & Wesson. I lay back down with the pistol in my hand.

My body ached from the attack and the active day, but I felt relaxed for the first time since I'd gotten home.

I held up the pistol and thought about how things change. A week ago, I hated guns.

Chapter 34

As usual, Mrs. Thompson was on the phone when I arrived at the Legal Aid Society Monday morning. My awakening had been easier than the morning before, and I'd allowed myself to doze past the alarm. It was just past nine as I opened my office door.

Behind me, Mrs. Thompson said, "I just don't know yet, Irma. I'll find out today and let you know."

Before I could get to my desk, Landry shouted, "Tammi, is that you?"

I put my purse and briefcase on my desk and went to Peter's door. He was sitting behind his walnut desk. There was a large rubber plant behind him on either side. The floor was covered with thick carpeting and the walls were paneled in rich pine. Mommy and Daddy had paid for all that.

He leaned back in his leather chair. "Got a message for you. Mrs. Thompson was on the phone, so I took it." He whispered, "Lucky for you."

True, I thought.

He picked up a pink message slip. "A man named Gilstrap called. He said he understood you talked to his secretary Friday. Said he'd be in Patsboro today and would drop by. Sometime around one. I told him I didn't know your schedule. He said he'd try anyway."

I was leaning on Landry's door with my arms crossed. Gilstrap wants to see me, I thought. Must be nervous. Good. Sort of. Meant Lucas was right. I thought of my purse on my desk and the Model 58 that was in it.

I said, "Thanks, Landry," and started to turn.

"Have a good time Friday night?"

I began to tell him I had enjoyed the symphony, but the whipped cream and Hershey's syrup afterwards were better, but stopped myself. The game wasn't fun anymore. I also thought that unless Landry was a total waste as a human being, which he wasn't, he must not know about Crowe. Good. "Yes. The symphony was beautiful."

He leaned forward and put his elbows on his desk. "Ought to hear the New York Philharmonic. We could fly up Saturday. Stay at the Plaza."

I pursed my lips. "Michael suggested the London Philharmonic for next weekend," I lied. "Have to think about it." As I walked back to my office I heard him saying something about the Bolshoi Ballet in Moscow.

I decided to check on my Yugo and was reaching for the phone when Mrs. Thompson came in and sat down. "Have a nice weekend?"

"Yes," I lied again. Mrs. Thompson rarely came in to chat. What'd she want?

"I guess you heard what happened on Farris Street Saturday evening."

That was my street. "No," I lied for the third time that morning. I leaned back and checked my nose.

"Aren't you living in the old Milsford place on Farris?"

"I live on that street. I don't know if it's the old Milsford place or not. I know it was a boardinghouse before Professor Gatlin bought it."

She sniffed, obviously miffed that I didn't know the house's heritage. "A man was shot and killed in a house on Farris Street Saturday night. The newspaper said he was raping a woman. I thought you might know something about it."

I realized what her phone call had been about. She couldn't wait to spread the word.

Landry hadn't heard, and Mrs. Thompson didn't know who was involved. I knew the event wouldn't stay secret, but at least for now it was holding. Of course, with Mrs. Thompson on the trail, I was sure that would only last till noon.

I surprised myself by saying, "Mrs. Thompson, survivors of rape deserve privacy. It's a traumatic experience and does not need to be exacerbated by public gossip. Surely even you can understand that."

Her face expressed shock. I'd never spoken to her that way before, though I'd thought it often. A sense of shame welled up. Why'd it take my being a victim of her gossip for me to finally express my opinion?

She worked her lips, as if she wanted to respond, but didn't. She sniffed again before walking out. She must have been desperate. She went immediately to Landry's office and asked him.

I called to check on the Yugo and the man said it'd be a while before it was fixed. They were having trouble getting parts. The tab on the Geo was building every day, so I called Fain Insurance and told Eric Fain that the loss-of-use bill was running up. He might want to check on the problem with getting parts. He said his company wasn't responsible for that, that a week was long enough to have my car fixed.

He picked the wrong time to be obstinate. I told him that it was too bad that the car he had insured decided to hit a Yugo, and that without question, I'd see him in court, that it wasn't the usual idle threat. I had free representation by Bernard Fuchs, one of the nation's premier attorneys. I suggested he think about the cost of his legal fees if he wanted to continue to argue about what was a clear-cut case. I wished him luck and hung up.

The phone rang immediately and was disconnected by Mrs. Thompson. When it rang again, I grabbed it, and Fain said he'd check on the situation and not to worry. His company always fulfilled its responsibility. I thought about the poor folks who didn't have Bernard Fuchs as a friend.

I called Teal General to see how James Cleveland was. A nurse at the station on his floor said he was quiet, as usual. His mother and brothers were there. I called Dan and asked him if he'd go with me to the hospital that afternoon. He agreed. We talked about the KKK meeting that night. He said he'd talked to Mitch. He said Mitch was practicing saying things like, "Damned niggahs takin' over. Time we whiteys reasserted our rights." I told Dan to tell Mitch the Klux probably didn't say things like "reasserted." Dan said he'd pass that along.

I got ready for the eleven o'clock meeting with the planning committee of the Anti-Airport Coalition. We were going to discuss our tactics for countering the presentation by the Atlanta Regional Commission on the environmental impact of the new airport that was scheduled for the next day. The coalition was focusing on environmental concerns because it seemed that at this point, that was the only chance we had of stopping the airport. The problem was, we hadn't been able to find our spotted owl.

Michael had joined the coalition too late to be on the committee, but I tried to call him to see if he could come anyway. His office said he wasn't there. I called his home, and Barbara said he'd left early that morning in his fishing clothes. I should have asked him earlier.

By 11:05 all the members of the committee were sitting around the table in our conference room. As I looked around the room, I again realized how slim our chances were.

The committee was made up of ten men and one woman. None of them owned more than fifty acres of land, and all of that was inherited. Money and influence were nonexistent. The only thing they had going for them was an intense desire to continue operating their chicken houses as their fathers had.

Kurt Riley suggested we tell everybody to bring their shotguns to the meeting. Maybe that'd get the message across. Another farmer said some rope might be useful.

After I let them vent their frustration, I told them that I'd been in touch with a professor at Catledge University who specialized in ecosystems, and that he had agreed to attend the meeting tomorrow. We'd listen to what the commission had to say, then meet with the professor to plan a court challenge based on the environmental damage the airport would cause. The rest of the meeting consisted of their dividing up a calling list to be sure we had a large crowd at Friday's meeting.

As we were breaking up, I heard Kurt Riley ask one of the other members if he was going to the rally that night at Elysian Fields. It hadn't occurred to me before that I was representing members of the Klan.

After they left, I walked to Woolworth's and had a turkey and cheese club sandwich with a pile of potato salad. I was back in my office by one o'clock. I didn't want to miss Radar Gilstrap, but I shouldn't have hurried. He wasn't there at one.

Bernard had taken my cases for the society, except James's, and there was nothing to do on the airport until tomorrow. I didn't have anything to do while I waited.

I didn't need time to think. Time to think brought visions of Crowe. The feeling of him . . . the feeling of being violated.

I *had* to concentrate on getting *them*: Fish—probably Radar—and Tackle, whoever he was. I was sure they'd brought Crowe here. I had to focus on that.

I made a promise to myself. I knew I had to deal with my feelings about Crowe. But first, I would deal with Fish and Tackle.

How should I handle Radar? There was no real evidence that he was involved with Reeves's murder. No evidence other than that which would undoubtedly convict James. We'd found nothing in Reeves's house to indicate what they were looking for. The only hope of finding anything else was that they'd still be nervous about my continuing to investigate the case. And that maybe they hadn't found what they wanted at Reeves's. We were left with waiting for *them* to do something else. Something incriminating.

With Radar, I had to make him think I knew more than I did.

I looked at the clock on my wall. One-fifteen and no Radar. I was alone in the office. Mrs. Thompson had gone to another funeral, and Landry and Bernard were both in court. I thought of Daddy's pistol in my purse. I didn't think Radar would do anything in here, but I wanted to be ready anyway.

I stood and looked out the window to the street below. I could hear the *tick, tick, tick* of the clock hanging next to me. Where was he?

I heard the front door open.

"Hello. Anybody here?"

I walked to the lobby. Radar Gilstrap was standing at Mrs. Thompson's counter. He looked just as he had four years ago. He was wearing a lightweight navy blue suit with a thin blue tie that was loosened at the collar. He was just a little taller than I, but was broad at the shoulders and the waist. A straight line down each side. His dark hair was combed straight back in a fashion that accentuated his widow's peak. His pockmarked face was jowly.

I started to greet him, but realized I didn't know how. "You know, I don't know what your title is now."

"No rank. We're called agents," he said. "It's good to see you again, Miss Randall."

"Come on in." I led the way to my office and indicated a chair for him to sit in across the desk from mine. I didn't want him in the side chair, which afforded a view of my purse.

He crossed his legs and said, "Lois said you called Friday. I had to be up here anyway and thought I'd stop by and see what you needed."

"I appreciate that." I leaned forward, resting my elbows on the desk. "I'm defending a boy on a murder charge. I have reason to believe Buddy Crowe was involved in it."

"Crowe?" he asked with a puzzled look. "Jarvis's Crowe?"

"The same. My client ID'd him. Others did too, though not at the crime scene."

"Wouldn't think he'd come back here."

"No doubt he came back. He was killed Saturday night."

"Killed? You sure?"

"Reasonably. I killed him."

That felt funny. First time I'd said that out loud since telling Meg on the phone.

"You?" he said in surprise. Was the surprise genuine? Seemed so. "I hadn't heard that. What happened?"

I told him of the attack, but left out the details.

"The bastard. I'm sorry for your sake, but I'm glad he's gone."

Maybe for more than one reason, I thought. Don't have to worry about Crowe as a witness. I couldn't tell if Radar was telling the truth about not knowing. If he was, Tackle must be out of the loop. That said something about McDaniel, too. Of course, for Radar to be involved in all this, he had to be a consummate liar.

"Don't know how I missed that," he said.

"The local papers reported him as Melvin Kroanel. Atlanta papers didn't pick it up. I don't want them to."

"Oh," he said. I looked at him and he looked back. "What'd you want from me?"

"At the time I was still trying to establish that he was here. I just wondered if you'd heard anything. Maybe from Jarvis. Of course, it's a moot point now."

Would he deny seeing Jarvis? That'd tell me something.

He crossed his legs. "I did see Jarvis recently. Had business at the federal pen and thought I'd renew an old acquaintance while I was there."

He told the truth. If Lucas was right, Radar knew I'd talked to Jarvis, too. With his years of experience, Gilstrap must know lying is a number-one way to get caught. Better to have a plausible reason for your actions than to deny them.

"How was he?" I asked.

"Arrogant as ever." He cocked his head at me. "So you think Crowe did the killing. That your client's charged with, that is."

"No doubt about it. In my mind, anyway. Nobody else seems to think so."

Did I see relief? Maybe, but I may have been looking too hard. Mostly his face was impassive.

"What motive would Crowe have to come back here and do that?"

I leaned back in my chair. How much should I tell him? The answer came quickly. If the purpose of my hanging out in the wind was to try to make something happen, I had to tell him everything. Except for the part where we figured he was Fish. So I did.

When I finished, he shook his head. "You've drawn a lot of conclusions on pretty slim evidence. You sure you're not reaching a might in this defense?"

I shrugged. "You do the best you can with what you got." I leaned forward again. "But I can guarantee you this: I *will* find Fish and Tackle. Soon as that happens, things ought to clear up considerably. You can take that to the bank." I glanced down at my purse. I could see the Smith & Wesson clearly.

"Well, I wish you luck," he said and rose. "Let me know if I can help you with anything."

I stood and extended my hand. He took it and held it. "What brings you to Patsboro?" I asked as I extracted my hand from his grip.

"Klan rally tonight. Gonna have wackos from all over the country here. Governor wants to be sure it stays peaceful and contained in Elysian Fields."

Like sending the fox to guard the chicken coop, I thought. Another trite aphorism came to mind: In for a penny, in for a pound. "Might see you there."

"At the Klan rally? Why?"

"I have some indication Reeves's murder may have been Klan related. My client, a black boy, may have been set up as a cover. Gonna see what I can find out."

For the first time his face betrayed something. What, I didn't know, but something. "Be careful. The Klan's not too fond of liberal lawyers."

"I'm always careful. But surely they wouldn't hurt a woman. Would they?"

Chapter 35

"Oh Lord. If my sainted mama saw me now she'd die. I ain't believin' this." Mitch was standing in Meg and Dan's bedroom and was draped in white. I was wrapping him from his elbow down in gauze.

Dan was on the other side of the room, looking at himself in a full-length mirror. He had on a pointed hat, and a mask of white covered his face. Two holes, shaped like eyes, allowed him to see. "Know now why they like to meet after dark. This outfit'll kill you in the summertime. Hotter'n hell under here."

It was an hour before the rally was set to begin. Dan and I had gone to the hospital and met James's mother and two of his brothers. James seemed to be in better spirits than before, though it was hard to tell. He never said much.

After his family had left, Dan, in an attempt to make conversation, said, "You know, Bear, I've wondered about you and your brothers. George is so short and Jerome's tall and thin. You, you're sort of in between."

"Well, you see, Doc, George's daddy, he be short and Jerome's daddy, he be kinda tall. My daddy, he be 'bout like you."

On the way home, Dan said, "It hits me every day. I don't know how these kids make it at all."

At eight-thirty, Dan said we'd better be going. "Oh please, Lord," Mitch said as we pulled him to the garage where Mitch's rented car was sitting. Dan's van and Mitch's Mercedes were too conspicuous to drive to the rally. I followed them to Elysian Fields in the Geo.

Elysian Fields was a twenty-minute drive north of Patsboro. We joined a procession of pickups bouncing over the rutted roads to a large field where a bonfire was blazing. There was scaffolding set up next to it. I parked beside the Chevrolet Caprice Dan and Mitch had driven and waited for them to get out.

That took a while because Mitch was trying to put on his headdress before he got out, for obvious reasons. The tall hat kept hitting the ceiling of the car. Finally he disappeared as he lay down to get it on, then slithered out the door. I stayed a few feet behind him and Dan as they walked toward the fire, which was the gathering place for the participants. Mitch was having trouble. His robe was slightly too long for his legs and he kept tripping over it. Finally, he picked it up, like a bride walking up steps. I heard him say, "Oh please, God, forgive me for my sins."

When we arrived in front of the scaffolding, we joined the milling crowd dressed in white. About half wore masks. I looked around for Radar, but didn't see him. A row of Teal County Sheriff's Department cars was parked a few hundred feet away on the road, and I thought he must be up there, watching. Or else, he was in a robe.

A table was set up to the right of the fire and Klansmen were filling out name tags.

"Name tags?" Mitch asked in wonder.

Dan shrugged and they fell in line. When they returned, instead of a name under HELLO, MY NAME IS, Dan's tag read *West Virginia* and Mitch had written *Vermont*. I followed them away from the fire to an area that was empty.

"So what do we do now?" Mitch asked.

I said, "Mingle. We want to find somebody who knew Reeves."

Mitch picked up the bottom of his robe. "Maybe the Grand Lizard of Patsboro."

"Wizard," I said.

"Whatever."

"I'll follow you," I said. Mainly I was there as bait. Hopefully I would make somebody nervous. But I didn't want to be alone.

There were other women there, but they were at the campers that had been set up in an area a hundred yards from the fire. Children were playing among them. Raising them right, the Klan way. Instill irrational hatred as early as possible. The whole scene made me shiver.

Mitch and Dan approached a group of men whose tags indicated that they were from Teal County. They turned as we approached.

"Welcome to Teal County. Name's Clint," one said to Dan and Mitch. "Where you boys from?" he asked while moving his head to try to read the tags through his mask.

"West Virginia," Dan said. "And my friend Grif's from Vermont."

"Vermont?" the Klansman repeated.

"Yaup," Mitch said in a New England accent.

The others stopped their conversation and turned toward them. The first said, "Well, you ought to win the prize for being the one from fartherest away."

Another stepped forward and said, "You hurt yourself?" He was looking at Mitch's hands.

Dan laughed. "Had some trouble last night in North Carolina. Grif picked me up and we stopped there for a cross burning. Some nigger'd tried to join my brother's church up there. Grif here accidentally burned his hands."

The Klansmen hooted. "Boy, you gotta be dumber'n a stick," one said.

Another said, "Only thing dumber'n a nigger's a Yankee."

"Yaup," Mitch said. "Need to be mighty careful at cross burnings. Learned that right enough."

"Hey, boy, you're awright, though. Wish we could get more of y'all in the brotherhood. Hell, y'all need it more'n we do."

"Yaup."

"Listen," Dan said, "Since you boys are from Patsboro, I want to ask you something. Few months back we had a fellow named Reeves, called himself a doctor, come up asking a bunch of questions. Y'all know him?"

The laughter stopped. Clint said, "Yeah, we knew him. Got killed by a nigger a few weeks back."

"Oh. Guess it don't matter anymore," Dan said.

"Guess it don't," Clint said. His voice was guarded.

"Just wondered what he was doing."

I didn't hear the reply because a voice behind me said, "Ain't you that lady lawyer who keeps niggers outta jail?"

I turned to find a masked Klansman a foot away. I had to look up to see his eyes. No, not eyes, holes. This whole scene was weird.

Before I could answer, another next to him said, "She's all right. Helping us with the airport." I recognized the voice. It was Kurt Riley.

The first said, "Well, you need to be over there with the other women." The two turned and walked away. When I turned back to Mitch and Dan, they were gone. I walked around, but couldn't find them. The field was filled with white robes, and I had to get close to each one to look for gauzed hands. Finally, I went back and sat on the hood of my car and listened to speeches about how the white man had to reclaim his rightful place in America.

It was close to eleven o'clock before I saw two Klansmen walking toward me and figured one was Mitch from the way he was picking up the bottom of his robe. I had got off the hood to meet them when Mitch suddenly tripped on his robe and fell forward to the ground. His hat and mask flew off.

Most of the robed figures were either around the fire or drinking beer at the campers, but a couple were a few feet from Mitch. One of them looked around when Mitch fell.

"*Nigger!* There's a nigger here!" he yelled.

"Oh, sweet Jesus," Mitch yelled as he grabbed his hat and ran toward the pickups and scattered cars.

Klansmen were turning their heads from the fire to watch the running figure. The Klansman who had screamed began running toward Mitch.

Dan ran behind the Klansman and managed to step on his robe. They both tumbled down in a heap. Dan stayed on top and yelled, "Get the nigger! Get the nigger!"

The rest of the Klansmen were too far away to hear. The first jumped up and yelled, "Goddamnit, he's gettin' away. Can you believe that? Shit!"

I turned to see Mitch's rented car racing down the road. The Klansman put his hood back on and returned to the fire.

After waiting a moment, Dan approached me. "I think I need a ride home. Mine seems to have left."

When we were out of Elysian Fields on the road back to Patsboro, Dan said, "Well, that was a bust. Liked to got Mitch killed for nothing."

"Nothing?"

"They seemed to think Reeves was writing a history of the Klan. That's all. Didn't appear to mind. Didn't appear to have any animosity. Mostly thought Bear ought to be lynched for killing him."

"Dead end," I said.

"Dead end," Dan replied.

"Damn."

Chapter 36

Mrs. Thompson cluck-clucked when I arrived late for the second morning in a row. Amazingly, I didn't give a damn what Mrs. Thompson thought. That's not to say I wasn't polite. In fact, I was overly kind. Being raised southern means that'll never change. The difference was that I no longer cared about what she thought of me.

I arrived late partly because of the debriefing Dan, Mitch, and I had carried out at Dan's house after the Klan meeting. The discussion hadn't lasted long, but we had begun on the other side of midnight.

There wasn't much to go over, except for Mitch's moment of terror. Dan and I fell over laughing as Mitch repeatedly offered to fly us to Newark for a tour of his old neighborhood. He kept saying, "Fair is fair."

The only conclusion we reached was that either the Klan was more adept at keeping secrets than we were ready to believe or that they had nothing to do with the Reeves murder. That left us at square one. We had to keep looking for Tackle. I kept thinking about Officer McDaniel.

Thinking about McDaniel didn't keep me awake after I was home in bed. Thinking about Buddy Crowe did.

By that afternoon, the puffy white clouds that had started the day had thickened and multiplied. As I left my office for the three-block walk to the Teal County Courthouse for the meeting with the Atlanta Regional Commission, the clouds to the west had towered into the classic anvil shape that preceded a thunderstorm. The air was again hot and heavy. I was thankful for the additional penny sales tax we were paying that provided funds for the courthouse renovation, including an air-conditioning system. Only a year ago the primary cooling for the seat of government was provided by barely moving ceiling fans.

I was shifting gears as I walked along Peter Street. I was walking out of James Cleveland's case and its nightmares and into the effort to save Teal County from the noise, pollution, and threat to the quality of life that a giant airport would bring.

The commission obviously anticipated our move to work against them on environmental grounds. It had announced this meeting to explain the steps that were being taken to insure that the airport would meld with our agricultural industry and the ecosystem in general.

Ought to be interesting, I thought. Sort of like explaining how a couple of chicken houses next to the Fox Theater on Peachtree Street in Atlanta would blend right in to the urban landscape.

I thought about a foreign exchange student Dan had told me about. The student was from Copenhagen and his host family had brought him to register for school two weeks before the school year was starting. Three days later, the family called and said he wasn't coming after all. He couldn't stand the smell of chicken houses near their home and had asked to be moved somewhere else.

Right. If the farmers of Teal County had to live underneath screaming jets, the folks in Atlanta could live with the smell of chicken houses.

Of course, real life doesn't work that way.

I was deep in thought as I walked up the courthouse steps and didn't notice Dan until I heard, "You in there?"

"I'm sorry. I was thinking about the meeting. This one, I mean."

"Ought to be interesting to discover how the airport's gonna produce fatter chickens."

"I was thinking the same thing. It should make fascinating science fiction." I looked down the street. "Have you seen Mitch?"

"Nope," was all Dan said.

The hall that led to the room where the county commissioners usually met was filled mostly with men in overalls and T-shirts. As I walked past them, I wondered how many had been at the meeting last night at Elysian Fields. That's something an attorney needs to get used to—the cognitive dissonance inherent in the job. An attorney who represented only people she thought innocent or held only values she agreed with would not only go hungry, but would operate contrary to constitutional principles.

Still, sometimes it was hard.

The ecology professor I had recruited for the committee was sitting in the front row. Michael was sitting next to him. Dan and I joined them. I sat next to Michael. I told him how much I had enjoyed the trip to the mountains.

He nodded and said flatly, "Me, too."

I told him I enjoyed talking to his mother.

He nodded and said nothing. Was this the moodiness Meg had talked about?

I looked to the front of the room. An easel was set up to our right. Two slide projectors rested on a table in front of a screen. A podium had been placed next to the projectors. Just as I looked at my watch, the mayor appeared at the podium and asked everybody to sit. I looked back at the crowded room.

"Gonna be hard to do," I said to Dan. "Unless they sit on each other."

The room was packed and began to—there's no other way to put this—stink. I turned around to find Kurt Riley sitting behind us. I looked at him and sniffed.

He laughed. "You said we couldn't bring shotguns. Didn't say we had to clean up from the chicken houses this mornin'."

Hell of a tactic, I thought, and tried not to breathe. It was evident that Kurt Riley thought along the same lines I did about some things.

Through a strained voice, Dan said, "God Almighty! Forget the air conditioning and open some windows."

I looked at Michael. He was staring straight ahead.

Mayor Darnton stood and called the meeting to order. Only he said, "This meetin' is called to odor."

I laughed, but soon realized that that was how he said the word.

The mayor introduced three men who were sitting where the commissioners usually did. The chairman of the environmental impact committee stood. He was of medium height, not quite six feet, and wore sideburns that were twenty years out of date.

The chairman went to the podium and took a deep breath. The room quieted when he said, "Ladies and gentlemen, I grew up on my granddad's farm in South Carolina. For the first time in a long time, I feel like I'm home."

I leaned over to Dan and said, "Brer Rabbit."

The chairman explained that the purpose of the meeting was to allay our fears of what the airport would do to our community. He ended by saying, "The fact is this airport will be quite small. Designed only for flights terminating and originating in Atlanta. The Atlanta airport will continue to bear the major traffic."

Somebody in the back said, "I'd like to see your granddaddy's farm if you think ten thousand acres is small."

Brer Rabbit smiled and said, "Just my point. Most of that land is buffer to isolate the problems the airport will bring. Oh, I admit, there'll be an impact. But it's our job to minimize possible problems and Dr. Porterfield is going to tell you how we're planning to do that."

A plump man with a full white beard walked to the podium. He talked about the need to blend the airport into its surroundings and ensure that the natural habitat not be disturbed. He pointed to a chart on the easel that listed the agricultural products produced in Teal County. Behind that chart was another that listed animals native to the area. That was followed by a third chart listing indigenous plant life. Dr. Porterfield provided examples of airports that coexisted with such activities in other locations.

The farmers grew restless. They wanted to grow chickens. They didn't give a rip about saving the Cherokee rose.

Porterfield turned on one of the slide projectors. An aerial view of the northeast quadrant of the 10,000 acres appeared on the screen. The other projector came to life and displayed an overlay that contained symbols representing landmarks on the actual photograph. Its purpose was to clarify what we were seeing. He used a pointer and talked about decibels and particulate matter.

My mind drifted. I'd seen this part at the meeting when the site selection committee made its original announcement. I thought about Big Jack. The man showing the slides resembled him.

The slides continued to flip.

Had I been wrong about Big Jack? I shook my head. I was just trying to justify my not liking the man who my mother planned to marry. The guy was a lecherous creep. Some things you just have to live with. I forced myself to think of something else.

James Cleveland.

I retraced everything that had happened since Lucas's phone call that Friday night. Was I missing something? I put my elbow on the armrest between Michael and me and rested my chin in my hand. Tackle had to be somebody in Patsboro. The more I thought about it, the more McDaniel made sense. Maybe he had a relative from Patsboro. Had Dan seen the name McDaniel in the yearbook at all? Even if it wasn't our McDaniel. I opened my eyes to whisper that question to Dan, but didn't.

Dr. Porterfield's words entered my consciousness. "And this area, in the southeastern quadrant, is made up mostly of wet-lands." He pressed the button that lit the second projector containing another overlay of symbols. "Our plans are to leave it just as it is."

Michael said, "*What?*"

I stared at the screen. My mind clicked. "That slide. I need that slide." I said quietly.

Dan said, "What slide?"

I pointed to the projector with the overlays. "The one in there. It's the key, Dan. It's the key to the whole thing."

Chapter 37

Finally, the presentation was over. Dr. Porterfield was hesitant when I asked to borrow the slide of the overlay that symbolized the features of the wetlands.

The mayor was standing next to Porterfield when I made the request. "We all know your agenda, Miss Randall," the mayor said. "You want to stagnate this county's growth for the sake of a bunch of chicken farmers."

Before I could reply, somebody from behind me said, "When you and I was in school, Harold, before you got to be the high and mighty mayor, I seem to recall that your family raised pigs." I looked around and saw it was Kurt Riley. "I'll take chickens over pigs any day. Let her have what she wants."

When Riley took a step toward him, the mayor said to Porterfield, "I don't suppose it'd hurt to let them have one little bitty picture."

"Let's go," I said to Dan after getting the slide. When we were outside, I realized that Michael was with us.

"What is it, Tammi?" he said from behind me. I was nearly running.

"Something we've been working on. Need to get down to the police station."

"I'm going with you."

I stopped.

"Michael, this has to do with my work," I said.

He put his hands on my arms. "You were hurt real bad because of your work. You haven't said that, but that's what I suspect. I'm going with you." Whatever mood he'd been in had changed, but I had more important things on my mind.

"Fine," I said and turned again.

The Patsboro Police Station was across the street from the courthouse. I marched past Molly Sheridan, who was behind the counter. "Hey, wait a minute!" she exclaimed.

Michael and Dan followed me through the swinging door and down the hall to Lucas's office. He was sitting at his desk.

I said, "Lucas, we've got to go to the Reeves house."

He stood. "What's going on?"

"Tell you when we get there."

"Now wait a minute. First, I don't know what the hell you're talking about. Second, we turned the house over to the family. We can't just go barging in."

The tension, fear, anger, and nightmares I'd been living with for the past ten days broke loose from deep inside and invaded my brain. I felt them rise and leap out.

"*Damn* it. I will *not* wait a minute! I *know* what they were after in Reeves's office. I just have to confirm it. We do that, and we've got 'em. I *know* it!

"Lucas, this has gone on long enough. This has got to end. *Today.*"

Lucas looked past me at Dan.

Dan shrugged.

Lucas rubbed his hand across his face. "OK. We'll go over there. See if somebody will let us in. If somebody's there."

That was good enough. I didn't care if anybody was there or not. At least we were moving.

I followed Lucas through the halls to the back of the station. Dan and Michael were behind me. We went down two sets of stairs to a door that led to a parking lot filled with police cars. Lucas got in a light green Buick Regal. I got in beside him. Dan and Michael sat in the back.

Lucas looked back at Michael.

"He's with me. Let's go," I said.

Lucas glanced at Michael again before starting the car.

The trip to Bond Street took just less than ten minutes, but it seemed like hours. Lucas parked in front of the Reeveses' house and I jumped out and ran to the door. I hit it with my fist, then rapped it with the brass knocker.

Nobody answered.

"Not here," Lucas said. "Not surprised."

"Open it, Dan," I said.

"What?" Lucas said.

Dan walked around Lucas, squatted in front of the doorknob, and peered at the lock.

Lucas said, "Look, Tammi, I know you've been through a hell I can't even imagine, but there's no way we're breaking into this house."

"No breaking," Dan said. "Just entering."

I said, "I know the problems you could have with this. Go on. We'll call you."

Dan had his wallet out and was going through it. "Don't need much for this," he said. "A credit card will do."

Lucas looked at me again. He made a decision. "Guess if my old teacher says it's all right . . ."

"Not so old," Dan said as he slid a credit card between the door and the jamb.

Just as Lucas was saying, "That's not what I meant," the lock clicked and the door creaked open. Dan went in first, but I passed him and ran up the stairs.

I *had* to be right. I *knew* I was. I ran up the stairs to Dr. Reeves's study and went directly to the fireplace.

"Turn the light on," I said. I held up the slide and tried to compare it to the abstract painting on the wall. I turned around and said, "I need a lamp on the mantel or something. It's still too dark."

Dan looked at me, at the slide, then at the painting. A look of recognition crossed his face. He turned and walked to a closet to the left of the door. "Saw this the other day," he said as he opened the closet and started rummaging. He turned around with a slide projector.

"Yeah!" I said.

Dan unwound the cord and plugged it in. I gave him the slide and he put it in the lighted slot. An unfocused image washed over the painting above the fireplace.

He said, "Take the painting down and move it to the left. I'll focus the slide to the right."

"I still don't know what the hell's going on," Lucas said as he walked toward the painting.

Michael was standing at the rear window. His face held a quizzical look.

Lucas removed the painting from its hook and moved it to the left. Dan pulled the projector toward the wall as far as the cord would allow. When he focused it, the image was about twice as large as the painting.

I concentrated on the lower right-hand portion of the slide, comparing it to the painting. "You see it, Dan?"

He walked closer and looked. His head was moving from one to the other. "Yeah. *Yeah!*"

"What?" Lucas asked.

I went over to the fireplace. "Look, Lucas. About here." I outlined an area on the slide. "These symbols represent landmarks. Here's a structure of some kind. This is a grove of trees. Big ones, like oaks. Here's the main creek running through. This is an area of . . . uh."

"Briars," Dan said. "Blackberries, maybe."

"Yeah. And so on." I moved to the painting. "Look." I pointed. "There's a structure. The trees. Water."

"A map?" Lucas said.

"Right. A map."

"Coincidence?"

"Look at it. It's a match. No way it's coincidence."

Lucas looked at Reeves's paintings of beaver ponds on the wall. "So it's a map. The guy liked beaver ponds. That's an area of beaver ponds. What makes you think it's connected?"

"The airport," Dan said.

"Right," I said. "Something happened a long time ago and something happened a few months ago." I had been looking at the paintings on the walls, but now turned to Lucas. "The decision on the airport was made in April. Reeves changed a few months ago. Radar got quieter . . . distracted. Reeves gains a whole new theoretical perspective and is writing some kind of article. He's killed. Looks like he was being interrogated. The killers were looking for something."

"Minerva wrote that Bait, who was Reeves, had the evidence. He was going to do something with it," Dan said.

"Wait a minute," Lucas said. "You're saying this painting is a map that leads to the evidence Hildegarde wrote about?"

"Exactly," I said. "It was right in front of Crowe's face and he didn't know it."

"How does Crowe fit in?" Lucas asked.

I shrugged. "Maybe the evidence will tell us. Whatever it is."

I looked at Michael. I'd forgotten he was there.

"I don't know what you're talking about," he said in response to my look.

"It's a long story." I turned back to the painting. "The question is, where is the evidence? Which mark on the map?"

Dan stepped back from the projector. "You ever been in a beaver pond?"

I shook my head.

Dan said, "I have. Long time ago. Bud Freeburg and I used to explore one on my father's farm. It's like a swamp. Got lost all the time." He walked toward another painting. "It's not like people think. A pond, I mean. There's usually a stand of water, but behind it the water backs up into the woods. Everything in there looks the same. Reeves wanted to remember this place."

He walked to the painting. "This black blotch in the middle. That'd be what he was interested in." He backed up again. "Look at the other paintings. Bet they depict what surrounds the black patch."

I looked at the landscapes. One featured a chimney rising from the ground. A house of some kind had been abandoned long before the beavers arrived. Another showed a distinctive tree trunk. Split in two at some point in time, it had grown back in the form of a figure eight. Each of the pictures showed something with a distinctive feature. I walked quickly from the room and ran down the stairs to the kitchen. In less than a minute, I was back in the study with a knife.

"Whoa, now," Lucas said.

"We need these. You think the family's gonna mind if they lead to information on who killed their relatives?"

"The family figures we got him."

"They're wrong," I said and took down a picture. I cut the canvas from the frame. "You didn't see this, Lucas."

He sighed and sat in a chair next to where Michael was standing. "See no evil."

Dan helped me until we had all the paintings cut out, rolled up, and bound by some rubber bands we found in Reeves's desk.

"Let's go," I said when we were finished.

"Need to change your clothes," Dan said.

I looked down. The dress and pumps weren't exactly beaver-pond gear. "You're right. Let's go by my house first."

I looked at Dan and Michael. Dan was in his usual jeans and knit shirt with tennis shoes. Michael was wearing a tailored suit and leather shoes. "You want to go, Michael?"

He looked indecisive. "I still don't know what you're talking about, but I want to be with you. I don't want you to get hurt again."

"We'll go by my place, then Michael's. OK, Lucas?"

"It's your show. What you say makes some sense, but I'm still not convinced."

"No way to know till we look. What else have we got? Except hoping Radar or Tackle does something stupid."

Lucas nodded. "We'll give it a shot."

Lucas and Dan got in the front seat of the car, Michael and I in the back. I was tapping one of the paintings on my knee and Michael took my other hand. He squeezed it and I looked at him. He was looking out the car, staring at the passing scenery.

Chapter 38

My dress, pumps, and panty hose were tossed on the floor of my room. I pulled on a pair of old jeans and replaced the lacy bra I'd been wearing with something more substantial. I found a paisley linen dashiki I'd bought at a yard sale. When I bought it, I wondered when I'd ever wear it. This was it.

I was trying to put on my second tennis shoe while walking toward the door. I fell over my purse, which I'd thrown on the floor, barely avoiding impaling myself on an umbrella in its stand.

What's the hurry? I thought while I put on the shoe. When it was tied, I stayed on the floor with my arms resting on my knees.

What's the hurry?

I was convinced there was something in that beaver pond that would help me understand what was going on. For some reason, Reeves knew where the evidence was and the others didn't.

Had he hidden whatever it was?

No. That didn't make sense if the airport being built made a difference. And I was sure that it did. Gilstrap and Tackle had to know where the evidence was.

But not exactly.

They knew it was there somewhere, but not exactly where. I thought back to the slide and the scale imprinted on it. The wetlands covered over a thousand acres in the southeastern quadrant. A lot of area to search.

What's the hurry?

I thought of Gilstrap. He was in Patsboro yesterday. What if he was to find it?

That's the hurry.

The thought of *any* possibility that Gilstrap would escape was too much. I was convinced he was responsible for Crowe being here. Responsible for my . . .

I grabbed my purse, threw it on the bed, headed for the door, but stopped. The weight of the Smith & Wesson lingered in my arm. I walked to the bed and removed the pistol from the front pocket of my purse. Buddy Crowe's image appeared, but was replaced quickly by the visage of Radar Gilstrap.

Never again.

But where to put it? Carrying a purse in a beaver pond wouldn't work. I ran across the room to the closet where I had made my escape just a few days ago, and pulled out the box that held the useless stuff I couldn't bring myself to throw away. The fanny pack I used at swim meets was at the bottom. I strapped it under the dashiki, pulled on the Velcroed cover, and slid in the gun.

I dashed out the door, not taking time to lock Dan's new dead bolt. I climbed into the backseat with Michael. Nobody said anything on the way to his house. When we arrived, my watch read 2:45.

Michael went inside. While we waited, Dan and Lucas examined a map of Teal County. Lucas said that New Liberty Church Road would get us closest to where Reeves's painting matched the commission's slide. Michael emerged from his front door in dirty boots, khaki pants, and a short-sleeved shirt with epaulets. He looked like he was ready for the jungle. His mother came out behind him, shouting something I couldn't understand. Michael waved his hand without turning around and got back in the car.

"Use your siren?" I asked Lucas as he entered Partridge Drive from Michael's driveway.

"No need." Lucas glanced back at me. "Look. I've already violated my oath of office twice today. If we don't find anything, I don't want to explain why I screamed through Patsboro. Besides, there's no hurry. Plenty of daylight left."

You're not the one waiting to be attacked again, I thought, and took a deep breath. No sense getting mad at Lucas. I looked at Michael. He was staring out the window. I could see his jaw working. It seemed strange to have him here with Lucas and Dan. He belonged in a different life. Not this one.

Suddenly it struck me.

Why *is* he here? I thought back. What had he said?

You were hurt real bad because of your work, at least that's what I suspect.

Why would he suspect that? I'd told him about James Cleveland and the Reeves, but nothing else. I had never mentioned Crowe's connection to anything.

The airport? Michael must've known about the possibility of Teal County being selected for a long time. The commission's work went back five years. All of a sudden he wanted to stop it.

What else had his mother said? He'd got mad when she found an envelope in his room. An envelope ready to be mailed. It just needed sealing. Why would he be mad about that?

Reeves's calendar. He had entered a deadline for an article to be submitted. Hildegarde wrote that Bait had one last thing to do. Write an article? An incriminating article? I knew Bait was Reeves and that Reeves was a scholar.

I jumped when I felt something on my hand. I looked down and saw Michael's hand over mine. I looked up at him. He was looking at me, his gray eyes peering into mine. He squeezed my hand and smiled.

I saw my room in them. Our laughing and his gentle touching. His unselfish lovemaking.

Paranoia was a typical result of rape. I'd read that enough. You begin not to trust anybody.

Michael is a guy who cares about me and doesn't want me to be hurt again, I thought. He sees no sense in having his own place when a castle is available, but doesn't want his mother taking care of his business. And like everybody else in the county, he never dreamed Teal would be selected for the airport. Early in life, he'd gone through a time of depression. Who didn't at some point in his or her life? He was just man enough to admit it and take care of it. And besides, he went to Jeff Davis Academy, not Patsboro High.

I smiled and squeezed back.

Relax, Randall, I thought. Don't get weird.

In the front seat, Dan and Lucas were discussing the best place to stop so that we could begin walking toward the gray mass on the painting. They decided to park the car at an abandoned store on New Liberty Church Road. Lucas turned onto weed-filled gravel. The store was a rotted wooden structure with a faded sign that read J. R. EDWARDS. Bits and pieces of a Coca-Cola advertisement were barely evident on one side of the store. The windows were cracked and broken.

The air-conditioned car had been a haven from the cotton-candy air that blasted in when the doors were opened. The sky behind us was dark with clouds. A bolt of lightning cut through the gray haze on the horizon. As the thunder rattled what was left of the store's windows, I pointed to the storm and asked, "Where's that going?"

"Somewhere other than here, I hope," Dan said. His hands were full of Reeves's rolled-up paintings.

"Just love being up to my knees in water in the middle of a lightning storm," Lucas said. He was standing behind the open trunk and was strapping on a black holster containing a pistol. The belt also held a flashlight, along with a row of extra ammunition.

"What's that for?" I asked. "Think somebody might be out there?"

"Snakes," Lucas said. "Hate snakes."

"Snakes? What kind of—"

Dan interrupted, "Snakes shouldn't be a problem, but be careful around briars. Rattlers like to get up in them."

"What about moccasins? All that water." I asked.

"Don't have moccasins above the fall line. Might see some water snakes. They're thin and black. Harmless." Dan was at the edge of the woods. He pointed with one hand and held the abstract with the other. "We head this way."

I walked to Dan and picked up the paintings of the beaver pond he'd dropped at his feet. Michael was behind me, and I gave him two of them and kept two. One for each hand was enough.

Dan entered the woods and Lucas, Michael, and I followed. For about fifty feet, the pine trees and oaks were well spaced, but the undergrowth thickened. A mixture of briars and vines soon surrounded us. Dan held branches away from him until I grabbed them and held them for Michael and Lucas. I was trusting that Dan knew what he was doing and where he was going. I couldn't see beyond five feet, if that.

The ground began to soften. Dan found a sturdy branch to hold down the sticky, stinging vines. He laid it down, and I stepped over thick masses of undergrowth. I let Lucas and Michael fend for themselves.

Abruptly the underbrush was replaced by a layer of water surrounding oaks, yellow poplars, and a few southern magnolia. There were isolated clumps of bushes and, rarely, a formation of boulders. The dense canopy above blocked the sun, causing a midday twilight in the swamp below. Thunder reverberated in the distance.

As we stood on the edge of the dark brown water, Dan pointed straight ahead. "See that poplar with the split trunk?"

I followed his finger and saw the tree fifty feet away. It divided in the middle and rejoined five feet above the split.

"Yeah," I said.

"We'll walk to that first. It's easy to get lost in this stuff. I used to find myself walking in circles and backtracking where I'd been before till I learned to follow landmarks." He looked up and said, "Can see enough of the sun from time to time to keep it just to our right until it's time to choose another target."

"Let's go," I said.

Chapter 39

━ ━ ━ ━ ━ ━ ━ ━ ━ ━

Dan stepped into the water. I lifted the dashiki, stuck the paintings in the back of my pants, and glanced back at Michael. He was looking at the fanny pack on my waist.

"Come on," I said. Michael looked in my eyes, not moving.

I turned and followed Dan, and heard Michael and Lucas splash behind me. The water was warm and knee-deep and filled with debris on the bottom. It was slow going. Dan carefully felt his way along and I tried to step where he had. Occasionally, my tennis shoes slipped on a slick limb and I would drop an arm in the water to catch myself. It'd come out covered with small brown flecks of organic matter and slimy algae. By the time we reached the doughnut tree, I was damp to my neck from falling and splashing. I thought about the paintings. They were oil. Water shouldn't be a problem. I remembered the gun. I had no idea what water did to a pistol.

When we regrouped, I said to Dan, "You used to do this for fun?"

"Yeah. And to look. It's beautiful in here."

I looked around at the dark water covered here and there by a greenish muck. "To each his own."

Dan glanced up, presumably to find the sun, then pointed again. "Head for that fallen tree." He was pointing to a tree that had snapped five feet above the water. We began again. Halfway to the new objective, an ear-piercing screech sounded overhead. I looked up, took a step, and landed on nothing.

The world turned black.

Hands grabbed my flailing arms and pulled me out of the water and back to where I'd been.

I spit water and tried to get goop out of my eyes. I was breathing hard.

"You all right?" Michael asked.

"Yeah," I said as I pushed my sodden hair out of my face. "Got distracted. What was that noise?"

"Owl," Dan said.

"I thought they slept during the day."

"Insomniac," Dan said and laughed.

I spit again, and wiped the goop off my face.

After picking out two more landmarks, Dan started again. As we headed away from the second, the water began to deepen. At one point, it was chest-high and I was practically swimming. I felt things hitting me under the water, but kept telling myself it was my imagination. By the time we reached the large pile of fallen trees we were aiming for, the water was less than knee-deep again. After climbing over the logs, we were confronted by a thick stand of golden reeds that stood at least eight feet tall.

"The splotch of gold on the map painting," Dan said.

He moved his hands in breast-stroke fashion to separate the reeds. The overgrowth above thinned and Dan kept the sun to our right. The sound of thunder was still far away.

The sun disappeared again as Dan stepped out of the reeds.

"This is incredible," he said.

He stepped aside and I looked ahead.

It *was* incredible. A sea of white filled the space between the trees in front of us.

Spiderwebs. Some were well-crafted webs with thin strands in symmetrical concentric circles that spanned more than six feet. Others were thick strands in a ghetto-like jumble. The New York City of spiders. I moved closer and found a lone occupant for each structure. Some had large bodies with legs that extended an inch or more. Some were small and fuzzy. Still others glistened with rich hues of red, yellow, and blue.

"A testimony for coexistence," Lucas said from behind me. I turned. Michael was beside him. He remained silent, as he had throughout the trip.

Dan unrolled the map painting. He pointed to a series of crisscrossing lines above the splattering of gold.

"On the right track," he said. "Problem is, we have to walk through this to get there." He pointed to the patch of gray that was our objective. It was beyond the crisscrossing lines.

I took a deep breath. Lucas hated snakes. I hated spiders.

Dan found a slender stick on the ground and waved it in front of him as he headed through the maze. I followed closely behind him with my arms crossed in front of my chest. I thought about King Kong.

Despite Dan's efforts, webs fell across my face and in my hair. My jeans were soon covered with white strands trailing behind. Occasionally, I had to shake a former inhabitant off my arm. We were through it within a couple of minutes, but it seemed like hours.

When the webs disappeared, so did the underbrush. The trees began to thin as the ground began to slope upward. Soon the trees were gone, replaced by head-high briars filled with berries. Some were red, others black, still others a mixture. Standing on my tiptoes, I could see that the area was surrounded by trees, with an occasional oak among the bushes.

"This is it," Dan said. He pointed to the right. "Need to go around. My guess is the chimney is over there."

We walked, still in single file, between the trees and the black-berry bushes. In places we had no choice but to push through the thorny briars. My arms were soon covered with scratches, some oozing blood. Twice Dan pointed out rattlesnakes resting near the top of a bush. I'd just as soon he had kept that to himself. Lucas removed his gun from the holster.

The briars ended. To our left, the ground rose slightly before dropping again to form a meadow. Except for a rare tree, it was covered by bachelor's buttons and Queen Anne's lace to our left. Kudzu covered the rest. Dan cut across the open space to where the forest began. Out in the open, the dark clouds behind us were evident again. The meadow dropped sharply, almost cliff-like, and narrowed to a peninsula that extended into the trees. It was surrounded by water. At the end of the peninsula sat a crumbling chimney. I reached behind me and retrieved the paintings. Lucas and Michael opened theirs.

I had the one with the chimney and held it up to compare it with the real thing. "Need to move to the left."

The four of us shifted like a group would at the direction of a photographer. Twenty side steps later the perspective looked right. From there it was easy to match the other paintings to their models. We stood in a tight group and looked around.

"Something buried?" I asked no one in particular.

Dan said, "No evidence of fresh digging."

"Who could tell with all this kudzu?" Lucas wondered. "The stuff grows a mile a minute and eats oil for breakfast."

"Whatever happened, happened a long time ago, anyway," I said.

Dan sat on the ground and rested his elbows on his knees. "Like a needle in a haystack."

"Yeah," Lucas said. He was standing with his hands on his belt and holster.

I turned around, looked at the terraced landscape behind me, and sank to the ground.

All this for nothing, I thought. *Damn.* I gazed at the darkened sky above the trees on the horizon. A flash of lightning cut through the black clouds. The air reverberated with the sound of thunder.

I stared again at the meadow before me. It was flat for about fifty feet. There it rose twenty feet before once more becoming flat. The kudzu covered the terrace and had spread ten feet beyond it. The paintings had been made here. I *knew* this was the spot.

I walked toward the terrace in front of me. I stopped two feet into the kudzu. The thick, leafy vines were hard to walk through.

Something caught my eye. In one spot, the kudzu fell like a curtain over a window. I walked to it and pulled apart the vines. There it was. A hole in the ground. A big hole.

At first I thought it was a cave, but as I pulled the kudzu farther I saw the beams.

Dan was standing behind me. "Bingo," he said. "An old mine."

Lucas pulled the flashlight from his belt and approached the entrance. "Mine? What kind of mine?"

I glanced at Michael. "Maybe a gold mine."

"Gold mine?" Dan said in puzzlement. He pushed the kudzu away from the other side and examined the supports.

"Michael says some people mined gold here a hundred years ago." We all looked at Michael. He nodded.

Lucas turned on his flashlight and walked into the mine. Dan followed. They and the light soon disappeared. Before entering the mine, I looked back at Michael. He was standing ten feet away with his hands in his pockets. "You coming? This may be one of the mines you've been looking for."

He looked at me for a moment. "I guess. I don't like enclosed spaces, though."

I looked at him questioningly.

"If I found one, I figured I'd hire somebody."

"OK. You don't have to go."

"No. I'll go."

I moved ahead quickly in the dark, trying to catch Dan and Lucas. I didn't know the mine turned and when I ran into the wall, dirt fell across my head. Michael bumped into me and I took his hand. We felt our way until the shaft straightened again and Lucas's flash came into view. Michael let go of my hand when we approached Lucas and Dan.

The mine widened and a single beam of light cut through the darkness about ten feet from where Lucas was standing. I knew absolutely nothing about mines, but reasoned it must be coming from an air hole.

Lucas had the flashlight pointed at the floor of the shaft. A stream of water was flowing across the mine.

I moved around Dan, bent, and felt the water. It was cold. After standing again, I peered into the black ahead. I extended both hands and walked slowly. I stumbled on some rocks and something touched my face.

"Shine the light over here, Lucas," I said.

It was a rope, with a noose at the bottom. Lucas moved the light to the ground.

I jerked back reflexively. The rocks I stumbled on weren't rocks.

In front of me was a pile of bones and a skull that was undeniably human.

Chapter 40

Dan gripped my shoulders. I leaned against him and covered my mouth with my hand.

"There're three of 'em," Lucas said as he moved the flashlight from one pile of bones to another. The anxiety he'd expressed at the idea of sleeping snakes was replaced by a professional tone of voice. Now he was doing his job. Sort of. I doubted that he often found three skeletons in an abandoned mine.

Lucas moved the beam of light to the ceiling. Three noosed ropes were hanging from one of the timbers overhead.

The bones were in heaps beneath each rope. Clothes were intertwined among them. Lucas reached into one of the pants pockets. When he did, the material tore easily.

"Rotted from the damp," he said. "If this was a dry place, they might still be hanging. With this humidity their ligaments decayed. There was nothing left to hold 'em together."

Lucas felt the pocket of a flannel shirt that was in the pile farthest to the right and pulled out a laminated card. "Library card for Patsboro High. Wayne Roberts."

Dan squatted next to Lucas, who now was leaning down, examining the back of one of the skulls.

I moved around them so I could see. Strangely, once I was used to the idea, these bones seemed no more real than the plastic models we had in our high school biology classroom. It was a different feeling from the one of fresh death that dominated the Reeveses' house.

Michael was standing away from us, beneath the shaft of light I'd noticed earlier. Shadows under his eyes gave him a ghoulish look.

Lucas pointed to one of the skulls. "Chipped and fractured. Looks like they were shot from behind before they were hung."

"Or vice versa," Dan said.

I shuddered. Gilstrap and Reeves had done this?

Why?

It couldn't have been for money. It was obvious these people wouldn't be carrying much. The fragments of clothing looked cheap and worn. That didn't happen just sitting in the mine. The clothes were old when they were killed.

"Lucas," Dan said, "Let me have the flashlight." Dan pointed it at the front of the skull and wiped away the debris. "My God," he said quietly.

"What?" I said.

"I can't *believe* this. Initials. In the bone. Carved."

"Initials?" I said, unable to comprehend.

"Marks in the skull. This one has . . . *L-K-G.*"

"Lawrence K. Gilstrap," I said.

Shot in the back of the head and hung. Initials carved in the forehead. Before or after?

What the hell difference does that make? My mind was trying to block the notion that such a thing could happen.

Dan moved to the skull that belonged to the middle pile of bones. He wiped away the dust and said, *"G-R-R."*

"Reeves," I said, before kneeling next to the third skull. "Then this one is . . ."

"Tackle," Dan finished.

I took the flashlight and glanced back at Michael. He was still in the light. His hands were in his pockets and his head was down.

I shined the flashlight on the remaining skull and focused on the last initial engraved on the forehead.

"M," I said. "McDaniel?" I looked back at Michael again.

He was staring at me.

"Can't be," Lucas said. "I checked his file. His dad was military. He was everywhere in the world but here when this happened."

I said, "We'll look in the yearbook again. Maybe 'Tackle' means something else. Maybe they weren't all fishing terms."

"Wait a minute," Dan said. He brushed off the left side of the skull. "Look at this." He pointed to the first initial. "That's clearly an *M.*" He pointed to the last initial. "It doesn't look like this one."

He was right. They were different and the first one was definitely an *M.*

Dan said, "This last one's an . . . *H.* Made with a shaky hand."

That feeling again. My stomach sinking to my feet.

The initials read *M-R-H.*

I looked up. "Michael?"

"What?" Dan said.

"Michael R. Hutcheson," I said. "That's his name."

Dan said, "The *R* stands for . . ."

"I don't know," I said.

"Roderick." I was blinded by the light. It flooded the excavation from the direction of the entrance. A human form was outlined behind the light. "Roderick, as in Rod. As in rod and reel. As in Tackle." The figure walked beyond Michael and stood to his left. He put the portable fluorescent lamp at his feet. His features became visible.

It was Radar.

"Michael!" I said. His face was clear in the light from above. I started to move toward him.

"Stay where you are!" Radar shouted.

I stopped. Debris fell from the top of the mine.

Radar had a blackened pistol in his hand. He said flatly, "We finally found them, Michael."

I looked at Michael. He didn't say anything.

Radar, Reeves, and Michael had killed the people piled behind us and carved their initials in their foreheads. I was trying to understand, but my mind wasn't working.

Lucas said, "Radar, you need to put the gun away."

Radar laughed. "Right." He shifted his weight from one foot to the other. "I don't think so. What you need to do is take off your gun belt and throw it over here. In front of me."

Lucas didn't move. Radar pointed his pistol at me.

Lucas said, "Your intentions are clear. You can't let us go."

"True. But, there can be a difference in how it goes down." He didn't have to explain more. Lucas unhooked his belt and threw it in front of Radar.

I was looking at Michael. Did I see glistening eyes? It was hard to tell. The shaft of light shining on him disappeared, reappeared, then disappeared again.

The storm's coming, I thought. Clouds covering the sun. I squeezed my eyes shut. When I opened them, the light was back. I tried to visualize the first of the storm clouds covering the sun. Thinking about the storm was better than thinking about what was going on in here.

"You're going to have to kill us," Dan said matter-of-factly.

"*No!*" Michael said forcefully. I looked at him. He was staring at Radar. I looked at Radar.

"Don't do one of your numbers on me, Michael. Not again. They can't leave here and you know it."

I tried to focus. Michael *couldn't* be involved in this. "What . . . ?" I was trying to understand.

Michael still had both hands in his pockets. He looked shrunken. "It was Fish."

"What do you mean?" Dan asked.

"It was his idea. We were drunk. Gary and I didn't want to do it." He hung his head.

"Do what?" I asked.

"Do that," Michael said and pointed to the bones.

"Who were they?" I asked.

"Niggers," Radar said. "Goddamn niggers who were destroying us."

"How's that?" Dan asked. He was sitting on an outcropping of rock, almost reclining, as usual. His voice was calm, as though this were a therapy session.

"Wouldn't stay in their place."

"Wouldn't stay in their place? This happened twenty years ago. You were seniors in high school. How'd they hurt you?"

"They came to *our* school when they had their own. Ol' man Hutcheson even built the nigger school a gymnasium. Most of 'em did stay. Not these three and two others."

"Freedom of choice," Dan said.

"What?" Lucas asked.

Dan sat a little straighter. "First school integration plan of the South. Everybody could choose where they wanted to go. Of course, when black children chose to go to white schools, their parents suddenly couldn't find work. Rent was increased. Police followed them around. The courts caught on eventually, and freedom of choice was disallowed." Dan nodded at the skeletons, and said, "History."

"Ruination of the white race," Radar said.

I was still focused on Michael. "You didn't even go to Patsboro High."

"Yes he did," Radar said. "At least until his senior year, when these three and the others came. After that, his daddy sent him to Jeff Davis Academy. My folks couldn't afford it."

"Reeves's parents could," Dan said.

"Reeves's parents were fools. He knew it. Then, anyway."

"How'd your picture end up in the yearbook?" Dan asked. He was looking at Michael. "We saw it in Minerva's house. You signed it. It would have been your senior year."

Michael shrugged.

Radar said, "Hildegarde sponsored the yearbook. That picture was taken after a ball game. She got it in." Radar glanced at Michael. "It was after a football game. I played. Gary and Michael were in the stands."

I looked at Michael. "I thought you played football. For the academy."

Radar laughed. "He did for about three days. Ran away from camp in the middle of the night."

The story he'd told in Athens. It was about himself. I looked at him. Tears were running down his cheeks.

"And the marines?" I asked. He had mentioned Parris Island.

Radar laughed again. "Michael? In the marines? You gotta be kidding. When he drew a fourteen in the draft lottery, his daddy arranged for a Four-F. Vietnam was hot. No way his kid was getting killed by a bunch of gooks."

"So, it was after a football game . . ." Dan prodded. Now he was sitting with his elbows on his knees and his fingers intertwined. That was his counseling pose. He wanted to keep Radar talking.

Why did Dan want to keep him talking? Radar would never let us leave this mine alive. I knew that. Dan was playing for time, hoping something would happen. Anything. Part of me just wanted it to be over. Just get it over.

"Yeah," Radar continued. "We went to Michael's house. His folks were out and we raided the liquor cabinet. After that we went to the Burger Chef. These guys were there." Radar motioned to the skeletons. "We'd lost that night. Pell County beat us. Mainly because of a kid they called an Indian. Wasn't no Indian. The nigger was good. I'll give him that. Anyway, we got these three in the car. Offered 'em some Wild Turkey. Get 'em every time. Of course, Ripple would've been better."

Michael said, "Stop, Fish."

"Why? They wanna know." Radar looked at me and said, "Don't you?"

I nodded, but didn't know if I did or not.

"Gary's dad owned all this land. Bait hunted out here. He led the way and we ended up in here. By the time we got here, they were dead drunk."

"So were we," Michael said.

"That's why you didn't know where this place was. You came at night and you were drunk," I said.

Radar lowered his gun slightly. He was enjoying the story. "Pitch black. Couldn't see squat."

"We were drunk," Michael said again.

Dan said, "I'm trying to understand this. You're telling us that these three black guys followed you all the way through the beaver pond and into this mine and you were carrying a *rope?*"

Radar laughed. "That's a hell of a thought." He held a hand as if he were carrying rope over his shoulder, laughed again, and shook his head. "Like I said, they were dead drunk. They didn't give a shit where we were going. We were in my GTO. I told them I was putting the Wild Turkey in a PE bag that was in the trunk. Had some rope back there and my dad's gun. Stuck them in the bag with the booze."

Michael said, "We were just going to mess with them. Bring them out here and make them find their way back. Make them realize that they needed to go to their own school. If Radar hadn't found that gun and rope . . ."

The room fell silent. Lucas broke it by asking, "How'd you find the mine this time?"

"Followed you. Actually, I followed her." Radar pointed to me. "Which is something *I* wonder about. How the hell did you find it?"

Michael said, "It was there all the time. Gary painted a picture. It was a map. Hanging right on the wall."

Radar shook his head and pointed his pistol at Lucas. "What the hell are you doing here? I thought you had James Cleveland all wrapped up."

"That's what we wanted you to think."

Radar didn't respond. He didn't like that.

Something had changed. It *was* important to find out what all this had been about. I needed to know everything. I needed to know *why*. I squelched the thought of ending up like those behind us. Anger replaced my fear.

I said, "So years ago, twenty years ago, you did a horrendous, drunken thing. Murdered three blacks because they had the audacity to go to your school. All these years you knew they were here with your initials engraved on them. Surely you knew they'd be found someday." When I leaned toward Radar to point my finger at him, my arm brushed the fanny pack at my waist.

The fanny pack—Daddy's pistol. The pistol that had been erased from my consciousness first by consternation, then by terror. Now it hung heavy.

"The initials . . ." Michael said plaintively. "They . . . they were already dead."

Radar's gun was pointing to the ground. "The initials didn't concern me till later, after I started learning about forensics. Didn't know till then how soft bone tissue really was. When I found out, I thought about my Barlow. I kept it sharp. Real sharp. When I realized those marks might still be there, I talked to Gary about it. He kept saying better to let it lie. I didn't push it because I knew how hard it was to get in here and I knew nobody remembered this old mine. I mean nobody. Gary's old man and his mother were dead, and I couldn't find anybody who remembered it. Michael kept trying, but I figured if I couldn't find it, nobody could."

"I don't think that's why you didn't push it," Dan said.

Radar stared at him.

I had to find some way to get out the Smith & Wesson. How?

I sat on the cold stone floor with my elbows on my knees and said, "Didn't anybody notice three of the five black kids who chose to go to Patsboro High had disappeared?" I lowered my right arm to my lap. When Radar didn't react, I crossed my left arm over the right.

Radar pointed to Michael. "He took care of that. Surprised the hell out of me. Got a note one of them had written from his pocket. He copied the handwriting and wrote another one that said they were tired of being the only blacks in an all-white school. That they were gonna take off. Of course, nobody really cared except their mamas and the preacher."

"Hard for blacks to complain twenty years ago," Dan said.

"Still is," I said automatically. My right hand was on the fanny pack's cover, gripping its tab.

Dan looked at me. "Kids disappear every day. Even today, nothing much is done. I see that a lot. Police just figure they've run away."

"That's usually the case," Lucas said defensively.

I was incredulous. I turned to the bones, saying, "*This* was different! Even with the note Michael wrote, these three disappear and nobody cared? My God . . ."

Dan held up his hand. He said quietly, "You had to be there, Tammi." He looked at Radar. "The airport changed things?" Dan was still keeping him talking. Good. I gripped the tab on my fanny pack harder.

Radar scratched his forehead with his gun. "True. It became imperative to find these bastards."

"So you went back to Reeves," Lucas said.

"I didn't. Michael did. Gary'd changed. Got eaten up with the liberals. Turned into a nigger lover. Wouldn't tell us where they were."

"And he wouldn't be persuaded." Lucas said.

I pulled on the tab slightly. The sound of the Velcro tearing in the enclosed space screeched in my ears, so I stopped. I glanced at Michael. He was staring at me.

Radar shrugged. "Start building an airport, digging, find those," he pointed with the gun, "and a big investigation starts. We needed to get these bastards out of here—the skulls anyway. The problem was that the Reeveses owned thousands of acres. Finding this place was like finding a nigger on a dark night." Radar waved toward Michael. "He kept looking, but I knew it was useless."

Michael took his eyes off of me. "They weren't even going to touch this place."

"What?" Radar said.

"That's what they said today. They're not going to mess up the ecosystem."

"Shit," Radar said.

I said, "So you panicked. Made a deal with Jarvis. He provides Crowe. In return, you guarantee an early parole provided by your friend Jerry Moreau when Jarvis is moved from Atlanta to the state pen in Reidsville."

For the second time, Radar looked startled. "Lois has a big mouth."

I realized what that could mean. "She didn't tell me anything. Just that you were fishing with Moreau, who happens to be head of Pardons and Paroles. I learned two-plus-two in first grade.

What I want to know is what the *hell* did you need Crowe for?"
My anger was obvious.

"Crowe was good. He'd eluded even me for four years.
Might've done different if I knew he was crazy."

"You didn't *know* that?" I said with incredulity. I pulled the
Velcro cover from the fanny pack without thinking. My raised
voice covered the sound. It also caused dirt to rain on my head.

It hit me. The dirt *and* the thought. What would the noise
from the Model 58 do to this mine?

"I knew he was meaner than hell. That's what I wanted—to
scare Gary."

The fragility of the mine was a probability. Radar's intentions
were a certainty. My hand slipped into the pack and palmed the
pistol.

"But you couldn't do it yourself," Dan said, more to himself
than to anybody else.

I looked at Michael. "Crowe did more than scare him, didn't
he, Michael? You were there."

Michael looked at the ground.

"You didn't know the map was hanging right in front of you,
but you did find something in his office. An article."

Radar shook his head. "The cocksucker wrote a confession.
Combined that with an investigation of the Klan. Found out
what I knew all along. The Klan's a joke."

"Trying to make a case for sociogenetics," Dan said.

"Something like that," Radar said. "It was bullshit. I burned
it."

I looked at Michael. "Not before Boots almost mailed it."

Radar looked at him. "Goddamn!" he said sharply.

Michael winced.

I was beginning to understand. Michael needed Radar's approval. Even today. It must have been even more important
twenty years ago.

"I should've known better than to involve you at all," Radar
said with disgust.

I was still looking at Michael. A sense of pity was recessed within me, but it was overwhelmed by anger.

I said slowly, "You let that *monster* do that to me." More dirt fell.

He looked up, his face stricken.

"I didn't *know*. After Gary was . . ." He hesitated.

"Killed," Dan said.

Michael blinked. "After that, I told Crowe to go. Go back to wherever he came from. He said he had something else to do. I didn't know what he was talking about."

"Go after Tammi," Lucas said.

Tears flowed down Michael's cheeks again. He started crying and rubbed his face with both hands. "I didn't know *what* he was doing until the day after the wreck. He said he'd arranged it to look like a nigger'd done it, but he missed. He said he was leaving. Too many people had seen him."

"Why didn't he?" Dan asked.

"He did," Radar said. "Went to Atlanta, anyway. I called him back."

"For God's sake, *why?!*" I screamed and cocked the hammer on the pistol.

I barely noticed the large rock that crashed to the floor of the ancient mine. A vision flashed through my mind—my office, when Bernard was in there talking about James Cleveland. Michael had been in the waiting room. I looked at Michael.

"You heard me talking to Minerva Hildegarde on the phone. *You* told Crowe."

"No," Radar said. "Michael told me. I told Crowe."

Dan said, "So you called him back to get rid of Hildegarde. Jarvis told you about Tammi asking him questions about Crowe."

"That's about it," Radar said.

My mind was reeling. If Michael hadn't come to my office that morning . . . how long was he there? Just a couple of minutes.

A quirk of timing that led to hell.

All my being wanted to jump up and run at Michael, but I

couldn't. My finger rested on the trigger. "Why didn't you *tell* me? Why didn't you *warn* me? How *could* you . . ."

"Oh God, Tammi," he whined. "I didn't know. I thought he was gone."

I gritted my teeth. "Michael, you *knew* he killed Hildegarde and blew up her house."

Radar waved his pistol. "Enough of this bullshit." He pointed the gun at Lucas. "Go on out, Michael."

"*No!*" Michael shouted.

The mine groaned.

Like a father talking to a recalcitrant son, Radar said through gritted teeth, "Get the hell out of here, Michael."

I was staring at the gun in Radar's hand, but saw Michael's movement. He reached under the back of his shirt and came out with a pistol.

Radar glanced at him, then back at us. "Put the goddamn gun away."

Lucas spoke. "Michael, you've got to think about this. You came out here with us. We disappear and you go back. They'll figure it out. Radar can't let you go back. No way."

"Bullshit, Michael," Radar said. "I met with them and you came with me. We don't have any idea what happened to them. Even if someday, they find three skeletons without heads and these three, it's a mystery to us. Remember who I *am*, Michael. We're home free—finally."

I looked at Michael. His eyes were vacant . . . undecided.

Dan said, "*Listen* to me, Michael. Mitch Griffith was following Tammi. We were taking turns. He *must* have seen Radar. Don't make it worse than it already is."

Mitch was following us! That's why Dan had been keeping Radar talking. He was giving Mitch time to get help.

It came from above. A voice I recognized. One I'd heard on the phone. It reverberated through the enclosed space.

"My boys—Fish, Bait and Tackle. Oh Tackle, you killed Bait. How could you do it? You were always my favorite, you know.

Fish was a mean one. It was all his fault. I know that. Let these people go, Tackle."

"Hildegarde!" Michael screamed. Muck rained from the ceiling above him.

Radar yelled, "For Godsake, Michael, don't you know who that is!? I'll get him!" A popping sound came from behind me.

I looked at Dan. His head dropped. Mitch was alone.

"Get Fish, Michael," the voice said. *"Now!"*

Michael raised his gun. Radar started to turn away from us, swinging his weapon toward Michael.

No thought was involved. I pulled the gun from the pack, rested my arms on my knee, and squeezed the trigger.

The pistol blasted in the enclosed space. Radar's middle flew backward and his arms flew forward. His gun skidded across the rocky surface. The timber above creaked, and I crawled forward on my knees before it crashed behind me. Through the fog of dust that filled the mine, I saw Michael staring at Radar.

"Michael," I said. I stood up and started for him.

He pointed his gun at me and I stopped.

Five feet separated us. He looked at Radar's blood-soaked body lying on the floor in front of the fluorescent lamp. We stood, our pistols aimed at each other.

"Put the gun down," I said. *"Please."*

He looked at me. "I'm sorry, Tammi. I'm so sorry."

Michael put the gun against his head and pulled the trigger.

The light disappeared. I was back on my hands and knees. Choking. Coughing. Each attempt to breathe filled my nose and mouth with dust. My eyes watered, trying to rid themselves of the grit. I squeezed them shut and held my breath.

The mine was cracking and popping. I heard a thud behind me. Another timber falling.

Air. Air! I had no choice. I had to breathe. I took a quick breath. A little dust, but not much. I opened my eyes and blinked quickly to rid them of the cleansing tears. The dust was settling. Mitch dropped from the shaft next to where Michael was sprawled on the mine's floor.

Michael! I crawled to him and put my hand to his chest. Nothing.

Dan was next to me. He placed his fingers on Michael's neck. "He's alive."

A slab of rock fell in front of us.

"We've got to get out of here," Mitch said.

Mitch and Dan grabbed Michael's arms and feet. I stood. "What about Radar?"

"Dead," Lucas said from behind me. "Let's go."

Lucas had Radar's fluorescent light and led the way. Timbers fell behind us like dominoes as we ran for the entrance. The path turned and light appeared through the kudzu curtain ahead. We entered the meadow, and seconds later the entrance to the mine collapsed.

The kudzu covering the opening fell apathetically, hiding any evidence of Radar being buried with his black schoolmates of so many years ago.

Chapter 41

"How'd you find us?" I asked Mitch.

We were sitting on my veranada. Dan, Mitch, and I were in the rusted metal chairs. Bernard sat in Aunt Ouida's rocker. Landry had dropped by, too. Mrs. Thompson had come with him and brought a pie. Landry and Mrs. Thompson had just left.

Lucas, Dan, and I had carried Michael out though the beaver pond. Mitch had stayed at the site until the police arrived. Lucas called from his car. Michael was still breathing when we arrived at Teal General.

Part of me wanted to stay with him, another part wanted to be shed of him.

The latter won.

Lucas had dropped me at my house. Getting cleaned up was the first priority. I wanted to wash the whole thing away. I wanted to be free of it.

All of it.

The bath had taken care of the dirt from the mine and the beaver-pond scum, but it couldn't clean my mind.

Before getting in the tub, I'd called Bernard and asked him to work on getting James Cleveland freed. He talked to the district attorney, who talked to Lucas. The district attorney was granted a nol pros from Judge Turner and all charges were dropped.

James was released. The speed with which that happened is one of the nice things about small-town justice.

Dan and Mitch showed up an hour later. We sat on the veranda and started processing what had happened.

After I asked Mitch how he'd found us, he looked at Dan, then back at me. "We weren't too excited about Lucas's plan to let you draw out the killers. So we took turns watching you. If Gilstrap or Tackle . . ."

The name Tackle stabbed through me. "Michael."

"We didn't know that. But if somebody came after you again, we didn't want you to be alone. Today was my turn. I didn't know what the hell was going on. I'm sitting in front of the courthouse in the Caprice and you come flying out. Dan and Michael are chasing behind you. I watched you run into the police station. I start to go in to find out what's going on when I see him."

"Radar," Dan said.

"Right. He runs from the side of the courthouse and jumps in a car. My job's to look for him and there he is. Only I'm going crazy wondering what you're so excited about." He pointed to me. "Fifteen minutes go by. Radar just sits. All of a sudden he takes off, so I follow. We end up at the Reeveses'. I don't know how he knows to go there."

Dan said, "Lucas ten-sevened when we got there. Radar had a radio."

"Yeah. Guess so," Mitch said. "So we sit there. I'm down the street, trying to be sure Radar doesn't see me. I don't see you come out. Radar takes off, follows you here, and then to Partridge Drive. After that we head out of town. Radar stops on the side of the road and I'm half a mile behind him. I mean there ain't nothing out there. Nowhere to hide. Lots easier to follow somebody in Newark."

"You followed him into the beaver pond," I said.

"Right. Kept panicking, too. I mean, I'd lose him and everything looked the same out there. I don't know where I'm going and keep expecting him to pop out from behind a tree. I see him again. I watch him heading across that meadow, and I have to stay back in the blackberries. Nowhere to hide out in the open like that. All of a sudden he disappears."

"He found the entrance to the mine," I said.

"I don't know that. I finally decided to chance it and start walking around in the damned kudzu. You ever walk through that stuff?"

I nodded. Once. Today.

"I keep tripping, getting tangled up in it, and expecting to get shot, or something, and wonder where the hell he'd gone. I hear voices. I can't tell where they're coming from. I think I'm going crazy. Keep walking around, listening. The voices get louder, then diminish. I turn and hear 'em again. Finally I find it. A hole in the ground, under the kudzu. The voices are coming from the hole. Not much bigger around than me. I slide into it."

I thought back. When the shaft of light disappeared and reappeared—that had been Mitch.

He continued, "A ledge opens up just beneath the ground. I get on it and listen and try to figure out what to do. I hear Dan say, 'You're gonna have to kill us.' Figure he's talking to Radar. Figure he's got a gun."

"You were right," I said.

"I don't know what to do, so I just keep listening. Figure out what's going on with Michael. He was in on it. He doesn't sound too stable. That's when I think of Minerva Hildegarde. I have to do something, and that's what I do."

"Provided the distraction Tammi needed," Dan said.

Bernard had been listening quietly, but now asked, "How did you know her voice?"

Mitch looked at him and said, "Like I told Tammi and Dan, she bought the AV equipment for the schools at my store. Good customer."

"And Mitch never forgets a voice," I said.

The sound of a car door slamming came from the street. Lucas appeared between the bushes and came up on the porch. "Y'all all right?"

Bernard nodded and the rest of us shrugged.

Lucas half-sat on the veranda's railing. "Just came from the hospital."

"How's Michael?" I asked and thought, Damn you, Michael, why?

"Still alive. Still unconscious." Lucas folded his arms. "Weird doctor working with him."

"Emergency room doctor?" I asked.

"Yeah. He's supposed to be an expert in trauma treatment. He told me Michael really pissed him off. He said they ought to teach people how to shoot themselves. Maybe in school. Said a gun to the side of the head's one of the worst ways. As often as not they survive, but turn out—this is what he said—'like a tomato.' He said something about doing it in the back at the base of the neck is much more efficient. Seems awkward to me."

"Was the doctor's name Bates?"

"Yeah. You know him?" He squinted his eyes. "Oh, yeah."

I nodded. "Sounds like him."

Lucas stood and said, "Well, just wanted to let you know."

"What about McDaniel?" I asked.

"Oh, right." Lucas leaned on the railing again. "I talked to him, too. It seems he wants to be a detective. He thought if he could get Bear to confess, that'd help in his ambition. He figured if he scared Bear, that might do it."

Bernard spoke again, "Is he aware of the problems extant with coerced confessions?"

"I explained the facts of life to him. Didn't really need to, though. He was shook up. Not only because of that, but because of what James did. McDaniel's really a good man, I think. He just screwed up."

"He called to tell me about James's attempt. He also told me there'd be no record of police officials talking to him. After James identified him, I wondered why he said that."

"Guilt, I think," Lucas said. "Anyway, that was the extent of his involvement."

I was glad. Michael was enough.

Lucas stood again. "Well, I've got to get back to the beaver pond. We'll be excavating all night."

Bernard stood too. "I must be going as well." He squeezed my shoulder. "Let me know if you need anything."

"I will," I said. "Thanks, Bernard."

He nodded and joined Lucas on the sidewalk. They disappeared behind the magnolias.

Mitch, Dan, and I sat in silence. I moved to the rocker.

Mitch said, "This is rough, Tammi."

That's all it took. The shock was wearing off. Now came the pain. Just like with Crowe. Except this pain wasn't physical. Mitch's and Dan's images blurred. I cried.

Mitch and Dan held me, one on each side. I took their hands, brought them to my face, and squeezed. Why? I kept thinking. What have I done? I squeezed their hands harder, trying not to feel so alone.

Finally, the crying stopped.

Dan said, "Tammi, you've been able to shut down your pain by focusing on getting those guys. But that's over. You need to deal with this. Need to talk to somebody. I can set it up for you."

I nodded. "I know. I will. It's just that . . . I want to figure out some things first. By myself."

Dan nodded. "Yeah. I did, too. With the twins."

Early in his career, two of Dan's students had killed themselves. He had felt responsible. "It helped me to write it down. See it in black and white. You might try it. I found the exercise to be cathartic, and it helped when I started talking about it. My mind was clearer after doing it." He leaned forward. "While you're thinking, you might consider *De malo, bonus*—From evil, good."

From evil, good, I thought. I was angry. "What every woman needs is a good, old-fashioned rape, right?"

Dan kneeled in front of me and put his hands on mine. "Of course not. You know me better than that. I'm just suggesting that we can use even horror to grow."

Time passed. "I'll be all right. I need to be alone for a while. You understand."

They both said, "Yes."

Mitch said, "Besides, I'm late for a meeting."

"What meeting?" Dan asked.

"With the Big Lizard," he said.

"That's the Grand Dragon," I said.

"Whatever," Mitch said and added in redneck, "Gonna make sure no more niggahs *in*filtrate the secret meetin's of the Grand Knights. Gonna *in*stitute blood tests. Make damn sure it all flows white."

I laughed and shook my head. "One of the things that really bothers me is that I thought we were through with all that."

"It's getting better," Dan said. "Listen, two of the three old-time southerners who hanged those people couldn't live with it. There was a time when that'd never happen. Minerva even wrote about it. Twenty years ago, she'd have shot Earl Warren, not asked God to bless him."

I'd forgotten about that.

"And you were at the Klan meeting the other night. A national gathering only attracted a few hundred of them. Overgrown adolescents dressed up in costumes." He paused for a moment. "When those two Klan members showed up at school, not one student joined them. Every kid I heard, most born and raised in Patsboro, was disgusted that they were there. The bottom line is, Radar was a throwback."

Mitch said, "Still got a ways to go, though. Governor Maugham helped me, but it was for the money, pure and simple. He doubled his investment. Doubtful that Bear's going to be that lucky."

"No doubt about it," Dan said. "But it *is* getting better. I see it every day at school."

"I guess you're right," I said doubtfully. We were silent for a moment. "I still don't understand why Radar brought in Crowe. Why didn't he do it himself?"

Dan leaned forward, his elbows on his knees, and said, "He couldn't hurt his friends. Not directly, anyway. Nobody is all bad. . . ."

He saw the look I gave him.

"Crowe was a sociopath. Radar wasn't. Loyalty was important to Radar. That's what I realized as we talked in the mine. He was an effective policeman with a fatal flaw—an ingrained hatred that wouldn't go away. He was also a survivor. He would have killed us, but it wouldn't have been easy for him."

"It'll take me a while to sort all that out."

I didn't understand Michael, either. Manic-depressive, maybe. Arrested development on top of that. With a strong father and domineering mother, and who knows what else, he never really grew up. And there was something else I knew, but had lost track of. Southern gentry hide weakness. They're raised that way.

I knew I'd talk about all that someday. I had to. But not today.

Dan and Mitch left. The twilight was diminishing and I walked into the house and into my room. I opened my briefcase and pulled out a yellow legal pad. I heard a knock on my door.

I sighed. I didn't want any company. I wanted to start writing it down. I went to the door and opened it.

There stood Big Jack Pelham.

Anger returned. I said, "Big Jack—"

He held up his hand. "Now wait a minute. I want to tell you somethin'. Drove all the way up here to do that. If you want me to leave after that, fine. Just want to say somethin'."

"What?" I said, the disgust clear in my voice.

"On the way home the other day your mama told me why we had to leave. I couldn't stand it. Been tryin' to avoid it, but if that's what you thought, I had to tell you."

"What?" I said again. I didn't want this. I didn't want him here. I was tired of dealing with sick men.

He reached behind him and pulled out a case. He took out a pair of glasses and put them on. The lenses made his eyes look like specks. They were the thickest glasses I'd ever seen.

He grinned through his beard and mustache. "Couldn't stand the thought of bein' called four-eyes. Problem is, I can't see diddly without 'em. But it killed me when you thought . . ."

I was leaning against the wall. I slid down, laughing. I tried not to. Really tried, but couldn't help it. Pain and anxiety flowed out as I laughed, looked at Big Jack, and laughed again.

His grin faded. I said, "No, Big Jack . . ." but couldn't quit laughing.

He removed his glasses.

I took a deep breath. "Listen. I'm not laughing at you. It's just that . . . I needed that. Needed some man not to be—" I stopped. I didn't want to talk about it. "Put 'em on, Big Jack. You look fine. Really."

Big Jack grinned again and replaced the glasses.

"Long way back to Maytown. Wanna spend the night?" I asked.

"Shore would. If you don't mind, that is."

"I don't mind. Come on in. Have you eaten supper yet?"

"Nuh uh. Picked these up," he touched his glasses, "and drove straight up here."

"I'll order a pizza," I said and headed to the phone.

"Make it two."

Big Jack and I sat on the veranda. I ate two pieces of the pizza and he ate the rest. After we ate, we sat and talked.

He told me selling Mama's house was her idea. She thought I'd be mad so she blamed it on him. That sounded like Mama. He said he'd talked her into keeping it. He had his guitar. He played and we sang. Stuff like "John Henry."

Finally, I said, "Big Jack, I've got something I've got to do."

"Go right ahead, Tammi. I think I'll sit out here a while longer, if you don't mind."

"No problem." I walked to the door, but stopped before reaching it and said, "Good night."

I thought about adding "Daddy," but didn't. Maybe someday. I looked at him.

He was grinning.

The cloudy skies had cooled things off. The air conditioner was off. The window in my room was open. I heard Big Jack strum his guitar. In a haunting, slow voice he sang:

Southern trees bear a strange fruit.
Blood on the leaves and blood at the root.
Black bodies swinging in the southern breeze.
Strange fruit hanging from the poplar tree.

I laid the pillows against Aunt Ouida's headboard, reclined, and put the legal pad on my bent knees.

Pastoral scene,
Of the gallant South,
Of the bulging eyes and the twisted mouth.
Scent of magnolia, sweet and fresh,
And the sudden smell of burning flesh.

I picked up my pen, but held it without writing. Instead, I listened to Big Jack.

Here is a fruit for the crows to pluck,
For the rain to gather and the wind to suck,
For the sun to rot and for the trees to drop.
Here is a strange, and bitter . . . crop.

"Big Jack," I said through the window. "Sing that again."
"OK, Tammi," he said.
Dan was right. If Big Jack Pelham could sing that song with such feeling, things have changed.
And I know this, too: I am changing. Only I don't yet know if it's transformation or mutation.
A strange and bitter crop . . .
Big Jack began again and I looked at the pad in front of me. Where to begin? Just write what happened, I thought.
I wrote: *Within ten days I killed two men. Both deserved it. For the first time in my life, I hope my mother's right and there is a hell. The savagery I suffered demands that those men now scream in horrible pain.*